SICK
&
BEAUTIFUL

A PSYCHEDELIC NIGHTMARE

JIM QUEEN

Copyright © 2022 Jim Queen

The moral right of the author has been asserted.

Apart from any fair dealing for the purposes of research or private study, or criticism or review, as permitted under the Copyright, Designs and Patents Act 1988, this publication may only be reproduced, stored or transmitted, in any form or by any means, with the prior permission in writing of the publishers, or in the case of reprographic reproduction in accordance with the terms of licences issued by the Copyright Licensing Agency. Enquiries concerning reproduction outside those terms should be sent to the publishers.

This is a work of fiction. Names, characters, businesses, places, events and incidents are either the products of the author's imagination or used in a fictitious manner. Any resemblance to actual persons, living or dead, or actual events is purely coincidental.

Matador
Unit E2 Airfield Business Park,
Harrison Road, Market Harborough,
Leicestershire. LE16 7UL
Tel: 0116 2792299
Email: books@troubador.co.uk
Web: www.troubador.co.uk/matador
Twitter: @matadorbooks

ISBN 978 1803131 481

British Library Cataloguing in Publication Data.
A catalogue record for this book is available from the British Library.

Printed and bound in Great Britain by 4edge Limited
Typeset in 11pt Minion Pro by Troubador Publishing Ltd, Leicester, UK

Matador is an imprint of Troubador Publishing Ltd

*To the people I love. For inspiring my
dreams and enduring my nightmares.*

SICK
&
BEAUTIFUL

PART ONE
PREMONITIONS

CHAPTER
ONE

My relationship with Rachel Garland was born through an act of intentional violence.

It started in Knightsbridge, in the Paxton's Head, when the landlord passed the phone across the crowded bar. It was my editor, Eleanor Wither. Minutes earlier, she received a report that a man had fallen from the eleventh-floor balcony of the Mandarin Oriental, Carriage Drive's most extravagant hotel.

"Be quick, David. The victim might be famous."

I smiled. The Mandarin was only a two-minute dash from the boozer. The timing of this event, my proximity to it, felt like fate. It felt like I was supposed to be here, to be there. Jesus. It felt *cinematic*.

"I'm on my way," I said.

"You know your role, David. Good luck. And Happy New Year."

She hung up the phone.

By the time I sunk my gin and tonic and jogged to the death scene, ambulances and police cars congested the hotel's cobblestone forecourt. Hypnotised by their flashing ruby-blue lights, seduced by the promise of violence, intoxicated tourists and office workers battled to the front of the crowd swelling outside the lobby. Eleven storeys above, revellers in tuxedos rutted for a premium view on the balcony, poised precariously over the balustrades, pinching the stems of their cocktail glasses.

I felt a familiar excitement pervade the oxygen. Bored by London's dismal landmarks and turned out of the pubs after last orders, this audience converged under the cloud to leer at the human who tumbled out of the sky. It wasn't a death we would elect for ourselves, a death that was private and painlessly dignified. This was *entertainment*, reality TV, hardcore pornography. This was the closest thing anybody could find to the giddy thrill of a public execution.

According to one spectator, the victim sailed through the air like an Olympic diver before he torpedoed through the glass veranda and collided with the marble steps of the exorbitant lobby.

"Thank God it wasn't me," concluded the spectator, shaking his head sadly.

"Thank God," I agreed.

I looked around me. The grimace of every onlooker was hung with an irrefutable question: *How could the human body – moulded by divine hands, refined by millennia of evolution – be as fragile as a cheap plastic toy?* It was poignant. It was frightening. The scene reminded us that we would all fall victim to the same inescapable prophecy. But what could drive somebody so (presumably) wealthy to end it this way? I needed to know the answers.

I elbowed confidently to the anterior of the crowd to take a closer look at the body. There was almost nothing perceptibly human left. A shapeless suit and two carefully polished shoes, crumpled in a pool of blood and broken glass, like the dregs of a toppled over Bloody Mary. I glowered at this alien autopsy, these ruptured components, unable to comprehend how they ever slotted together.

Out of professional reflex I photographed the scene, performing my small role with rehearsed detachment. Two detectives searched the pockets of the cadaver. A cigarette case. A leather wallet, gorged with money. A pellucid baggy of white powder, illuminated by a knife of torchlight. Car keys. And so on. Every item salivated with gore. In the background, a policeman ushered guests down the lobby steps, past the human spillage. Some bowed their heads like mourners passing the open coffin of a distant relative. Others looked grateful, almost *gleeful*, it wasn't their own remains decimated on full public display. I examined the trauma in their perplexed expressions, searching for witnesses.

That's when a woman wearing a floral dress and sunglasses floated down the steps and knelt beside the body. Her hand hovered over the mutilated shape, contemplating touch, contemplating contact. *What's she waiting for?* I wondered. Was she afraid of its viscid textures? Or was she afraid that a shattered arm might reanimate, clutch her wrist and drag her into the claret, into the ground? I photographed this extraordinary moment before she retracted her hand, stood and vanished into the crowd. I decided to follow her. She turned right, pacing towards Hyde Park Corner, and then disappeared through the doors of the Lanesborough Hotel. But get this: she was barefoot, without a raincoat or umbrella, inviting the bite of the cloud's acidic verve. *What a character*, I thought. These enigmatic details – they intrigued me. *She* intrigued me. I smiled. I couldn't wait to interview her.

Minutes later, I found her at the deserted restaurant bar, stirring crushed ice and mint leaves inside a sweating highball. She was soaked, audibly dripping rainwater from her barstool. I sat next to her and ordered a gin fizz, subconsciously adapting to my bombastic surroundings. The bartender nodded silently, unconcerned with my half-cut condition (it was New Year's Eve in London, after all). I gripped the edge of the counter, patiently waiting for the universe to stop pirouetting. I needed to focus. I needed to raise the questions that mattered. *Where were you when the accident occurred? Who was the victim? How did he fall? Was he under the duress of drugs or alcohol? And where are your shoes?* The interview, the trajectory of our discourse, was clear in my mind. It felt intrinsic.

But I didn't open with any of the above. I didn't get the chance.

"You look quite unwell," she said. "Have a sip of your drink."

Obediently, I sipped.

She lowered her sunglasses to analyse me: face, suit, shoes, soul.

"You're not police," she said confidently. "And you're not a PI. Their appearance is always more purposeful, more *authoritative*. Let me guess. You're a journalist, aren't you? Yes. I can see it now. It's unmistakeable."

"Photojournalist," I said, holding out my hand. "My friends call me David."

She stared at the hand until I tucked it back inside my overcoat pocket.

"I report for *The Daily Sun*," I continued. "Crime scenes. Traffic accidents. Men falling from the sky like raindrops." I paused. "I'm curious. How did you know that I'm a journalist? Is it really that *unmistakeable*?"

"Bad posture. Unshaven. Unable to maintain eye contact. Look at you, with your creased suit and camera. You're practically a caricature." She smiled, revealing an abyss of crooked teeth. "Don't take it personally. I know what your kind looks like, David. I've studied your habits."

I smiled too, determined to conceal my discomfort at her accuracy, but I suddenly felt detached. Detached from my role. Everything was off-kilter. I was adrift in an unscripted daydream. I wasn't in control of the dialogue, the motion. She was both interviewer and interviewee, so what was I? What was my purpose in this scene? Was I even really here? I traced my fingers over my damp forehead, the concaved cheeks, my parted lips, to confirm that I existed inside this moment.

"I know why you're here, so let me make this easy for you," she said. "I'm going to tell you what happened on the eleventh floor of the Mandarin Oriental. I'm going to tell you what I saw, how the action transpired." That grin again. "I hope you're ready, David. You might not believe a word of it."

I took out my biro and notepad. She lit another cigarette.

"The victim was a movie producer named Rupert Wreath," she said. "The studio execs rented the hotel penthouse for NYE. Rupert was intoxicated, but he didn't fall off the balcony. Someone pushed him."

"This is good," I assured her. In fact, it was *fantastic*. Murder? What a twist. "Who pushed him?"

"A man in a bowler hat."

"What did he look like?"

The way her head sank, the way her hands began to shake. Something shifted in her demeanour. Something drained and summersaulted within. It clearly took a lot of courage to tell me this next part.

"Black suit. Black overcoat. Hair like cobwebs. He was dressed like a pallbearer, except he was smiling. But it wasn't a warm smile. It was a grimace. It was pain. His mouth was like a wound filled with barbed teeth." She paused. "He had a camera too, just like yours," she added, pointing at the Praktica Super TL2 around my neck. "He was stood next to Rupert, staring at me, *into* me, as if he knew me. As if he knew everything about me. It's so strange, David. I felt a connection."

I wrote these details down – *Bowler hat. Smile. Jagged teeth. Camera.* – wondering if, in time, a hidden meaning would emerge.

"And then what happened?" I asked.

She smirked, as if this part was obvious. "He pushed him."

"But why?" I insisted. "Was there an argument? An altercation?"

"No. Perhaps his motives will become clearer over time."

"Perhaps," I conceded.

I waited for more (more specifics, more data), but after a passive shrug and an incurious sigh, it became evident that she was pained by my prosaic questions. Hidden behind her sunglasses, did she sense how attracted I was to her complex energy? The waterlogged dress. The bones that ached to tear through the surface of her skin. The strange cadence of her accent. The way her incisors and canines overlapped, competing for light. All these traits infatuated me.

"What happened to the man in the bowler hat?" I asked. "Did anybody try to restrain him?"

"No. They were too busy trying to get a view of Rupert's body. There was shouting, screaming, shoving. He vanished in the chaos." She paused, perhaps refining the words in her mind. "I want to believe that I imagined him, but I felt him. Jesus. I could *smell* him. This stench of decay. I can't deny his existence." Another cigarette. "So, there's your scoop, David. It's obscene, isn't it? But it doesn't sound like front-page stuff to me. Rupert wasn't even famous. Just another human sacrifice for the famished city. And Christ knows there are enough producers on this planet. There will be a dozen more Ruperts waiting to take his place, queuing in the rain."

She was right. It wasn't *front-page stuff*. But the piece still had value. It was still *news*. I felt confident that the gruesome details of Rupert Wreath's death and his mysterious assailant would happily furnish the ephemeral middle pages of tomorrow's tabloids, but I just couldn't get excited about the snuffed producer and the sneering apparition. These characters bored me. I wanted to know more about *her*. Cryptic. Quotable. Beautiful. The witness had depth. She oozed potential.

"And who are you?" I asked. "What's your role in this ugly episode?"

"I'm an actor," she said. "Rupert and I worked on a number of movies together. Our relationship was sexual as well as professional, but it wasn't love. We simply existed in the same time, the same space."

"What kind of movies?"

"Mostly horror. I've landed small roles in over 100 pictures. I played a paysan at a lynching in *Mary Shelley's*

Frankenstein. An extra in TV miniseries of *Body Bags* and *The Tommyknockers*. I was also a zombie in *Braindead*. I turned down a speaking part in *Army of Darkness* for that last one."

I nodded, jotted, tutted approvingly.

"And how did tonight make you feel?" I asked. "This wasn't a horror movie. This was real life."

When she removed her sunglasses again, her emerald pupils contracted like evaporating oceans.

"I'm ashamed to admit this," she said, "but the scene excited me. The gore. The sound of the body connecting with the city's impassive corners. The shrieks and the traffic choking the boulevard. Being photographed behind the police cordon like a movie star. But the way Rupert exploded on the steps like a binbag filled with paint and prosthetics. It almost didn't look *realistic*. It was sick and beautiful, vividly and concurrently."

I wrote this down. *Sick & beautiful*. I added a question mark before scribbling it out again.

The next thing she did surprised me: she grabbed my hand. The strength of her grip – it was startling. But it was tangible. She was really here, we both were, fingers entwined, sticky sweat amalgamating.

"Is death supposed to make you feel so *alive*?" she asked. "It's like true love. It burns. I almost can't endure its caustic intensity."

"True love. How would you define it?"

"It's helplessness," she said. "It's the inability to function without that person. The desire to be a part of them, whatever the cost. It's forever."

"That notion. Does it frighten you?"

"Yes. But it intrigues me too. Just like tonight. I'm conflicted. I'm still unsure how to dissect what I've felt, what I've witnessed."

Although she seemed enchanted by death's sardonic poetry, her body language suggested that she was underprepared for the consistency of warped flesh, the psychedelic hues of internal organs, the odour of blood mixing with downpour. It was all unfamiliar to her. I felt compelled to appal her.

"I photograph the dead almost every day in this city," I said. "Slow-motion traffic accidents. Stabbings. Shootings. Alcohol poisoning. Overdoses. People tripping over their shoelaces in front of trains and buses. Asphyxiation from house fires and bungled sex acts. I even saw a woman crushed underneath a billboard advertising life insurance. What I'm trying to say is, death always surprises us with something innovative and awful. The human race has come so far, but we still can't stop dying in the most painful and peculiar ways. Somehow, it *never* feels realistic. After a while, it's like going to the cinema or watching TV. It becomes empty, effortless."

But this wasn't entirely true.

I didn't want to admit that repeatedly observing the unravelling of the human form terrified me. It made me feel unsafe, insecure, as if consciousness itself was loosely strapped into a malfunctioning rollercoaster carriage on the cusp of falling apart. This shuddering vessel of flesh and bone becomes incrementally unreliable and unpredictable, an ephemeral cage of complex agony. Even if we learnt to understand death, nobody can escape the draconian finalities of this stampeding human abattoir. This was the truth I wasn't prepared to confess (to myself, to anybody). But it's

OK. Because she was lying too. I could feel it. Her story didn't add up. Something was wrong. I wanted to know her secret.

"Tell me something," I said. "A person you knew, a person you knew *intimately*, is dead, shoved off a balcony by an evaporating boogeyman, and you're just so– *relaxed*. It's spooky. It's as if you're not even shocked."

"I would have been shocked with Rupert's death if I hadn't already seen it," she said.

"I don't understand–"

"Last night, in my dream, the man in the bowler hat pushed Rupert off the balcony. But when he hit the steps, he opened his eyes again, sprouted feathered wings and floated into the cloud. Rupert was covered in blood, weeping and smiling, as he climbed up towards Paradise. He looked petrified."

"That's very interesting," I admitted.

As I began to scrawl this down, she snatched the biro out of my hand and scribbled something across my notepad. It was an address – *Casa del Mar, Venice Beach, California.*

"I'm boarding the first flight from Heathrow to LA tomorrow," she said. "If you have any more questions, ask for Rachel Garland. I'll be by the poolside bar, early in the morning and late at night. Happy New Year, David."

She abruptly exited the Lanesborough Hotel in the same way she had entered it – silent and barefoot, passing through the building's brick walls with the unobtrusiveness of a ghost. Her wet footprints, the drained highball and fag-jammed ashtray, were the only traces of her presence.

"Rachel Garland," I whispered.

I wrote her name down. I underlined it. I circled it. I gently tapped it with the nib of my biro.

Rachel Garland.

I wasn't prepared to believe that our dreams could be premonitions from the future or the past.

I also wasn't prepared to admit that last night – before we met, before we knew that we both existed – I dreamed about her too.

Her and the man in the bowler hat.

CHAPTER
TWO

The dream I experienced that night, even for dreams, bordered on insanity. Somewhere between reality and a nightmare.

I'm in my flat, in my dream, on my sofa.

Outside, rain pummels the windows. Wind screams across the balcony.

The sky is black, devoid of stars or moonlight.

When I look at the television, I can see a monochrome image of a figure pressed against the glass. The face is wrought with distress: hollow eyes, sharp teeth, torn lips, a bowler hat. The face is staring at me with a mixture of fear and sorrow. Tears spill down its lacerated cheeks, onto the camera hung around its neck. The grin is contorted into a grimace. I smile back, wondering what I can recognise in its compassion.

Behind the figure is a double bed. A watercolour painting of a beach and an ocean hang above it. Like mine, the room is mantled in darkness. Sat on the edge of the bed is Rachel Garland, covered in blood. She smiles, waving with a broken hand. Flies crawl over her face, into her mouth, around the deep wound in her abdomen.

I wave back, fascinated and paralysed. There is no sound. Just the pictures, the faces.

I pick up the remote control on the coffee table. When I press the power button, the television doesn't turn off. I tap the remote in my palm. I check the batteries. I press the button several more times. Nothing.

The figure bangs its fists on the inside of the television screen. Almost imperceptible, it sounds like an echo from an immemorial reality.

My breathing intensifies. It's short, sharp, as if I'm running, sprinting from an unspeakable fate.

On my hands and knees I crawl towards the television set, entering the radioactive halo of its anaemic smoulder. I press my hands against the glass. The figure on the other side does the same, splaying its fingers over my own. I can almost feel the warmth of its flesh, the rhythm of its pulse. Inches from the screen, the image sears my eyes, bleaching my peripheral vision in iridescent fire.

The figure mouths the same words over and over again. I try to turn up the volume with the dial on the television set (no success). I squint, determined to decipher its inaudible message. It slows its words, accentuating the syllables with its split lips, the pained click of its ulcerated tongue.

Something– go to–
Don't? Don't go to–
Don't go to pyre dies?

It doesn't make any sense.

"What are you trying to tell me?" I shout at the screen, pointing at both ears with my fingers.

The figure's mouth gapes open in mute laughter. When it thumps its bandaged fists on the other side of the screen, the glass begins to crack. Before I can pull back, before I can *react*, its arms break through. It clamps its hands around my neck. It forces its fingers into my mouth, into my eyesockets. It unhinges my jaw, sinks its thumbs into my eyeballs. I feel blood flow down my face, brittle bones snapping, as I'm hauled into the television set, into an ocean of burning static.

I hold out my arms, hoping that somebody will grab my hand to rescue me.

If they did, I would drag them in with me. Yeah. I'd tow them into oblivion.

CHAPTER
THREE

I didn't repeat this disturbing imagery to Rachel Garland, but I did describe it to Eleanor Wither.

In fact, I described it in incredible detail. Confessing my nightmares had become a biweekly habit. Somehow, tragically and quite gradually, my editor had become my therapist. As far as I knew, I was her only patient.

Underground, in the bowels of *The Daily Sun*, in the comfort of Eleanor Wither's uncomfortable office, we sifted through the rubble of my personal life. We even discussed the odious weather, the congested public transport, soaring living and dying costs, and the fact that Leonard Lynch, a young undergrad from King's College, was promoted from unpaid intern to political correspondent in just one calendar year (an esteemed role with a salary and responsibilities that significantly outweighed my own). Eleanor Wither and I shared things. Dreams, though, were her preferred topic. *Especially* the nightmares.

We stared at the photographs on the desk: Rachel Garland knelt beside the remains of Rupert Wreath, playing the role of the bereaved widow. Eleanor Wither tutted unsympathetically. It was New Year's Day. She looked impatient, hungover. Always, she looked impatient, hungover.

"And what happened when you woke up from your nightmare?" she asked. "How did you feel? What could you see?"

"I was on the floor, fully-clothed, in front of the television," I said. "Erect. Upright. Screaming into the darkness. I was trembling violently, drenched in cold sweat and static. And get this, Ellie – I don't even remember turning on the TV."

Eleanor Wither clamped a pencil in-between coffee-stained incisors. She leant back in her chair (deliberately, thoughtfully), the fingers of both hands linked behind her head. We were illuminated by the green glow of the banker's lamp on her desk, the lightbulb hanging limp and naked from the cracked ceiling. She seemed to savour this contemplative pause while she listened to the radio on the bureau behind her – a car accident on the Victoria Embankment, but no confirmed fatalities. With lost interest, she offered an apathetic shrug.

"Your sick dreams are like bad porn," she said. "An abstract echo of contemporary life. You and I are culpable witnesses to the daily déjà vu of humanity's ferocity. Motorway pileups, atomic bombs, ethnic cleansing, royal sex scandals, institutional racism, neverending wars. Violence is everywhere, flourishing in the tall shadow of our intrinsic vitriol. Your dreams reflect that reality, David. Dreams *mean* something."

"I don't believe dreams mean anything," I countered. "They're a tombola of arbitrary objects, false recalls, past experiences, unrealised ideas. Like you suggested – they're a mirror to a blurry reality."

Eleanor Wither simpered. "Perhaps," she said. "But I still believe there's allegory hidden in their unsettling content. Here's my professional opinion. The man in the bowler hat is a messenger from the past or future. Rachel Garland symbolises the present, the duality of purpose and despondency, a metaphorical crossroads. And the television, it seems, conducts memories like electricity. Like a gateway to abandoned and unexplored eventualities. It's obvious, really."

Eleanor Wither's eyes twinkled with the smug satisfaction of a gifted detective who had finally solved a baffling cold case. Most notably, she used the adjective *professional* with devout sincerity. In many ways, I believed she enjoyed assuming the role of cowboy psychiatrist. The act was probably a welcome respite from over four decades behind that news desk, proofing daily tragedies, scything widows and absolving typos. In another life, another reality, she might have been perfect for the part, adept at solving my catalogue of personal issues or, perhaps, those of the entire human race. I was always impressed with her creativity, her ability to conjure meaning out of thin air.

"Let's talk about something else," I suggested.

Eleanor Wither sighed, gazing up at the pipes and airducts humming noisily above.

"Sure," she said, but she sounded disappointed. She anticipated what was coming next.

"Ellie, I'm afraid I haven't got what it takes to write anymore. To write *anything*."

In fact, I couldn't even write the accompanying 300-word article for my photographs. I had the headline: *HOLLYWOOD PRODUCER PUSHED OFF 11TH-FLOOR BALCONY*. I also had Rachel Garland's bizarre testimony.

I even had a photograph of Rupert Wreath, pre-death, taken at a movie premiere six months ago: extortionate suit, un-London tan, white teeth, mane gelled back, bones unbroken. I had everything I needed for the article, but I still couldn't imagine writing it, because that would require a semi-sober effort that wasn't worth thinking about.

I stared at the first draft in my hand: a blank page, worthless and wordless, a reflection of my blank expression. If the article fell through (not an impossibility), I could still sell the grisliest images of Rupert Wreath to my old university friend, Richard Hayes, a perverse collector of macabre objects and souvenirs. I looked at the photographs on the desk and smiled. Yeah. These photos were totally his bag. I squeezed the sheet of paper into a tiny ball and watched the ceiling fan whip the torrid air and cigarette smoke. I pinched the bridge of my nose in-between my thumb and forefinger, aghast with my lack of ability.

"I fear my current role is ebbing away my creative talents," I continued. "Once they're all dulled and dried out, what will be left?"

"Don't be so dramatic," she said. "You're just burnt out, badly dehydrated. This profession can sap the soul. If you want to survive, it's simple – sleep more, drink less, collate material possessions. And no doubles before noon. No exceptions, excluding exceptional circumstances like airports, state funerals, royal weddings and national elections. The intolerable events which necessitate a numbing of the senses. Just find a balance that respects reality without bowing to its dreariness. Earthlings in relationships last longer than the lost and lonely, so adhering to the basics is crucial. Leonard Lynch follows these rules like religion, but I'll concede that he takes a pride in his physical and emotional wellbeing that you evidently lack."

Silhouettes passed the frosted glass door of her office like ghosts. Outside, endless copywriters were hunched over obsolete computers on endless rows of desks, surrounded by stacks of unedited scandals. Like Eleanor Wither, they were tethered to this purgatory (married to their roles, annulled from reality). The muted din of clicking-clacking keyboards and the eternal, high-pitched ring-ring of convulsing telephone receivers punctuated our discourse. I imagined Leonard Lynch behind one of those desks: straight back, relaxed shoulders, writing with pace and elan, working diligently.

"I appreciate the advice, but it feels like all of this death is having an awful effect on me," I said. "It's transforming reality into a nightmare, distorting my memories into a carousel of violence. Every day that darkness is intensifying. It's growing bolder."

"In that case, I prescribe an unpaid holiday," she said. "Explore life beyond the city limits. Jump on the Piccadilly Line tonight and board the first flight from Heathrow to Mexico. In the Seventies, I spent three months on the Gulf of the Yucatán Peninsula. Underground, they have cenotes instead of sewers and tube stations. Above, the Mayan temples stand taller than the council flats in Kensal Green. Out there, nature is so rapacious they can't even build roads or infrastructure. Trees punch through the concrete like the undead clawing out of their coffins." Eleanor Wither balled her fingers into a fist to illustrate this metaphor. "I'm sure it's difficult to imagine how something so ferocious could be so beautiful. Look, you don't even have to fly to Mexico. There's Ireland. France. Germany. Jesus, there's Surrey and Sussex. Just go somewhere that's far away from *here*. The lust to discover new frontiers defines humanity. It's entrenched in our DNA, David. Embrace it. It's how we got this far. It's why we keep going."

"I haven't left London since my childhood. I have a memory of a beach and ocean. Chalk cliffs. Sand. My mother. But I can't picture her face. I can't even be sure if this is a recall or a daydream. It feels too idealistic. Staged like a postcard. I have no idea how many times I've revised this image in my subconscious, trying to construct meaning from its content. I don't ever want to leave the city again, Ellie. From everything I've read in the papers and seen on the TV, out there looks like Hell."

"OK, David," she sighed, growing exhausted. "If you don't want time off, what do you want?"

"Let me write an article on Rachel Garland. 5,000 words in the Sunday features section. If the piece widens in scope, we can serialise it."

We returned our attention to the photographs scattered on the desk. Eleanor Wither picked one of them up.

"What's the angle?" she asked. "She isn't even famous."

"Fame is irrelevant, Ellie. Rachel has a unique gift for verbalising the untold truths about our world. The story doesn't need context. Rachel *is* the story. I feel like the more time I spend with her, the more we'll learn about death, love, money, the movie industry, the human condition. You said it yourself. *Dreams mean something.* I can't explain it, but something's forcing us to collide. I can *feel* it. Call it journalistic intuition. The piece could be dynamite. Trust me. An angle will surface."

Did I really believe this? I wondered. Or did I merely want an excuse to get engulfed in Rachel Garland's orbit? She deluged me with an anomalous sense of hope. I didn't want her to escape. I didn't want her to fade away. *I* didn't want to fade away.

"Please, Ellie," I whispered. "I *need* this. I have ambitions, dreams. Just like Leonard Lynch. I want to achieve something incredible. I want to be remembered. I want the world to know that I existed."

"Welcome to the club," she shrugged. "I suppose you want to write a novel, just like every other fantasist in this building?" When I failed to answer, she laughed, mostly to herself. "How irresistibly vain, David."

Eleanor Wither picked up another photograph. There was a lasting pause, an absence of sound and motion. In the green light, her grey perm and cracked makeup looked like it was chiselled from stone, like the statue of a forgotten war hero eroded by centuries of London drizzle. Even her suit emulsified with the furniture's weathered upholstery. She cleared her throat, reminding us both of her sentience, her tangibility. Her expression softened. It suggested that she felt empathy.

"Sounds interesting," she admitted reluctantly. "Perhaps we'll learn something about your friend in the bowler hat too."

"Perhaps. Perhaps it'll make me famous."

"Perhaps. What's the title of the article?"

"*Sick & Beautiful.*"

"*Sick & Beautiful*?" she repeated.

"Yes," I nodded. "*Sick & Beautiful.*"

"But what does it even mean, David?"

"*Sick & Beautiful*?"

"Yes. *Sick & Beautiful.*"

We took turns saying the words – reciting them, chanting them like a prayer – waiting for their significance to emerge.

CHAPTER
FOUR

"Your picture was in the paper yesterday," I said. "You and Rupert Wreath."

It took me two days to contact Rachel Garland about the article. I called the Casa del Mar from the phone box opposite my flat, midnight West Coast time. I asked the receptionist if she could put me through to a guest named Rachel Garland. As promised, she was at the poolside bar.

"My picture is always in the paper, David. Do I look beautiful?"

"You look like a grieving widow. Sick. Forlorn. Vaguely ethereal. Were you acting?"

"To an extent we're always acting, playing vicarious characters in unknown roles."

The muted fracas of car horns and coastal winds echoed down the line. *Venice Beach, California*. A place I had only seen in magazines and daytime television. I imagined Rachel Garland in her floral dress, looking across the Pacific. Behind her, tall palm trees swaying in front of a halcyon horizon of pastel yellows, riotous teals and flamingo pinks. LA felt like a distant planet. An alternative reality. If Rachel Garland could escape the city with such painless autonomy, crashing through the sky 30,000 feet above, why couldn't I? I admired the sweating droves that fearlessly crammed themselves into unventilated aeroplanes, racing towards far-flung countries and continents I never aspired to visit.

"I spoke to my editor," I said. "She wants me to interview you for a big feature. Pull quotes. Full-bleed photography. The works."

"What's the piece about?"

"If I'm being perfectly honest, I'm not entirely sure. I'm hoping that'll become clearer in time."

"Your editor commissioned an article without a subject? It sounds intriguing, but I'm shooting a movie right now."

"What movie?"

"*Wes Craven's New Nightmare*. Another uncredited role. Perhaps it'll lead onto bigger things."

"Perhaps," I agreed.

But something suggested that Rachel Garland didn't want it to. I wondered if she had the talent for a starring role or if she chose to fade into the periphery. I analysed videotapes of the movies she said she acted in, examining blurred freeze-frames of extras adorned in fake blood and special effects, but I couldn't find her. Her face, her smile, the disruptive angles of her appendages and abdomen – she simply wasn't there. Rachel Garland was a ghost, an evader, a perfect actor. Would she agree to the interview if she knew how I obsessed over this violent footage, inches from the convex glass of the television set? It was impossible to know if my dedication would be misconstrued as addiction.

"How's LA?" I asked.

"Different," she said. "The air is brighter, denser. The ocean is emerald. The beaches are as white as pestled bones. And you can see the sky here. It's lucid cerulean. I haven't seen a single cloud since I arrived. It looks like Paradise. How's the weather in London?"

Outside, rain whipped the glass walls of the phone box. Under the ceaseless deluge, the city skyline and its concrete megaliths looked like a futuristic set piece, the backdrop to a dystopian fever dream.

"Predictably drab," I replied. "When are you flying back? *Are* you flying back?"

There was an agonising pause. Could Rachel Garland, almost 5,500 miles away, detect intonations of desperation in my voice?

"I wanted to talk to you about the man in the bowler hat too," I added. "I've seen him, Rachel."

"My plane from LA lands at London Heathrow Friday morning," she said at last. "Perhaps we can discuss your article then."

"Perhaps," I agreed.

I gave her my address.

She hung up the phone.

4PM, Friday afternoon: Rachel Garland was sat on my sofa, arched over the photo album on her lap. She studied the image of a man cowered in a shower. He was naked, knees tucked into his chest. His hands covered his eyes, framing a mouth ossified in agony. Both wrists were slit, from the base of the palm to the inside of the elbow.

"This is the first dead body I ever photographed," I said.

"Beautiful," she said. "The light– it almost looks *operatic*."

Rachel Garland had spent the last few hours examining

my photo albums. Images of billboards and road signs, derelict houses swathed with graffiti, buskers on crowded avenue corners, homeless people sleeping inside porches, Father's funeral, London commons in autumn, cathedrals, casualties of knife crime and gang violence, Christmas lights in Carnaby Street and Covent Garden, refuse sacks of industrial waste fly-tipped outside a sex shop in Soho, exotic plants in the Victorian glasshouses of Kew Gardens, a burning high-rise, butterflies fluttering above bluebells, fatal car collisions, Egyptian artefacts in the British Museum, televisions stacked in a shopfront window, movie posters in cinema foyers, unconscious junkies on park benches, commuters descending tube station escalators, cloud-throttled horizons. These weren't just photographs. They were evidence that my memories weren't delusions. They proved that I was really here, that my life really occurred.

Punctuated by bumps of coke snorted off the corner of my expired credit card, I exhibited these photo albums with surging intensity and enthusiasm, logging Rachel Garland's observations. I urged her to express herself as she turned their acetate pages, confident that these images had the power to evoke a childhood event, an unsung perspective, a forgotten recall, a unique hook for the article.

I sat opposite her, pen and notepad in-hand, waiting for a reaction. I felt the stillness, a subtle tension, like a breakthrough was imminent. But every time Rachel Garland spoke, I was unable to distinguish between unbridled brilliance and drug-induced blather.

"What makes us human?" she asked. "It's not the body – it's the memories that we leave in our wake. They're like passengers diving off the deck of a sinking cruise ship. They float on an ocean, like a message in a bottle, until somebody finds them, to be remembered or forgotten. But where do the lost souls migrate? Do they drift through reality, walking among us, utterly imperceptible, desperate to make contact? They can't all wash upon the shores of Paradise. These are the questions that we have to contemplate, David."

I wrote this down, aware that it might mean absolutely nothing.

"The man in the shower, in this photograph," she said, tapping her finger on its glossy surface. "What was his name?"

"I have no idea," I admitted after a short pause. "He was a student at my university. He died in the flat directly above my own. I don't know who he was, where he came from, who he wanted to be, the emotions that haunted him."

"This information matters, David," she said. "Names. Ages. Postcodes. NI numbers. You see a body, the violent repetition of existence, its inevitable finale. I don't. I see letters on headstones, family portraits, carbonised smiles, houses lining suburban streets, nursery walls decorated with sentient choo-choo trains and cartoon animals. Possessions, memories, favourite things. They all give death its purpose. They prove that we live in the future, present and past. That we are fluid, eternal. Jesus, David. No wonder you're so sick, so shaken. You've been living without context."

Fluid, eternal, I wrote. *Without context*. This assertion, these words, felt significant.

"I'm living without information, *without context*," I repeated. "It's why I don't know who I am, what I'm doing, where I'm going, why I'm here. I don't know the purpose of this interview, the core themes of the article, its audience, its publication date, the hard deadline. I've ignored detail my entire life. And, as a result, I know almost nothing about myself."

"We rarely do, David."

We had more coke. Rachel lit another cigarette. The wheels in the tape deck rotated lethargically.

"I don't know who you are either, Rachel."

Apparently moved by this admission, Rachel Garland stood, walked towards me and began to trace her fingertips over the topography of my face – the sunken eyes, the pub car park scars that decorated my cheeks and forehead – searching for similarities and disparities between my anatomy and that of the corpses in my photographs, evaluating if constant exposure to a violent world had caused my tissue to imitate its bibliography of lacerations, the wounds of secular stigmata. Satisfied, she tilted her head backwards and peeled off her hair, revealing the coarse black stubble beneath. She smiled, placing the wig on my own head. She stroked it lovingly, tenderly, like the tresses of a childhood doll. It smelt like sweat and cigarettes.

"Do you know what I love most about acting?" she said. "It's the liberty to alter my appearance, *my essence*, in seconds. Being somebody else is addictive. That's why I'm endlessly evolving in small ways, acclimatising to my surroundings. Nobody truly knows who I am, David. They never will. My anonymity is how I survive."

Rachel Garland gripped my hands and guided my fingers over her scalp. This gesture, I surmised, was an act of trust or, perhaps, another test, another psychological experiment. She closed her eyes, inhaling the flat's bouquet of mildew and fag smoke. I watched her, paralysed and captivated. Like a butterfly devolving into a pupae, there was an undeniable beauty in her debased physical state.

"Every day we're somebody different, somebody new," she continued. "Trillions of microscopic cells dying and regenerating at inconceivable rates. Our potential is limitless, David. We never know who or what we'll metamorphosise into next. We can be anybody or anything that we want to be."

Our potential is limitless.

What a line, I thought, scribbling it on my notepad. *What conviction*. In this moment, in this scene, I believed in Rachel Garland. I believed in the article. Jesus. I even believed in *myself*, in the possibility that I could charter a blueprint of meaning for my own life. A map towards Paradise. I was enamoured by her hope, her honesty. I felt compelled to tell her the truth too. Tears fractured my vision. I steadied my breathing, composing myself. I was ready. I wanted to confess everything.

"I've seen your death, Rachel," I whispered. "I dreamed about you the night before we met. You and the man in the bowler hat."

Rachel Garland smiled. That was her reaction to this revelation. *She smiled*. As if she had already experienced this moment.

"Tell me how I die," she said, holding the tape deck microphone to her lips like a consummate professional. "Do humans like me die quietly, in old age, surrounded by our loved ones? Or do we die naked and young, exhibited like a painting, in front of an audience unable to swerve its gaze?"

"You were behind *him*, in a room, on a bed, covered in blood. You smiled and waved. And you were dead."

"But that's impossible, David." Rachel Garland leaned closer, pressed her warm cheek against mine and whispered: "Do you know what the man in the bowler hat told me? He said it's possible to escape death. That we can live forever, like him, over and over and over again. He promised to show us."

"That's ridiculous." I laughed, even though this conversation, this notion, didn't amuse me. "How can you *escape death*?"

"That's his secret, David. He said to have faith in the script. That our roles would become clearer over time."

I held her tightly. Until this moment, I always acknowledged an irrefutable truth – *I'm going to die*. We're all going to die. Every eulogist would become a corpse, every coffin-maker a coffin-filler. Everyone, allegedly, except Rachel Garland and I. And the man in the bowler hat. The prospect was too much. It felt dizzying, suffocating. The possibility of eternal life, the unending, terrified me. *But what an angle*, I thought. Would Eleanor Wither believe a word of it? Part of me didn't care. And then I remembered our conversation on New Year's Day.

You and I are culpable witnesses to the daily déjà vu of humanity's ferocity. Violence is everywhere, flourishing in the tall shadow of our intrinsic vitriol. Your dreams reflect that reality, David. Dreams mean *something.*

"It's probably just a dream," I replied, mostly to myself. "And dreams probably mean nothing."

Probably.

PART TWO
PURPOSE

CHAPTER
FIVE

Rachel Garland leans across the backseat of the taxi, presses her cold cheek against mine and says: "I hate the book. It's like bad porn."

I silently absorb this statement (both sentences, its cruel monosyllables) as we crawl in the traffic towards Charing Cross Road. It's Boxing Day, almost one year since Rachel Garland and I first met, on the night Rupert Wreath tumbled out of the black sky.

Tonight, we're sparring over *Sick & Beautiful*. Always, it seems, we're sparring over *Sick & Beautiful*.

A sensitive chapter. An intimate truth. An inaccuracy or embellishment. Rachel Garland regards the final draft – which ballooned from a 5,000-word editorial into a 270,000-word nonfiction novel – as an atrocity. She sinks back into her seat, lights another cigarette. I stare at the printouts of *Sick & Beautiful* in the open briefcase on my lap. A4. 7.5pt. Calibri. Single-spaced. My address (*Eden Estate, Loughborough Road, Brixton, London*) centralised under my name. These elements (the formatting, my authorial credit) inundate me with an unfamiliar sense of fulfilment. Rachel, however, doesn't want this book to exist. To her, the notion of publishing a novel is a narcissistic impulse. A luxury for the white, the male, the privileged. But it's more than that. *Sick & Beautiful* isn't just an exercise in indulgence or entitlement. To her, it's an abomination. A violation she doesn't want me to forget.

"Some elements really make me cringe," she adds with playful disdain. "Especially the dialogue and sex scenes. They just don't feel realistic."

"Dialogue is difficult," I reply defensively. "Sex scenes? Almost impossible. I did the best I could."

Do you know why Rachel is acting so provocative, so spiteful? It's because the unthinkable has happened. I didn't just finish *Sick & Beautiful*. I received a letter from Paradise Publishing, a literary agency based on Cannon Street. Their director wants to meet me at 9AM tomorrow to sign a book deal immediately. Isn't it swell? I want to collapse in tearful euphoria. The restless nights, infinite redrafts and laborious interview transcriptions. All of it. It might all be worth it.

I found the good news on Christmas Day, buried under the usual tide of junk mail. But there is a detail in the letter that disturbs me. Here it is – the director's name is *Rupert Wreath*. Extraordinary, isn't it? I'm not entirely sure how to take it. It's utterly thrown me. For now, I've decided to ignore it. *Probably nothing*, I rationalise, determined to mute these anxieties. For one evening, I want to cave into happiness. I want to celebrate success. I want to believe that my dreams can become material.

"*Sick & Beautiful* could be a bestseller," I say optimistically. "It could make us famous, Rachel."

"Perhaps," she says, watching the hailstones melt into raindrops on the window. "Perhaps."

Whenever I make this argument, I always recall her statement: *My anonymity is how I survive.*

Fame was never Rachel Garland's ambition. She treats the details of her life like an anthology of secrets hidden behind a locked door. She doesn't want the world, with its cruel eyes, to peek behind it. She was willing, perhaps even content, to be interviewed for the article, but a novel is an entirely different reality. It has a permanence, *an immortality*, that disturbs her. I smile. Despite these vocal resentments, I'm confident that Rachel will soften her vitriol.

Tonight we're going to the Prince Charles, a former porno theatre on the corner of Lisle Street and Leicester Place that screens low-budget horror films, grindhouse marathons and badly dubbed martial arts movies. Rachel Garland hates public spaces, assuming that someone is always watching her, but the Prince Charles, with its perpetually vacant seats, antisocial hours and poorly-lit alcoves, provides the seclusion she craves. We share some of our most idyllic memories in the PC: that John Carpenter triple in May (*The Fog*, *Prince of Darkness*, *They Live*), the Paul Verhoeven double in April (*RoboCop* and *Total Recall*), and, of course, the 70mm production of *Braindead* back in January (the night I told Rachel I loved her). Gripped by the gore and nudity inside the margins of the projector screen, our differences always dissipate in the living tissue of this sacred place.

"When your literary agent asks you what *Sick & Beautiful* is about, what it means, what will you tell him, David? What's the blurb? What's the elevator pitch?"

"I'm going to tell him that it's a saga about hope," I say. "A universal fairytale that examines love and death. Humanity's eternal war with itself."

"How painfully unoriginal," she sighs. "Isn't every story about love and death? Give your readers something unexpected. Cleanse their palates with apathy, so they feel nothing at all. What could be more refreshing? It takes courage to reject love. Only truly gifted authors can escape its platitudes."

"I disagree. Love and death are the only things we collectively understand. We all hope to love. To feel loved. And we're all dying. Dying from the day we are born. It's the only thing humanity has in common. It's part of our struggle. It always has been. People *want* to feel something. They want to relate."

"You make me laugh, David. There's something beautiful about your naivety, your blind belief in the human race." Rachel Garland rests her head on my shoulder. And then she says this: "He visited me again, David. He's back."

As we pass the radioactive billboards of Piccadilly Circus, joining the slow-mo lumber of traffic wheezing up Coventry and Wardour Street, I feel a coldness, *a weightlessness*, envelop me. Rachel doesn't need to elaborate who *he* is. *He* needs no introductions.

"Where did you see him?" I finally ask.

"In another dream," she says. "I was trapped inside a crashed car, dripping with blood. He smiled and took a photograph of me. *Everybody* was taking photographs of me. You were there too, David."

I frown, registering this unsettling information. The man in the bowler hat forever roams in the periphery of our nightmares, but I constantly wonder (no– I *fear*) when he will manifest again in our waking reality. Is he finally making a comeback? *What a downer*, I think. I want to scream. But when we pull up outside the Prince Charles, my disposition, my scoured spirit, feels instantly revitalised.

CLIVE BARKER 35mm TRILOGY: CANDYMAN, HELL-RAISER & NIGHTBREED shimmers on the bulb-studded readograph above the cinema's marquee. The cabbie draws his handbrake and points to the meter. I pay him with a fist of shrapnel and step out the taxi, into the rain. The deafening hullabaloo of car horns, bad language, exhaust fumes and human motion shrouds us as we run into the foyer.

In the queue for the bar, I note that Rachel Garland is shoeless. Her left heel, perhaps cut from a shard of cracked glass on the pavement, gently weeps blood onto the foyer's scarlet carpet. I ignore this detail. Now, I always ignore this detail (the barefoot thing). It's all part of her bit, the uniform of her personality. It's intrinsic, expected. Rachel smiles, holds my hand. I smile too, feeling a renewed sense of hope. The man in the bowler hat? He's irrelevant. Me, on the other hand? I'm hunky dory. I'm on the verge of authorial stardom.

"The first print of *Sick & Beautiful* is only the start," I continue, vocalising this buoyancy. "Then there's second, third, fourth editions. New artwork. Forewords by contemporaries. Translations in French, German, Italian, Spanish, Portuguese, Mandarin, Cantonese, Arabic. Audiobooks. Interviews and editorials in global newspapers and magazines. Movie adaptations and TV miniseries. The UK premiere would need to be hosted right here at the PC, of course. And who knows what else? *Our potential is limitless.* Your words, Rachel."

"But what if people don't *get* the book?" she says. "Not just your writing style. The story itself."

I sweat as fear looms over me like the shadow of a crashing zeppelin. It's the fear of everything that I am, the shame of everything that I am not. It manifests in every sound, every surface, every quizzical expression. What if Rachel Garland's right? What if *Sick & Beautiful* really is *bad porn*? The probability is unbearable. If I hate the book too, even intuitively, I refuse to admit it. Not until it fails unconditionally. Burying my distress, I grin as I order our tickets with two medium popcorns (two thirds sweet, one third salt) and two double gin and tonics.

"Meet me in the back row," Rachel Garland whispers. "It'll be easier to take the drugs there."

I nod, but when I turn around she has vanished.

I descend the staircase and enter Screen One. Inside, the projector casts an eerie glow over the theatre like a haunted lighthouse. Every row is virtually empty, only a dozen seats occupied with the silhouettes of dozing pissheads and nightshift workers. I note the vacuity, the musk of scorched dust that clots the stale air. Rachel waves from the centre of the deserted back row. I walk towards her, set our drinks in the cupholders and sink into my seat.

"*Candyman* starts in 10 minutes," she says. "An incredible picture. Virginia Madsen carries it, in my opinion. She is a rare talent in this genre."

"Clive Barker is a rare talent too," I say, racking up two lines of coke on the cover of my notepad. "Authors are rarely able to adapt their novels, but *Candyman*, *Hellraiser* and *Nightbreed* are sublime. All of them. I pray I have the flair to pen the screenplay for *Sick & Beautiful* when the time inevitably comes. I always believed it had big-picture potential."

"Clive Barker also has vision," she says, chewing a handful of popcorn. "Drive and focus. I read your final draft of *Sick & Beautiful*. The prose is riddled with adverbs, overcomplicated synonyms. It kills the flow. And the story has no thematic threads holding it together. You were happy to jettison plot points and structure because you'd rather talk about being a novelist than actually writing one, but I'm not telling you anything you don't already know." She pauses. "Why are you crying, David?"

"I'm not crying," I reply, tears on the cusp of rolling down my cheeks. I lean forward, snort both lines of coke, neck my gin and tonic in two acidic gulps and storm out of the theatre, into the gents toilets. Experiencing the abrupt uptick of the sniff, I unload my frustrations on the man facing the urinal behind me.

"Rachel Garland has a catalogue of the crippling inadequacies that define the marrow of my being," I begin, talking with volume. "But she simply doesn't understand the pressures of writing a novel. She thinks I'm some kind of anti-artist. A pro in maladroit dialogue and vacant metaphors. A pretentious pound shop peacock, incapacitated by his pompous, self-imposed fallacies. Clive Barker understands his genre, its intricate rules and ribbons. And he isn't afraid to embrace the notion that we are all victims of reality. That the human body is a frail, flawed machine, shabbily conceived by a creator who has abandoned us. He accepts the cosmic casino and its broken logic. He accepts death happens to us all. So, where am *I* going wrong? *Sick & Beautiful* asks the same questions too, but I'm not sure if it answers them. I'm not sure if I understand the medium, the genre or audience. And in writing this novel, I've learned nothing about myself. It didn't absolve the devils that plague me."

The man behind me patiently listens to this meandering tirade, tutting sympathetically, waiting for me to reach the crux of the argument. When he realises that there's no punchline, that I'm done talking, *that that's it*, he disintegrates into a fit of laughter. He slaps his palm on the wall, practically choking, groping for breath.

"Don't be so dramatic," he says. "I used to be like you, David – lost, devoid of purpose. That was before I knew what I know now. Before I accepted myself and the world around me. Until you do the same, you won't know the truth about Rachel Garland or yourself. The galaxy will remain a complete mystery to you. That's why you see ghosts every time you look in the mirror. You're sleepwalking in a terminal dream."

I hear his footsteps behind me, walking towards the sinks, the sound of running water.

"I've seen you attempt this life before, over and over and over again," he continues. "You won't believe me, but you and I have had this conversation a thousand times, in this dreary lav, in this time and space. And you never listen. You never do things differently. You never *fucking*– I'm sorry, David. I don't mean to rant. It isn't your fault. You're following the script, reciting your lines, just like you're supposed to. Just like you always do. This is your role. And you're doing good, padre. You're putting on a real show out there."

I turn my head so I can see him. He's facing away from me, leant over the sink. He squirts soap into his palms, conjures it into lather, rinses, squirts, lathers, rinses, over and over again. He whistles a broken tune as he does this. A discordant melody that causes the droplets of cocaine sweat on my upper lip and forehead to turn cold. He is washing his hands so frantically, so ferociously, they begin to bleed, causing the foam to turn pink. He composes himself, clears his throat, brushes the lint off the shoulders of his overcoat. He's acting like a real person, but the movements look extrinsic, badly practised. Perhaps he is drunk and drugged up like everybody else in this city, woefully attempting to appear human. He then adjusts his bowler hat, stroking the tendrils of hair that protrude beneath it. I can't see his face. I can only imagine it – anaemic, blistered, hideous, eyeless, grinning with acute pain.

"I haven't seen you since the accident," I say, attempting to sound conversational. "Rachel told me you visited her last night. And now you're here, in this bathroom, in this moment, in real life." I pause. "If you have something important to tell us, why not just say it? Tell me who you really are."

"Think of me as a messenger," he says. "An emissary from Paradise. I can take you there if you want, David. You and your friends."

A fly crawls across the back of his neck and disappears under the collar of his overcoat. I shudder, suddenly feeling chilly, detached from the scene.

"Enough of the bullshit," I say (bored by the riddles, emboldened by the coke). "Tell me why you killed Rupert Wreath."

"So we could meet Rachel Garland. So that we can be together in Paradise. All of us. It feels like I've been sailing through your memories for aeons trying to find her. Sunlit beaches, hospital wards, derelict hotels, labyrinthian corridors, the insides of crashed cars. It's been like a bad dream, but it can't last forever. Surely not? That would be too cruel. It's a vulgar joke, too insidious even for my tastes. But I still have faith in the script. I have faith that, in the end, it'll all work out."

The man in the bowler hat steps behind me, coughing, tittering. I can smell him now. The aromas of decaying flowers, rancid meat, medical waste, stagnant downpour. I feel diseased in his presence.

"Rachel doesn't believe in the book, but she believes in me, David. She still believes in Paradise."

"You're not real," I say confidently. "You're just a paper boy from my traumatised subconscious."

"How can you be so sure?" he asks. "Perhaps I'm real and *you're* the hallucination."

"Perhaps," I concede.

"Probably nothing, right?"

"Probably."

That's what I thought. Until next time, David."

When I turn around, the figure has vanished. The fetor lingers, but is this enough to prove that the man in the bowler hat is anything other than a manifestation of mine and Rachel's dilapidated imaginations?

I approach the mirror. I loosen my tie. I unbutton the collar. I wash my hands. I splash cold water over my face. I rub it on the back of my neck.

In the reflection, I look at the urinal he used. It's stained with streaks of black claret.

By the time I return to the theatre, the closing scenes of *Candyman* are playing out on the big screen (Virginia Madsen's violent transformation from female victim to male antagonist), but Rachel Garland has dematerialised. Where has she gone? I wonder. I check my pocket watch. Somehow I've been absent for almost 90 minutes. I finish the second gin and tonic as the credits roll, pick up my briefcase and exit the cinema.

I feel an ache of relief when I spot Rachel stood outside the foyer, smoking, watching a traffic accident transpire. On Cranbourne Street, a pedestrian, apparently hit by a turning night bus, drips blood onto the pavement. A small group of tourists have gathered around her to take photographs. The injured pedestrian looks blindly into their flashing cameras – delirious, surprised to be launched into such a vulnerable and communal dilemma. The violence looks unreal, like a scene in a movie. The tourists don't help her. We don't help her. She bleeds. They film. We watch. This is our roles.

These tourists, though. Where do they get off? They gravitate in dense throngs to ogle the most mundane scenery. Red phone boxes glazed with the numbers of call girls, rent boys and sex gabber hotlines. Bobbies and beefeaters in their spiffed-up titfers and bronze-buttoned uniforms. Hackney carriages and their flat-capped drivers dry-retching fag and exhaust fumes into the atmosphere. And all those piss-tinted, pigeon-swamped statues and monuments. Tourists sprint borough to borough, tinned inside gridlocked tubes and taxis, snapping photos next to these garbage landmarks. What's the appeal? I just don't get it. I just don't get *them*.

Rachel Garland stares at me, apparently concerned.

"What's the matter, David? You look deserted."

"I saw him, Rachel."

She smiles.

"What did he tell you?"

"That you never believed in the book. Implicitly, I think I always knew that you wanted it to be a catastrophe. You turned every interview into a ritual humiliation. You tried to vandalise my dreams for your abstruse motives. But why? Were you frightened to reveal yourself to the world? Or were you frightened to reveal yourself to me?"

Rachel Garland opens her hand to the sky and lets the rain collect in her palm like a polluted tarn, contemplating my question. Of this, she is a master – watching, waiting, writing the perfect dialogue in her head.

"Sometimes our dreams are incompatible," she says. "This might sound cruel, but we only ever shared one trait – the fact that we were both alone. It felt nice not eating alone. Not sleeping alone. Not going to the movies, just me. But for you and I, the future is a different place. A different reality. Your dreams are crystallised in an adrift past. They start and end here. And whenever I'm with you, I hear their strangled echoes reverberating. I feel like I can't breathe. I feel like my wings are broken."

This is where we differ. Rachel Garland is like a beautiful bird. She wants to migrate to warmer climes. She needs liberty, autonomy. It's the way she's wired – no wires at all. Conversely, I'm wired all wrong. I'm shackled. Sick, trapped, chained, tethered. London is a cage. It's an asylum. Even if somebody left its turnstiles open, I'd still be noosed to its gallows.

We only ever shared one trait – the fact that we were both alone.

I want to write this down. And then I want to vomit. I want this city to swallow me. My veneer is on the verge of cracking. I can *feel* it. I can feel myself summersaulting into blissful, self-indulgent pity, so I break her gaze and nod towards the congested high street. I don't have the tenacity to address her arcane statement, but I refuse to let her register my turmoil. I'm determined to save my dignity (assuming this still exists).

"Let's jump in a taxi," I say, summoning an untapped reservoir of equanimity. "We can discuss what chapters you're dissatisfied with at the flat. I can relay any feedback to my agent tomorrow. Perhaps there's flex to rework certain passages if you're willing to grant me a candid interview, but this could be beyond my control. The directors may believe the book is ready for the presses. Why else would they want to talk to me so urgently? Any amends now may compromise that polished product."

I open the back door of one of the taxis queued up on Little Newport Street, but Rachel Garland walks on, marching barefoot towards the floating lanterns of Chinatown.

"I must politely decline," she shouts over her shoulder. "It's a long walk to Paradise. And I need to keep moving forward – into the future and the past. When you find yourself, perhaps we'll find each other again."

Rachel Garland takes one look back – the smile is reticent and toothless, somehow both heartless and tender – and hopscotches the puddles with ethereal elegance. When she disappears, I slide into the idling taxi.

"Loughborough Road, Brixton," I say to the cabbie. "I need to sober up in time for my big meeting tomorrow morning."

I open my briefcase and slide a copy of *Sick & Beautiful* through the plastic barrier that divides us.

"I'm publishing a novel. I'm going to be an author. They'll interview me on the television. I'll crawl inside it, through the glass, and hide there forever."

The cabbie studies me in the rear-view mirror before turning his eyes back to the road. Illuminated in the glow of passing headlights, I watch tears cascade down the cheeks of my weeping reflection.

"Rachel Garland taught me how to cry. She taught me about true love."

Confusion, disillusion. Cabbies have seen it all before (in the back of the taxi, and outside of it). There is no advice to give. Polite indifference will suffice. Wordlessly, he turns on the meter, turns up the radio and swerves into the immortal traffic.

A newsreader broadcasts today's global disasters. A fatal school shooting in New York. Wars blooming in Africa and the Middle East. Earthquakes in the Pacific Ocean. Pubs permanently shutting their doors up and down the UK. Chaos and violence, it seems, infects every corner of our planet. And the death toll is rising. Day and night, it never ceases its ascent.

I slump sideways across the seats and close my eyes. But I can't sleep. I sit up again and stare at the architecture of Waterloo Bridge, Elephant & Castle, Oval and Camberwell until the cabbie pulls up outside Eden Estate on Loughborough Road. I pay the fare, step back into the rain.

I pull out my pocket watch. It's Father's pocket watch. I inherited it from him after he died nearly two winters ago. Whenever I look at its dial, I don't think of Father's life – I think of Father's death. I slide it back inside my overcoat. It's almost 2AM.

I wave as the taxi accelerates towards Herne Hill.

The cabbie doesn't wave back.

Presumably, he didn't see me.

CHAPTER SIX

"Death," said Father. "It happens to us all. Even you, David."

He reminded me of this uncomfortable fact from an early age. The last time Father recited these words, he used the vase of dying daffodils on the nightstand next to his hospital bed as a convenient metaphor.

"Nothing represents life quite like a bouquet of flowers," he hissed through his oxygen mask. "They blossom into something beautiful. And then, eventually, inevitably, sicken, wither and die."

We were in the cancer ward of St George's Hospital in Tooting. I kept staring at the gold crucifix around Father's neck, the mark it seared into the skin on his chest. Father started wearing it, almost religiously, after he got *the bad news*. His neighbour and oldest friend, Abraham Maher, also told me that my old man was spending more and more time in the hospital's chapel. When I cornered Father about it, he played it down.

"It's just in case," he said, lighting another cigarette. "I feel an inexplicable peace in that chapel. I can close my eyes and picture Paradise."

And that's where we left it.

The rest of the time we talked about the dire weather, my dead-end job at *The Daily Sun*, his various disappointments (with the world, with myself) and his Persian, Osiris, who Abraham agreed to foster. Father had an uncharacteristic affection for Osiris and demanded that he was taken care of when he left us. We all knew that Father wasn't coming home. Not this time. I decided his imminent death was the perfect opportunity to tell him that I loved him. Before it was too late.

As I said the words, *I love you, Dad*, his face scrunched up with unconcealed aversion.

"Save it, David. Jesus. Everything isn't about you. I'm the one on my deathbed, dying."

"Sorry," I whispered.

"Don't be sorry. Just listen. I've got something to say."

"A confession?"

"If you like." Father winced as he pulled down his oxygen mask. "Every time you have sex," he said, "it could be the last time you have sex. Don't ever forget that, David."

Father sobbed as he remembered the last time he had sex.

"She was beautiful. An angel. She–" He stopped. "Jesus, David," he snapped. "Aren't you writing this down?"

I pulled the notepad and tape deck out of my briefcase. As soon as I clicked the *REC.* button, Father continued detailing this graphic sex scene. It turned out to be the story of my conception. He was talking about *her*. About Mother. Yeah. He really opened up.

"She put my pocket watch on the mantlepiece," he said. "And when she knelt down, naked, I forgot about the awful things I did in the war, in Paradise. I remember how the morning light poured through the window, illuminating her face like a death mask. She looked unreal, like a hologram."

Father pointed at the cloud, thundering away on the other side of the window.

"Can you imagine it, David? *Sunshine.* It felt like hope. Your mother. She was sick. But she was beautiful. *Unbelievably* beautiful."

And so it went on.

The inaugural tenderness of this unprotected sex scene sounded something like true love. But these details quickly degenerated into morphine-hazed delusions, crude gynaecological diagrams, fevered gyrations. Even now, I'm not certain why he felt inclined to share this information. Was he confident that, over time, the subtle metaphors of his narrative would become more poignant? It's impossible to know, but I've learned to treasure the tale of my sweating creation with a detached fondness. Despite the explicit content and gaping plotholes, Father's story confirmed my existence. And it's the only time I can recall him talking about Mother with such strokes of affectionate, fuzzy-eyed reverence.

Two cassettes and one 20-deck of cigarettes later, Father curled up into an embryonic ball and shut his tired eyes.

"That cloud followed us from Paradise," he whispered. "Don't ever try to find it, David. No matter what *he* says. No matter what *he* promises. And don't forget to feed Osiris. He's a very special kitty."

"Who's *he*?" I asked.

But it was too late. The tension gently floated from Father's face, revealing a forgotten softness. His breathing became thinner, shallower, and then it stopped completely. All that remained was the sound of the rain. Weeping, I photographed Father from the foot of his hospital bed.

The next morning, an appropriately glum solicitor notified me that Father wished to be cremated (repackaged for eternity, incinerated at over 1,000 degrees Celsius). He then handed me a shoebox containing his war medals, his pocket watch and the keys to his Loughborough Road flat. A shoebox in its own right, but one with a fully-paid mortgage.

There was also a note.

David,

Scatter my ashes outside the city. Beyond the reach of the cloud. Take me back home. I still believe in Paradise.

Until next time.
Yours sincerely,
David.

Where is home if it isn't the city? I wondered. It suddenly occurred to me that I hardly knew my father. Who was this man before his war? Did I only ever meet a carapace of bitter memories?

Two hours after Father's funeral in Lambeth Cemetery (Abraham Maher, Osiris and myself the only mourners in attendance), I pushed the crucifix, medals and pocket watch across the counter of a pawn shop on Brixton Road. With Father tucked under my arm in his urn, his new ceramic condo, the pawnbroker examined these artefacts. They listlessly twinkled beneath the neon gleam of the *CASH-4-GOLD* sign above the door.

"Condolences for your loss," he said as he filled my palms with a roll of tens and some dulled shrapnel. It wasn't much (the medals were silver and the rood mostly nickel), but it was enough to pick up a gram of coke (*good* coke) and a new television set for my new flat – superior in inches, depth and definition to Father's obsolete appliance.

I decided to keep the pocket watch, though. It ticks. It tocks. It has a face with an unwavering objectivity that I found prepossessing. There was something admirable about its stoic disposition, the weight of this object in my hand.

Pleased, I popped it inside my overcoat and walked out into the rain, whistling a broken tune.

CHAPTER
SEVEN

That cloud wept relentlessly during Father's funeral and outside the pawn shop.

Just like tonight.

Just like always.

But it's not just the pocket watch that conjures these dour memories. It happens every time I unlock my letterbox in the lobby and thumb through the post addressed to my expired Father, my namesake, Mr David Temple. Insurance scams, unpaid bills, badly punctuated leaflets for cowboy builders, cruises, stray pets, stray people, Jesus junkies promising exclusive access to neverending Paradise. Briefcase between my feet, I toss these letters into the trash, where they belong, with wilful contempt.

Tonight, the lobby's discoloured wallpaper and furniture has a baleful ambiance. In the corner, a moulting Christmas tree strangled with fairy lights flashes with ominous regularity, causing shadows to dance with sinister intent. My eerie encounter with the man in the bowler hat has left me feeling vulnerable. I laugh nervously, striving to console myself. And then I discover something significant – a letter with *David T.* penned on its beige envelope. I rip it open and pull out the note folded inside.

David,
Have you lost your mobile or disconnected your landline? You're like a phantom. Pellucid, impossible to summon.
Meet me at the Boneyard. 10pm. Wednesday. Private party. Free bar. And an irresistible surprise.
Please find your invite enclosed.
Use the East Entrance. And don't be late.
We have lots to talk about.

Unsigned, undated, this is how the letter ends. But I recognise the handwriting. And only one person I know calls the Natural History Museum in South Kensington the *Boneyard* – my old university friend, Richard Hayes. Richard and I haven't spoken since Rachel Garland altered our realities forever. I did, however, make a point of posting him a copy of *Sick & Beautiful* with a note of my own: *You said I'd never finish the book. Enjoy it. And never doubt me again. Sincerely, Bestselling Author David Temple.* Until now, I was happy having the last word, the last laugh. But Richard Hayes, it appears, has finally responded.

I dip my hand back into the envelope and pull out an iridescent invite the size of a business card. The flickering fairy lights shimmer on its surface like stars on a silver ocean. The invite offers a simple promise (four words): *ONE ADMISSION TO PARADISE*. I slip it into the breast pocket of my overcoat.

As Richard Hayes presupposed, I did misplace my mobile (I threw it, quite deliberately, into the depths of a storm drain) and I haven't paid my landline in months, so I exit the lobby and run to the phone box opposite my block of flats. Wind and rain wallop its glass panels as I dump a handful of coppers into the coin slot and unhook the receiver. I dial the number for Richard Hayes's apartment, Arcadia Gardens on Clapham Common.

The intentionally seductive, playful language of his letter has irritated me. Richard Hayes knows that I would struggle to resist his offer to talk, but I'm determined not to attend his precious party. A conversation on the phone, I convince myself, will be adequate. For all I know, his invite has been sat in my letterbox for weeks, the cocktails and candlesticks of his soirée glugged and extinguished.

When he doesn't pick up the phone after several protracted rings, I hang up and dial for the front desk of his apartment complex. When the concierge picks up, I ask him to put me through to Richard Hayes.

"Tell Richard it's David Temple on the line. Yes. It's urgent."

These is a long pause before the concierge takes me off hold.

"I'm afraid that Mr Hayes isn't answering his intercom. In fact, I haven't seen him for a few days. He's quite a distinctive fellow, as I'm certain you already know. He's probably shooting at the studio or attending another casting."

"That's very interesting," I say, hanging up the phone. I sigh, almost relieved that I don't have to deal with Richard Hayes or his tedious psychological games. I'm unsurprised that he would lie to his concierge about his profession, feigning his dream of making movies is a reality instead of a passive fantasy. But he isn't a director. Or a producer. Or a screenwriter. Richard Hayes is just another King's College dropout, pursuing his hollow aspirations. He is an actor playing a role. A socialite feeding an unhealthy obsession with movie stars. Fearless idealists like Rachel Garland.

I check for change in the coin return slot (empty) before running back across the street into the 24-hour cafe. I buy a polystyrene cup of coffee and add two large spoons of sugar. Absently stirring, I look through the window, contemplating the premature brightness of the night.

It's strange how it's never pitch black in London. Even when the moonlight is blotted out by the cloud, there's always streetlights, headlamps, the scarlet-teal flutter of ambulances and police cars. It's coarse, constant. Humans don't mind, but it drives the nocturnal population doolally. No wonder the pigeons and foxes are so jittery. They're on edge from decades of sleep deprivation. These night critters see the things we do when we think no-one else is watching, but the fauna have still adapted nicely. It's more than you can say about the flora. It can't keep up with humankind. The tempo is too savage. Too self-indulgent and destructive. While we repair ourselves with plasters, crutches, splints, stitches, headplates, pacemakers, porcelain teeth, glass eyeballs and syringes of morphine and collagen, the plant life swoons and wallows, bored to death with the world we've relegated. Soon, it will just be us, the cloud and the rubble of civilisation. We can't stop it now. It's inevitable. It's no longer a question of *if* – the question is *when*.

In the grip of these bizarre ruminations, I linger by the window, watching the hailstones dissolve back into raindrops.

The storm is really expressing itself. It bullies, bulges, turns uglier. I can imagine Rachel Garland floating in that sky, tiptoeing on the surface of floodwater. She's a totem summoned by the squall. She's a ballerina on the bitumen boardwalks. Rachel performs. Disembodied, dancing and dreaming.

"There's no use waiting for the tempest to pass," says the woman behind the counter. She nods to the television mounted in the corner of the cafe. It's an image of a weatherman frowning in front of a weather map.

"*There'll be no peace tonight,*" says the weatherman. "*No peace for the foreseeable future. Looks like the cloud is here to stay, David.*"

I step back outside and walk across the forecourt of Eden Estate. The cars parked closest to the building are surrounded by empty tinnies, broken glass and the fetid viscera of binbags hurled from the balconies of the most hostile tenants. Two windscreens have been smashed by raining spirits bottles. I gaze up at my second-storey flat. A hard glow radiates from my sitting room window. *How odd*, I think. I don't remember leaving any lights on when I left for the Prince Charles this evening.

"Probably nothing," I mutter.

And then I gasp, dropping my briefcase and coffee onto the wet concrete. I cup my hands around my eyes to shield them from the rain. My jaw cramps, forcing my lips to curl with stark consternation.

Somebody is pressing their face against the inside of my window. A white mask, a smile gaped open like a septic orifice. Two hands are cupped around the dented eyesockets, mimicking my own posture like an alien imitating human motion. The fingers and arms are grotesquely long, like the legs of a giant spider. The body bulges and pulsates, shifting out of its anthropomorphic shape with awful fluency. I have no doubt every movement is part of a provocative performance, like an animal ballooning its anatomy to accentuate its sexual opulence. Sensing my terror (*feeding* off of it), the smile trembles into a grimace, revealing an infinite grin of jagged teeth.

The intruder doffs his bowler hat, pleased I've spotted him. Pleased I'm horrified.

With a steadied hand, he finger-paints a smiley face in the condensation of my window, framing his own sick smile behind it. He watches, waiting for me to retaliate. I feel like a human making first contact with an extraterrestrial lifeform. (Drunk, high, saturated with cold sweat and downpour, I'm a commendable ambassador for our defective species.) Perhaps not fully in control of my body (the scene and the city appear to be beyond my autonomy), I wave at the figure inside my flat. He waves back, quite enthusiastically, before stepping away from the light and melting back into the shadows. I stare at the empty window, unable to move.

Did I just witness a trespasser? I wonder. Or a drug-fuelled manifestation that haunts my flat like a spectre? It doesn't feel like an altruistic entity. It feels like something material, something *sinister*.

I start to feel the bone-chilling dampness of the rain. I smell the odour of deluged drains. I hear the music of early morning traffic, airliners hurtling through the cloud. Blood and adrenaline slowly flood my limbs and extremities as my peripheral vision regains its focus. I pick up my briefcase, run across the forecourt and, with surprising vigour, vault the steps leading to the lobby. *The adrenaline.* It's really working its stuff as I sprint into the lift and punch the button to the second floor. As I rattle up its concrete thorax, it feels like I'm re-entering the womb, climbing towards a reverse engineered existence. When the bell dings and the doors open, the corridor is tarred in darkness. I suddenly feel the stamina departing me, *abandoning* me, in this vacant space. Panting, I tiptoe to my front door (number 34) and press my ear against it. I can't hear anything. Just the tempo of my heart, the thudding machinery of the human body.

"I'm coming in?" I say unsurely. I force a deep breath, turn the key, push open the door and step into my flat, holding my briefcase in front of me like a shield.

All the lights are off, but the television is turned on, bathing the room with monochrome static. I inspect the rest of the flat. Kitchen. Bathroom. Bedroom. Pantry. Balcony. I stand in the centre of the sitting room, listening to the storm, my deaccelerating heartbeat, the spume of white noise. There's nobody. Nothing. Nothing except the stench of death, the same tainted bouquet in the gents of the Prince Charles. I open the windows, inviting the aromas of rain and exhaust fumes to take its place.

I then examine the smiley face painted in the condensation of the window, dripping on its round edges, melting into a scream. Could I have imagined this was the man in the bowler hat staring back at me? I wonder. And could I have conceivably created this myself, perhaps to send a message from my subconscious?

Tell me why you killed Rupert Wreath.

So we could meet Rachel Garland. So that we could be together in Paradise. All of us.

I close the curtains, double lock the front door, draw the bolt, hook the latch, shed my dripping overcoat and examine the videotapes stacked against the wall. After a short pause, I pick *Braindead*. I slide the cassette into the VCR, sink into the sofa, drape my grimy duvet over my shoulders and roll a joint. I inhale with long, purposeful drags. I fix a gin (no ice), knock back an alprazolam, return to the sofa. I unbutton my shirt, allowing the mixer to drool down my chin and chest every time I sip. All these actions are rehearsed. They're instinctive, automatic. I barely notice I've performed them as the opening credits begin to roll. Father's ashes rest on top of the television – unscattered, gathering dust like every other object in this room, in this world – observing my ritual.

Within minutes, I feel the weight of the day, the weight of a lifetime, force my eyes shut. I won't make it to the closing scenes, I accept. I won't get to see Rachel Garland perform her uncredited role (smothered in blood, attempting to eat the brains of Lionel Cosgrove and his girlfriend, Paquita). Not tonight, unless Rachel Garland visits me in my dreams. Momentarily I feel safe, on the periphery of serenity, crossing the borders of insensibility. Hot tears bloom in my eyes as I attempt to cling onto consciousness.

But it's too late.

Reality dissolves into the oblivion of my dreamscapes.

CHAPTER EIGHT

In my dream, I wake up in my flat, on my sofa, and crawl inside my television set, into the ruins of a dead city.

I walk down a deserted avenue. Sunflowers, *thousands* of them, punch through the dilapidated buildings, the blistered tarmac, climbing towards the sun. The flowerheads turn towards me as I pass them, black and expressionless, like the eyes of a spider. Their leaves twitch and fidget, gripping my suit with the strength of human fingers. Ash coats the abandoned cars, the collapsed rooftops. The skyline is a canopy of fire.

"Hello?" I ask the forsaken world. "Is anybody out there?"

I reach a junction and rub the ash off of a road sign with my shirt sleeve. It says Borough High Street. "London," I whisper, turning onto Stoney Street, passing the decaying fruit and veg stalls of Borough Market. Is this a premonition of an encroaching apocalypse? Or a big-budget movie set constructed by my frayed imagination? It's impossible to know.

That's when I hear it, in the distance: the toots of trombonists and trumpet players, the clap of tambourines, cymbals, snare drums. I turn around. A brass marching band is limping up Southwark Street. Hidden behind the burnt out carcass of a taxi – the bones of the passengers still smouldering on the back seat – I watch the parade shuffle across the bitumen. I cup my hands over my mouth.

Horrible. It's just horrible.

I recognise the bloodied and mutilated faces of the band members. Car collision casualties with severed limbs. Wealthy businessmen with broken necks. Children perforated with knives and bullets. Bloated bachelors clutching their sternums from forgotten heart attacks. Addicts with glass syringes twitching in septic median cubitals. It's a procession of all the corpses that I've photographed, spilled over the rugs and roads of London. Strips of flesh fall off their frames as they wince towards the sun, stubbornly and courageously crawling, twanging and tonging their brass instruments as they unravel. A woman in a wedding dress with the side of her head missing pushes the remains of Rupert Wreath in a wheelbarrow. Father, in his oxygen mask and shit-stained hospital gown, grips a flugelhorn in an emaciated hand. His eyes are missing. The sockets twinkle with the moisture of traumatised tissue.

"David?" he says, blindly feeling his way through the sunflowers. "Where are you? I'm in pain, David."

And then I see her, trailing behind. It's Rachel Garland, soaked with blood, wearing her floral dress. She cradles a screaming baby in her arms. The umbilical cord swings in-between her legs to the tempo of the marching band. She gently rocks her child, smiling, crooning a discordant lullaby.

I slump behind the taxi, eyes closed, too terrified to move, too late to save them.

"This is just a dream," I pray breathlessly. "And dreams probably mean nothing."

When I open my eyes, the man in the bowler hat is standing outside the boarded up doors of a pub called the Market Porter. His hands are tucked inside the pockets of his tattered overcoat, the eyes concealed under the brim of his titfer. His presence can't be defined by our earthly constructs (it's something beyond our experience). He has an intolerable coldness. The absence of love. I fear his touch will cause my skin to scab, my blood to congeal, my organs to rupture inside their lockbox. As he approaches me, the camera around his neck swings like a pendulum. It's the same model as mine. A Praktica Super TL2.

"Where am I?" I ask.

He smiles with vile warmth. Flies crawl between his cracked lips.

"You're edging closer to Paradise. Everybody you love. They'll all be there, David. Waiting."

"This isn't real."

"They're with the others, David, marching towards the coastline, the beach we explored with Mother. And then they'll walk across the water, towards our terminus. I think we'll reach the shore by sundown, Paradise before the New Year. Do you remember the beach, David? Mother is still there, waiting for us."

"You're not real."

"Don't worry, David. You'll catch up soon enough." He snaps his fingers. "Oh yes, before I forget – best of luck with your meeting tomorrow. Rupert Wreath is quite a character.

We'll all be rooting for you. Watching and waiting."

"I'm not real."

The smile ruptures as his jaw snaps open, tearing the skin from the corners of his mouth to his earlobes. Blood cascades down his shirt. There is another face emerging. One with reflecting eyes and jagged teeth. It blooms like a flower. An unthinkable, newborn reality. When I see it, I scream, shrill like the sirens of an ambulance. It echoes through the wasteland as meteorites sail from the sky. Mushroom clouds erupt on the horizon, obliterating the doomed city in a tidal wave of fire.

CHAPTER
NINE

The morning of my meeting starts like any other.

I wake up on the sofa. My hair and pillow are matted with tepid sweat. Pallid sunlight collapses through the windows. The television spits nebulous static. I sit up disorientated, disembodied.

I enter the bathroom. I'm naked, wet, hunchbacked, like an underdeveloped foetus. I study the shower with mild disgust before deciding not to step inside. I observe my body in the mirror like the subjects of my photographs: flesh hanging off a brittle skeleton, an image of the city and the cloud that presides above it.

I enter the bedroom. I slip into a human-shaped suit. My jacket is ill-fitting, the shirt unironed, the tie intentionally inoffensive and uninspiring. I gaze at the bed in the reflection of the wardrobe mirror. Unmade and unchanged since Rachel Garland left in March, the shape of her body and the perfume of cigarettes and serotonin still cling to the linen. I turn around and lower my nose to the pillows, inhaling her redolent echoes.

I enter the kitchen. It then takes a breakfast of scrambled eggs, triangles of torrefied toast, coffee, modafinil and endless cigarettes to contemplate exiting the flat. But before I can re-enter reality, the kingdom of fatalities, assaults and accidents, I need to feed Osiris, Father's Persian.

Don't forget to feed Osiris. He's a very special kitty.

It's one of the small tasks I fulfil for my elderly neighbour and Father's oldest friend, Abraham Maher. I collect his post. I water the barren flowerpots cluttering his windowsills. I fetch the morning tabloids with his prescription of bliss-inducing antidepressants and paralysing painkillers, collected from the pharmacy on Tunstall Road. I even stay up with him in the early hours (smoking, drinking) while he talks about his childhood in Trinidad, his traumatic adolescence in the war. ("A white boy, born in the city, born in peacetime, could never understand," he always assures me when the topic presents itself.) In return, he lets me pocket some of his little white pills and borrow his dilapidated VW Beetle. He even reads *Sick & Beautiful*. It's two-way traffic with Abe and I. We're co-dependent, like father and son, teacher and pupil, patient and healer, coexisting like symbiotic parasites.

Don't get me wrong. I enjoy performing these small errands. It gives me a sense of purpose, an anchor to this ceaselessly gyrating planet, the sensation that I'm atoning for the affections I didn't spare my own old man in life or death. But I don't enjoy feeding Osiris. Not one bit. Rachel Garland, though, insisted that it was our role, our responsibility.

"Abe is losing his mind," she once told me. "He keeps muttering about clouds and Christ knows what else. It's sad to watch someone ebb away like that. Misplacing themselves, piece by piece. But we need to prioritise the welfare of that vulnerable kitty. If we don't care for him, who will, David?"

Rachel Garland is right about Abraham Maher. His mind and body have destabilised since Father passed away two year ago. Even hopelessly drunk, he keeps these emotions bottled up (tears in his eyes, lips puckered with misguided male pride). In reality, he is no longer fit for purpose, outmoded by three degenerating generations of humankind. He isn't qualified to care for any living organism, amoebic or otherwise. Even the fungus breeding in-between his bathroom tiles struggles to survive.

But Rachel Garland isn't right about Osiris. He's far from vulnerable. I don't continue to feed him because Rachel or Father asked me to do it. Here's the truth: Osiris scares me. He puts me on edge.

This will sound insane, but I'm going to put it out there anyway – Osiris can communicate. And I don't mean a few meows sandwiched in-between buttery purrs. I'm totally serious. *Osiris can talk.*

The clogged veins and arthritic joints groaning under his wobbling paunch suggest that Osiris is like most cats (piggish, complacent), but this isn't the case. He's measured. Vindictive and vengeful. I can't predict what he'll do next or when he'll do it. And I can't determine if his voice is a projection from my subconscious, or if it's real words, real sentences.

I swallow this nervous sickness and step onto my balcony. I then step over the guardrail. I close my eyes, enjoying the drizzle on my face. I feel incredible clarity here, over the edge, a calm I can't explain. To access Abraham Maher's next door flat (number 35), I need to traverse the two-metre gap that divides our adjacent balconies. It's a three-storey drop onto the forecourt or through the windscreen of a parked car. One slip could mean severe physical trauma or, perhaps, death. Yeah, I know what you're thinking. It would be irrefutably less dangerous for Abraham Maher to cut me a key to his front door, but to him the notion is laughable. Triple-locked, chained and bolted, this is the first line of defence against the neighbours waiting to ransack his flat. Granting anyone access, even *me*, he claims, poses a major security risk. The unlocked balcony door is the only logical point of entry. This, he reiterates, is the only way.

"What would they possibly have to gain?" I once asked him, scrutinising the pissed furniture and worthless bric-a-brac trashing his flat. "You're financially and spiritually broke, Abe. There's so much *nothing* in here."

"Ask the cloud," he replied. "I know it's conspiring up there. With them. With *him*. Watching. Waiting for their opportunity."

I take a deep breath. Like an intoxicated tightrope walker, I start to shimmy across the narrow ledge, using satellite dish wires and the building's decorative brickwork as handholds. *You're doing great*, I tell myself, inching further. Halfway across, clinging onto a waste pipe, I pause. I always do this – pausing for a few seconds more than necessary to peer down at the lobby steps or gaze into the cloud above. In this moment, I know that I'm one whoops-a-daisy away from a grisly finale. So, why do I feel so composed? Rachel Garland once told me that it's addictive being somebody else. Perhaps that's what I'm addicted to as well – being somebody else, someone in control, someone unafraid. This character rarely emerges. He's just too fucking cool. He's surreal. "He isn't me, this character," I whisper, feeling the fear rising up, building momentum. "He isn't me." I take another deep breath and shamble across the last few feet, stepping over the rails onto Abraham Maher's balcony. I open the back door, step inside and shut it behind me, muting the discord of the rain.

Abraham Maher is asleep in his armchair. The only sign of life is the whistle of oxygen entering and evacuating his body. He smells diminished. Stale smoke, dried sweat. The face is creased like a crumpled newspaper, contorted by unseen nightmares. The head twitches with distant panic. Flakes of dead skin cling to his black cheekbones like snow. In the glow of his reading lamp, he looks like a dummy in a deserted wax work, both lifelike and inanimate.

I pick up the empty tumbler teetering on his armrest and place it on the coffee table, next to a printout of *Sick & Beautiful*. I flick through the pages, randomly reading his dense annotations. *What is the purpose of this chapter? Elucidate the narrative arc. Consider swapping chapters 34/85 to build tension. Weak character, enrich or remove. Where is the structure here? Who is Rachel Garland?* The feedback is startling. I wonder why, even after I told him that I sent the manuscript to every agency in New York and London, Abraham continues to make these tweaks and recommendations? Perhaps he's trying to help me. Perhaps, in his old age, he cannot grasp that the book is already perfect.

"Morning, David."

I flinch, spinning around, staring into the darkened bedroom. The yellow eyes of Osiris slice through the shadows, like lighthouses floating on a tide of bedsheets. They narrow and dilate with slow disdain. He springs off the mattress with a heavy thud and steps into the morning light. Osiris takes his time, because cats underrate the preciousness of our precious, overrated time.

"Abe has been talking about the cloud again," he yawns, stretching on the carpet. "Nonstop. Do you really think it's plotting something sinister?"

I ignore Osiris and enter the kitchen, flicking on the light switch. The sink is congested with dirty dishes. I open the fridge, peer inside, quickly close it again. The odour of rancid food is unbearable. I gag, gripping the top of the fridge for purchase. My hangover, momentarily forgotten, curdles and intensifies, emphasising its presence.

"Abe knows that you took his car on Christmas Day. The council already sent him a fine in the post. Apparently it's on the double yellow lines outside the Hero of Switzerland. Abe was asleep, but I watched you practically fall through the balcony door at two in the morning to drop the car keys on the coffee table. Christ knows how your survived the climb here and back. But I get it. I do. You were just letting off some steam. Celebrating the book deal, no doubt? Don't look so shocked, David. Abe tells me everything about you. Even *Sick & Beautiful*."

Letting off some steam. This is an idiom I haven't heard Osiris use yet. Perhaps he heard it on the news or in a movie.

Osiris weaves around the legs of the breakfast table. I open the cupboard, pull out a tin of tuna, slide open the cutlery drawer and rummage for the can opener. I hack into the lid with difficulty.

"He told me a secret about you too, David. You and Rachel Garland. I'm not sure if I believe it."

I shudder as Osiris rubs his furry caboose against my leg, curling his tail around my ankle like a tentacle. I shut my eyes and clamp both hands on the worktop, feeling its laminate surface squeak between my fingers. My head tumbles. My body trembles. My temples pulsate with dull, constant pain.

"Relax, David. Don't be so tense. You're secret safe with me. With us. Who's going to believe a cat anyway? You'd need to be unhinged to listen."

"You're right about that," I say, involuntarily smiling.

Osiris jumps on the worktop. His purr sounds like the rumble of idling traffic.

"If you rub my tummy, I can tell you things about Rachel she'd never dream of telling you. It'll be the interview you always wanted."

I tip the tuna into the filthy bowl in the far corner of the kitchen before lobbing the tin at Osiris. He doesn't flinch as it strikes the wall (missing him by inches) and clatters into the sink behind him.

"Fuck you, Osiris!" I scream, throwing my fist into the wall. "Fuck! Fuck! Fuck! Fuck! Fuck! Fuck!"

Abraham Maher briefly stirs in his shallow dreams, but doesn't wake. I stare at the blood oozing from my knuckles. Osiris looks at me sympathetically before jumping off the worktop and sauntering to his bowl.

"Composure, David," he says, audibly chewing. "You'll need it for your big meeting. You don't want Rupert Wreath to smell your fear."

I turn off the light, storm out of the kitchen, lurch across the sitting room and swing open the balcony door. Gripping the handle, I look back at Abraham Maher, deteriorating in his armchair. A skeleton in its threadbare suit. I briefly imagine confronting Osiris, *killing* Osiris, but I can't do it. I just can't. He watches me sag, step out onto the balcony, into the rain, and close the door behind me. We both know I'll do nothing (we both know I am nothing). I climb across and re-enter my flat, flushed with phallic shame.

I then pull on my overcoat, grab my umbrella and briefcase, exit the flat and enter the morning transit, the manoeuvres of bodies and vehicles. I walk up Loughborough Road, towards Brixton tube station, determined not to be late for my meeting, determined not to lose my focus. I descend into the depths of the underground, into the living tissue of the city.

Publishing a novel.

I whisper these words over and over and over again.

I should feel elated, but the confrontation with Osiris and the remnants of my nightmare flood the packed train carriage. Bad dreams. No sleep. Absence of appetite. Reality has taken an emphatic toll. But I feel like I'm galloping towards my fate, much faster than I had ever hoped or anticipated. I'm David Temple. Earthling. Londoner. Journalist. Novelist. Bestseller. I can see it all so clearly. The meeting with Rupert Wreath almost feels inconsequential. A mere formality.

"He isn't me, this character," I say to myself. But he can be. He will be.

I allow the confidence to swallow me. Be unafraid. Be *too fucking cool.*

CHAPTER
TEN

Arid heat sucks away the oxygen, adding density to the sweltering lobby.

It feels like a waiting room for Hell. And I've arrived five minutes early.

A janitor in blue overalls mops the tiled floor. He whistles, occasionally dabbing the sweat on his forehead with a handkerchief. I leave a trail of wet footprints as I beeline for the reception desk. The janitor looks up, but he doesn't seem resentful for sullying his handiwork. He looks anguished, as if he feels sorry for me. He returns his focus to the tiles, erasing my tracks as if I never stepped across them.

"How can I help, sir?" asks the receptionist, folding his morning paper. *PARADISE PUBLISHING* is printed across the wall behind him (iridescent italics, in a font I do not recognise).

"I'm David Temple. T-E-M-P-L-E. I have a nine o'clock with Rupert Wreath."

"Very good, sir. We've been expecting you. Watching and waiting."

The receptionist crosses his legs with excruciating slowness, adding emphasis to this comment.

"Please make yourself comfortable, Mr Temple. Eve will escort you up to the 34th floor shortly."

I nod, retreating to the sofa on the other side of the room, once again dirtying the mopped tiles with my footprints. I light a cigarette, trying to get a grasp on why this scene and its characters make me feel so unsettled. It's like I've woken up in a different city, in a different reality, where something vital is absent. In its place is this torrid lobby, its polite receptionist, whistling janitor, vivacious ferns and fragrant leather sofa. It feels like a stage set. Performers and props tonelessly imitating real life. I hug my briefcase and umbrella, feeling insecure. *It's the pressure of the interview*, I rationalise. My inarticulate suit. Months of toil coming to a boiling crescendo. Or perhaps this lobby is a gateway, seducing me into an unexplored consciousness. It's impossible to know.

"Probably nothing," I mutter.

I pick up one of the magazines on the glass table in front of me. It's dated to last December. I flick through its dogeared pages. I'm acting now, desperate to appear relaxed.

"David Temple?"

I flinch and look up. A woman stands outside the open elevator doors. Hazel eyes. Blonde hair. Blue overalls. Clipboard. Lipstick the colour of spilt blood.

"Welcome to Paradise Publishing," she says. "I'm Eve. We've been waiting for you, Mr Temple."

"So I've heard."

She smiles, extending her hand. I shake it. She isn't surprised (or repelled) by the dampness of my palm.

"Right this way, Mr Temple."

We step into the elevator and ascend to the 34th floor in silence. I can feel Eve staring at me, assessing my appearance like the movements of a strange animal in an alien menagerie. Her stare? It's entirely objective. But I refuse to engage in eye contact or chit-chat. I focus on my saturated shoes, content to let the carriage flood with inaudible repose.

"May I voice something quite personal?" she says. "You look somewhat– *unwell*. Deserted." Eve's forehead creases with apparent concern. "Are you sick, Mr Temple?"

I bite my bottom lip, attempting to fight back the tears, the emotions. I focus on my shoes again. Rainwater is leaking out of them, dilating around my feet like polluted oceans. My socks feel soggy. *I* feel soggy, washed out, porous.

"It's nothing," I say. "Just nerves. And I haven't been sleeping well. Late nights. You know how it goes. And dreams."

"What kind of dreams?"

"Bad dreams. And they're getting worse. Weirder. Darker. More frequent. More threatening."

"Could these bad dreams be reverberations from your accident? Feelings of guilt or inadequacy? Dreams *always* mean something. They're like the missing pieces of a jigsaw puzzle. We can't see the full picture without them."

Before I can answer, the elevator doors open and Eve guides me through a long corridor. The walls are white, windowless. There are no people, no pictures, no furniture, *no details*. We reach a door. It's the only door. *RUPERT WREATH, DIRECTOR* is printed on the frosted glass. Eve opens the door. I enter.

"How do you know about the accident?" I ask.

"Mr Wreath will be with you in a moment," she says, ignoring the question. "Just breathe. Good. Compose yourself. Get your head around the role. You're an aspiring author. And you want this book deal more than anything else in the world. Breathe again. Very good, Mr Temple. Enjoy yourself out there. Don't act. Just *be*. Remember – you are David Temple. Say it."

"I am David Temple."

"And what are you?"

"An aspiring author."

"And how much do you want it?"

"More than anything else in the world."

"Very good, Mr Temple. That's perfect."

Eve gently closes the door behind her.

I stand in the centre of the room and study the office. In front of me, with the entrance to my back, is a vast walnut desk. On top of the desk is a computer monitor, keyboard, telephone, rolodex, lamp, a chaotic stack of annotated manuscripts. A mirror framed with gilded cherubs spans the wall behind it. On my right is a window. On the left, a minibar. On top of the minibar is an icebox, spirits bottles, crystal tumblers. There is chair behind the desk. There is a chair in front of the desk. Chinese evergreens, Boston ferns, American milk bushes and snake plants spill out of the vases that furnish the edges of the room. I smile. *This office.* This, I think, is the stage where deals are made, contracts signed, dreams realised. It's everything I wanted, everything I expected, except for the strips of sunlight that slice through the blinds covering the window.

I walk into the light, underneath it, inviting it to trickle over my face and fingers. When is the last time I saw sunshine beyond the partitions of my memories and nightmares? I wonder. With infantile fascination I feel the heat of an ancient star, millions of kilometres away, warming my skin. It evokes flashbacks from the depths of my subconscious: the beach, the ocean, my faceless mother, her floral dress. And the burning sun above the searing city in my dreamscape. I recoil into the artificial light of the office, backing up until I'm flat against the wall, crouched in-between the minibar and a towering rubber plant. As I inspect my hands for blisters, I hear the door gently open.

"David Temple?"

Kneeling on the floor, I cautiously emerge from my leafy hiding place.

A man in a burgundy three-piece and paisley tie stands in the doorway. Polished brogues reflect in the light. White teeth twinkle behind moist lips. Flawless skin radiates with an unnatural tan – a sheen that can only be acquired outside of the city, beyond the shadow of the cloud. He crosses the room with three authoritative strides and crouches in front of me. He holds out his hand, like a zoo keeper coaxing a frightened animal out of its burrow. I look at the hand, the face, stunned how he looks exactly like the man who torpedoed from the eleventh floor of the Mandarin Oriental almost one year ago. He squeezes my shoulder, sensing that my mind is elsewhere.

"Mr Temple?" he asks. "I'm Rupert Wreath. Please. Don't be afraid. We're your friends. Let's start that friendship right – with a drink."

Softened by the promise of alcohol (I *am* thirsty, feeling dangerously sober), I stand up, slowly unfolding my body, and shake Rupert Wreath's hand. When I wince and squirm, failing to match his power, an eerie satisfaction mounts his face. He releases his grip. As my wet fingers slither out of his vice, he wipes his palm on his trousers, as if he just touched something contagious.

"Welcome to Paradise Publishing," he says. He smiles again, convincingly. "We're glad that you chose us."

But *did* I choose them? I wonder. Just like I explained to Abraham Maher: I sent my manuscript, synopsis, covering letter and headshots to every publisher and agency in New York and London, but I don't recall posting a draft to Paradise Publishing. In fact, I've never heard of them. Although this detail intrigues me (but only slightly), it's inconsequential. Paradise Publishing was a beacon in the dead sea of rejections and radio silence. Nobody else wanted anything to do with *Sick & Beautiful*.

"Take a seat, David," he says, gesturing to the chair in front of the desk. Obediently, I sit. Perhaps intentionally, the chair feels as uncomfortable as it looks, digging its uncompromising angles into my flesh. I note the aroma of new leather, the wooden skeleton, its inadequate padding. I fidget before settling into an excruciating yet tolerable position. Rupert Wreath crosses to the minibar. The sound of glass and ice cubes jingles with pleasant harmony.

"May I call you David?" he asks.

"When people address me as David, Sir or Mr Temple, I find these titles redundant. Even gender feels too specific. You can't define me. It's not because I'm unique. It's because I'm *generic*. I'm just muscles, bones, teeth and connective tissue, fickle molecules like proteins, glycogen, glucose, lipids, hydroxyapatite, amalgamated in the human template. Trillions of cells that die in their millions every minute. The notion that we're unique couldn't be further from the truth. This is how Rachel Garland views our world. She can even reduce the city to cement, aggregate, asphalt, steel, glass, bricks and mortar, a circulatory system of plastic tubes and electrical wiring. We're a society of twitching atoms veering towards collapse or violent combustion. Obsolete DNA on the periphery of mass extinction. Everything can be dissolved into nothing. Once, I found Rachel's concepts demeaning. Now? This is how I'm programmed to perceive myself and my reality. It's comforting. But please. Call me David."

There is an unbearable silence. It's endless and empty. The sound of human disconnection. Why did I feel the need to share this insight? I wonder. How do I want Rupert Wreath to feel? Is this really my opening pitch for the book, an attempt to build a meaningful picture of the author and his work?

"That's very interesting, David," he says. "A remarkable perspective. A snapshot of a real mind."

A real mind. Whatever this means, I take it as a compliment. Rupert Wreath hands me a gin and tonic. It's furnished with crushed ice and a wedge of lime.

"My favourite," I say. "How did you know?"

"We know everything about you, David."

There is another pause while Rupert Wreath studies my expression, interpreting my reaction to his statement. Satisfied, he raises his glass. It's a neat whisky with ice and a shaving of orange zest.

"To success," he says.

The tumbler looks small inside his thick fingers. The skin is coarse, calloused, more like the hands of a brickie than a literary agent.

"To success," I echo.

I raise my glass. We drink.

"Beautiful," he says, sitting behind the desk. "Tell me, David. How was *Sick & Beautiful* conceived?"

"It started as a feature for *The Daily Sun*, but I lost my job and it grew into something bigger. In the end, it was for the best. My role on the paper was holding me back from my vocation, my true potential."

"How did you lose your job?"

"Creative differences." I nod. "Yes. It was creative differences."

Rupert Wreath winks, as if he doesn't believe me.

"Tell me this. What inspired you to write the book?"

"Rachel," I reply, quite naturally. "Rachel Garland has an understanding of human nature unlike anyone I've encountered. She believes she knows the secret to eternal life. It's almost *philosophical*. I felt like I had a duty to record it. I want to share her story. She inspired me to change, to be anyone else. It could inspire others too. *Sick & Beautiful* wouldn't exist if it wasn't for her. *I* wouldn't exist if it wasn't for her. I wouldn't be here. We wouldn't be here, in this room, having this conversation."

"And how would you summarise the story?"

"It's a saga about hope. A universal fairytale that examines love and death. Humanity's eternal–"

"No, David. The plot. What's the plot? What obstacles do the characters encounter and how do they overcome them? What's the conflict?"

"I never intended there to be a plot, a narrative arc, a conclusion. I wanted to capture what was said, the moments as they happened. I wanted to fulfil my role as an author, an observer. I tried to be objective. The story reflects real life. And real life doesn't always have structure or resolution."

Rupert Wreath nods. He looks sympathetic now, he really does, a bit like the janitor in the lobby.

"You seem troubled, David. Out of sorts. Please don't take these questions personally. I'm simply trying to get a feel for the material. Or is it something else? You can tell us what's wrong. We're here to help."

"Sometimes I can't tell what's real and what isn't," I admit. "Even this office, this chair, you and your desk. The plants and gold-leaf. My deceased father's talking cat, Osiris. None of it feels *real*."

Rupert Wreath looks at me for a long time – concerned, perhaps even touched by this revelation – before he explodes into laughter.

"You're fun, David," he says, slapping the top of his desk, wiping moisture from the corners of his eyes. "A *real* character. We can certainly do with more of those in this business. You have everything it takes to succeed. But first we need to discuss the manuscript before we can consider publication." The smile dissipates, the eyes suddenly look lost, disconcerted. "Your book needs a lot of work," he adds. His tone, his expression, are quite serious now. "I'm confident, though, that we can salvage something from the wreckage."

"What kind of work?"

"Let's start with the title," he says. "*Sick & Beautiful*? I don't get it. It's a story about love, death, humanity, hope. But *Sick & Beautiful* tells me nothing. It's like your prose. Obscure and ostentatious. How about something with more clarity and a broader appeal, like *Rachel Garland: A Biography*? Or even better – *Rachel Garland: The Shocking True Life Story*? These are just ideas. Take them away. Draft some alternatives. You're the writer, after all."

I pull my biro and notepad out of my overcoat and scribble this down. *New title? More clarity. More hyperbolic. Broader appeal.* I put them away again. I feel droplets of sweat on my forehead. I loosen my necktie. I'm suffocating. I'm drowning. I take an audible sip of my drink. Ice cubes chime inside the tumbler like the bells of a tiny cathedral. Rupert Wreath opens a drawer in his desk and pulls out a brown envelope.

"We need to talk about these too," he says.

Rupert Wreath frowns as he thumbs through a set of monochrome photographs, flicking them onto the floor between us with intentional disdain. They're the headshots that I posted with every copy of the book. Rachel Garland snapped them back in January. There I am, behind my desk, staring pensively out of the window towards the city, arched over Father's electric typewriter, smoking with worldly intent. Or stood with my foot planted on the desk chair, a serrated elbow poised on an acute knee, attempting to accentuate the hard angles of my frame. In my photos, I tried a variety of poses in a variety of suits, some with the tie uniformly winched, others with the top button adventurously undone. I tried everything, but nothing felt right, nothing looked realistic. I was frustrated, incapable of exuding the image I desired. Rupert Wreath and I examine the headshots on the carpet in silence. *Jesus.* Look at me. It's undeniable. I emit an uncertainty that infuriates me. A wide aperture and high exposure couldn't hide these introversions. Rupert seems to sense this diffidence too.

"Have you tried smiling?" he asks. "Try now. No. Not like that. Try again." Rupert frames my face inside his squared thumbs and index fingers. "No," he sighs. "That isn't right either. Please. Just stop. You look like you're in remarkable pain." He shakes his head sadly. "And those hollow eyes. My God. They really are quite frightening."

I look past Rupert Wreath, at the cherubs that decorate the corners of the mirror behind him. They're armed with bows and harps. They look heavy, purposefully expensive, almost threatening. My spectral reflection glares back at me in the polished glass. My eyes are frightening, but they're not hollow. They speak a cautionary tale. One about love, our swansong of decay, an abyss where hope and faith flourish like biblical Paradise. These faltered features are a testament to the folly of humankind and its cracked fun house reflection, gimped by a galactic bootlegger's botched recipe. It's the face of another victim of the human condition, at the dawn of our species' low watermark.

"Rachel Garland said it best," I say. "I look a lot like what normal looking people look like, but fundamental fragments are absent. Those spaces are flooded with an appalling glow. She considers her imperfections as a rebellion against genetic conformity, but she still can't stand the placeholders which occupy the missing pieces of my own psyche, even if they fascinate her. My sickness, she says, traps the good inside me like the frame of a family portrait. She can see beauty within if she studies the faded brushstrokes, but there's illness there too. I'm like dead flowers on a derelict gravestone. Deflated birthday balloons strung to the headboard of an empty hospital bed. But Rachel concedes that these faults are inherent in us all. Despite our bluster, our pollen is polluted, no matter how much we attempt to hide, numb and soften it."

Again. Why do I feel the need to explain these bizarre

details? Is this another teaser for the book? Or am I simply attempting to create context for Rupert Wreath's hurtful interjections? It's impossible to confirm. He winces as he finishes his whisky. Leaving the tumbler on the desk, he stands up, walks behind me and rests his hands on my shoulders. He looks into the mirror and smiles at his reflection.

"May I ask you a question, David? Is it all true?"

"Is all what true?"

"The book," he says. "The facts about Rachel Garland. Your final chapter. What *really* happened on the night of the accident? Let me be frank. You talk about objectivity, recording the moments as they happened, but I feel like you're holding back. There seems to be misplaced info. Lost data. The details that glue the story together. I need you to be bold, David. Candid. Fearless. The book and our professional relationship can't succeed without this. You know we can trust one another, right? The bond between author and agent is sacred. It's time you started to honour that ancient tradition."

"Telling the truth can be painful," I say.

"Understood," he says, patting me on the shoulder reassuringly. "But the truth might be all we have to work with here. Just try it. Say *anything*. Anything truthful."

"OK. Do you want to hear something wild? You might not believe it."

"This is good, David. This is progress. You have my attention. Shoot."

"On the night I met Rachel Garland, a movie producer named Rupert Wreath was shoved off an eleventh floor balcony in Knightsbridge. But get this. He wasn't just your namesake. He looked like you too. Before his death, he looked exactly like you. The face, the suit. It's uncanny. It's chilling. I can't move past it. I feel like I'm talking to a ghost."

"That's remarkable, David. Is Rupert in the book?"

"Chapter 41." I pause. "Did you not read it?"

Rupert Wreath seems to recoil at the notion.

"I don't *need* to read it, David. I don't deal with the churn. My role is to examine the author, to gauge the marketing possibilities. Here's my opinion. The structure of the book is shaky. The title is uninspiring. And the word count? It's just ludicrous. That's the bad news. The good news? We have the skeleton of a bestseller on our hands. And we have the team to help you reach your potential. Proofers. Printers. Retailers. PR. Translators. Illustrators. Solicitors. The works. But guess what? Yes. There's more bad news. That calibre of marketing muscle doesn't come cheap."

Rupert Wreath rubs his thumb and middle finger together to emphasise this point, as if he is attempting to conjure fire in the palm of his hand.

"Is reworking the book, the title, the answer, though?" I counter. "If *Sick & Beautiful* has bestseller potential, surely it just needs a bit of exposure. Reviews in newspapers and magazines. TV interviews. Billboards and tube stations advertising. Guerrilla marketing. The stuff that *counts*."

Rupert Wreath erupts into another fit of contemptuous laughter.

"Enough," he giggles, massaging my shoulders. "Enough of this begging, David. It's pathetic. And there's me thinking that we had an understanding. Mutual respect. You've misconstrued your value. And I don't believe you appreciate the true dynamic of this relationship."

Rupert Wreath clutches my shoulders in his hands so

tightly I drop my drink on the floor. I release an involuntary squeal of pain as I squirm in my seat, unable to pry off his powerful fingers.

"Please, Rupert," I squeak. "Please stop."

Rupert Wreath pushes his forehead against the back of my neck like a rutting stag, breathing with primal fury. I can smell coffee on his breath, cigarettes, the notes of aftershave dabbed generously on his pulse points. His face is red now, the hue of untamed rage. Our claggy sweat amalgamates. For one moment, I'm certain that Rupert is going to snap my clavicles.

"At Paradise Publishing, it's not all about money," he says, "It's about family. Trust. We're going to help you achieve your dreams, David. We can transform your reality. But first you're going to help us. Are we understood?"

"Understood," I whisper, almost inaudibly.

I let out a gasp of relief when Rupert Wreath unleashes his grip. I only feel safe once he walks behind the desk, stepping out of range. The florid ferocity in his cheeks vanishes almost as rapidly as it surfaced, as if a hissing pressure valve hidden underneath his suit has been released. I look down at the turned over tumbler. The ice cubes from my drink have already began to melt into the carpet.

"Beautiful," he says. "Perhaps there is still latitude to rebuild this friendship. Together, I'm certain we can find a mutually beneficial solution."

Rupert Wreath rummages through his desk, apparently at random. And then he snaps his fingers, triumphant.

"Perhaps we do have something that could work," he says. "But I need to ask you something first. How much do you want this, David? Be honest. How much do you want to be a published novelist?"

"More than anything," I reply, rehearsing the discourse I practised with Eve in the lift. "You couldn't begin to understand what I've endured to write this book." But I can feel myself going off-script now. The tears follow. "The accident, everything that's happened. It can't be for nothing, Rupert. It has to mean *something*."

"Beautiful," he says, clapping his palms together like a performing pinniped. "I like you, David. You're passionate with an endearing anti-charisma. A risk-taker with soaring ambition. And true grit. Someone willing to bend the rules of reality for his aspirations. Do you want to know how to open the gates to Paradise?"

Think of me as a messenger. An emissary from Paradise. I can take you there if you want, David. You and your friends.

The words of the man in the bowler hat scream through the forefront of my mind. I look at the door, contemplating if I could escape this room, this building, and what the consequences would be if I couldn't. I'm *this* close to refusing the offer, but it isn't fear that stops me. It's the requisite for reverence, money. *Publishing a novel.* The notion is irresistible.

"Tell me what you want me to do," I say, my voice suddenly more robotic than human.

"Beautiful," says Rupert Wreath. "What we *need* you to do is quite simple. There's an artefact we'd like you to collect. It's being sold tonight at a private fundraiser in the Natural History Museum. Your friend, Richard Hayes, is hosting the event. We assume you received your invite in the post?"

"How do you know that?"

"Like I said, David. We know everything about you. Besides, Richard is your friend, is he not? Why *wouldn't* he invite you?"

"Because we haven't spoken in months. Not since Rachel Garland."

"It appears that Richard is ready to heal. And it couldn't have come at a better time for all of us. We need each other, David. If we don't seize our opportunity tonight, who knows where the artefact may end up? Lost forever, most likely in the impenetrable mansions of the elite or the subterranean vaults of a private collector." He smiles. "Do you have any questions?"

"A couple," I say, although this is a gross understatement.

"Shoot," replies Rupert Wreath, but his tone and body language effuse irritation.

"Why can't Paradise Publishing bid for this artefact?"

"If only it were that simple. What if we get *out*bid? We risk everything. We have good reason to believe that there are nefarious forces that want to stop us acquiring it, like a rival agency. We're at war, David. You wouldn't believe the heinous precautions they are willing to take for a competitive edge. But we're the good guys. And everything works out for the good guys. Everybody knows this."

"What *is* the artefact?"

Rupert Wreath's eyes light up with an abominable knowledge.

"It looks like a photo album," he says. "But it's so much more. You'll know it when you see it, David. They say you can almost *feel* it."

"Who are *they*?"

"That, David, is not your concern."

"So, why me? It doesn't make any sense. Surely you would benefit from hiring a professional?"

"It's a private party and we're not invited," he says. "You

have the ticket to Paradise, David. We don't need a pro. We need someone we can trust. But you appear to have reservations. Perhaps you don't want this book to succeed as much as you imagined."

"Richard and I have history. We studied at university together. We shared things. Once, we really were friends, but Richard has an unhealthy obsession with death that became impossible to control. There is a perverse motive buried in his desire to reconnect with me, but I can't predict where it will lead me."

"Are you afraid of getting outmanoeuvred by Richard Hayes?"

"No," I say, scoffing at this ridiculous suggestion. "He's too self-absorbed. Hopelessly addicted to himself. I'd be able to steal the photo album if it was tucked inside Richard's pocket. It's just– *all of this*. It doesn't make sense. It's unreal. I feel like I'm watching myself, unable to control my dialogue or my body."

Rupert Wreath crumbles into another fit of laughter. I can feel his eyes burning through me (my tie, my shirt, my skin), harpooning my abraded soul.

"Do you know what?" he says. "Perhaps you're not the man for the role. We overestimated you, David. You came here and seduced us with your counterfeit ambition. But it's a mask. What made us hope you would be capable of joining the publishing elite? Rachel and Richard are right. You haven't got what it takes. We must be losing our grip on reality. The city does that, I suppose. Something to do with the bad weather, the pollution, the crowds, the way we live and die on top of each other."

I feel an anger incubating inside my chest, desperate to

claw its way out. It rises to the surface, like the bubbles in a pint glass. Picturing the face of Richard Hayes or Rachel Garland, I want to crawl across the desk and attack Rupert Wreath. I want to clamp my fingers around his neck. I want to sink my teeth into the bridge of his nose. I want to press my thumbs into his eyes. I want to shove my fist into his mouth until his lips split, until the jaw dislocates and the throat ruptures. I want to desecrate his body. I want to violate the freshly-created orifice in his defaced remains. I want to make him un-human. I want him to feel my pain. And then nothing at all. But Rupert Wreath is offering something that outweighs every doubt and apprehension – it's hope. Affirmation. I don't want this. I *need* this.

Without hesitation, I dive to the floor and crawl towards the desk, resting my head on the carpet like a praying disciple. Tears cascade down my cheeks. I wish that Rupert Wreath's feet were closer so I could kiss them.

"Richard assumes that every dream has been a tragic misfire," I blubber into the carpet's acrylic fibres. "But he doesn't understand my ambition. He doesn't know what really happened that night."

Rupert Wreath re-emerges from behind his desk and kneels in front of me. He runs his fingers through my hair with paternal tenderness. I close my eyes and pretend he is my father, soothing my childish inadequacies. Perhaps sensing this transpiring role, Rupert rises back to his feet with disgust, leaving me to rock and snivel in the centre of his office. He watches thoughtfully, compassionately, like a predator observing its wounded prey.

"Beautiful," he says. "Now drag yourself back together. Have a drink. Get some sleep. Slip into something more presentable. Something with a little *panache*. Do whatever you need to do to ready yourself for tonight. You need to focus and remember your vocation. We expect the photo album by 9AM Friday. That's exactly two days from now. Until next time, David. We'll be watching. Waiting."

Rupert Wreath walks to the window and stands under the sunlight knifing through the blinds. He almost looks empyrean.

"The sun shines on us, David. Consider it a good omen. A blessing from the cloud. Did you ever consider that, perhaps, we were always destined to find each other and send this plot into motion? Meeting Rachel Garland, the accident, the photo album – it's all designed, it's all connected. We're only beginning to understand the true purpose of our roles. I have a feeling things are going to get weird, but I have devout faith in the script. It's taking us places. Strange places. The right places."

Everybody, it seems, has faith in this allegorical script. I want to believe in it too. The notion is liberating. If everything is preordained, like Rupert Wreath suggests, then there is no space for fear. Fear of ostracism or failure. Fear of oncoming traffic and collapsing floorboards. Fear of nosediving airliners, lightening forks and random acts of violence. Fear of death itself. They are all part of the plot. Scripted preconcerts created for dramatic traction. It's completely outside of one's control.

I want to believe that the accident is a nadir in my narrative.

Providence has never had such vogue, vulgar sex appeal.

CHAPTER
ELEVEN

I suppose you want to know about *the accident*? Everybody, it seems, is talking about it.

The accident happened on Atlantic Road in Brixton.

Even now, six months later, the details glimmer with disturbing clarity.

It was July. It was early. In the wake of an afterparty for the premiere of *The Passion of Darkly Noon*. Before that night, looking through the lens of my camera, I always marvelled how anybody could cause a car crash in London. It's almost impossible to shift into first gear in the city's clogged infrastructure. Kinetic energy feels like a divine gift. But to pick up enough momentum to cause a collision, to un-idle? It's breathtaking.

The accident caused a huge amount of congestion in Southwark. It didn't get a byline in the papers or the morning rush hour report, but it was compelling content for *Sick & Beautiful*. Rachel Garland wasn't just in the car – she was drunk and behind the wheel too. In fact, she was *plastered*. You couldn't make it up. It was poetry, an unpassable opportunity to heighten narrative tension, but it came with an emotional and physical penance.

I woke up in St George's Hospital. Hooked to a drip, skull-eyed and hungover, I looked out of the window. It was dark. Still raining.

"Where's Rachel?" I asked.

Adorned in customary white coat and stethoscope, the doctor, yawning, read from a clipboard with clinical indifference.

"Radius and ulna fractures in the right arm. Nerve damage in the right shoulder. Seven broken ribs. Orbital and nasal fractures. Two incisors and one canine knocked out, found embedded in the dashboard. Whiplash. Concussion. Dehydration. You're quite fortunate to be alive, Mr Temple."

"How long have I been out?" I asked, massaging my forehead. "It feels like I've been unconscious for centuries."

"Since the early hours of yesterday morning. Do you not remember speaking with the police after they admitted you into A&E?"

I shook my head slowly.

He nodded knowingly.

The doctor produced a syringe from his top pocket, inserted it into my drip and pushed his thumb on the plunger.

"And do you remember anything about the moments before the accident?" he asked. "Anything that could help us."

"I guess we just lost control."

"I guess so. Your blood alcohol levels were astronomical. Do you remember telling the police that you swerved to avoid hitting a man stood in the middle of the road? A man in a bowler hat." When I didn't answer, the doctor ticked something on his clipboard. "Are you currently on any medication?"

"Prozac. Ultram. Xanax. Valium. Codeine. Some other meds. I can't remember the exact names. My neighbour, Abe, gives them to me."

He looked impressed, but only vaguely.

"Recreational drugs?"

"Just the usual," I shrugged, wincing at the distant agony coursing through my arm and shoulder.

The doctor nodded, underscored something on the clipboard, flipped the page, circled something else.

"We'll keep you in here for a few days while we run more tests," he said. "Just as a precaution. You might still experience nausea, vomiting, headaches, dizziness, fainting, chest pains, high blood pressure, fatigue, insomnia, seizures, weight gain, weight loss, breakouts, depression, dissociation, anxiety, nightmares. Even death. You name it. But this could also be a new start, Mr Temple. Think of the crash as a metaphor for life. You have the agency to salvage something from the wreckage."

The doctor nodded, mostly to himself, as he annotated several more boxes. He removed his spectacles and slid them into his top pocket.

"The arm will heal up in a few months. It's everything else, everything up here," he said, tapping an index finger on his temple, "that I'm not so sure about. The human brain is a fragile artefact. But that really isn't my remit."

Technically, it isn't Eleanor Wither's remit either, I thought.

"Until next time, David," the doctor concluded. "We'll be watching. Waiting."

He exited the ward, whistling as the sound of his footsteps echoed and faded down an unseen hospital corridor.

The doctor was right. I did salvage something from the wreck. Sitting on a damp bench outside the ward (a cigarette in one hand, my other arm winched in a sling across my chest), everything was distinctively sharper. Vision. Touch. Taste buds. My concentration. Everything. Mesmerised, I took in my surroundings with a newfound fascination. Was it the pills and alcohol finally vacating my system or a resuscitated pizzazz, a revival of focus? I knew this kaleidoscopic clarity wouldn't last forever. Like the flicker of a flame, it might even fade with the day's cloud-shrouded sunlight. Alarmed with this eventuality, I decided to discharge myself. I needed to act decisively.

Undetected, I exited the ward and lurched up Blackshaw Road, leaning on an elbow crutch for purchase. By the time I reached the intersection of Upper Tooting Road, I dropped the crutch and picked up the pace, cantering for the Antelope. I was dressed in the same mutilated suit from the night of the accident, but the universe looked revitalised. The brutal edges of the brutal buildings. Bubbles rocketing to the tops of beer bottles. Every hair and feather on the swarms of humans and pigeons. Even the raindrops looked like crystal kingdoms falling from Heaven. In this hypersensitive state, I could see the microscopic building blocks of reality. I couldn't determine whether it was the aftereffects of the morphine or a restored lust for reality's undiluted bluster. I felt no pain. And my vague memories from the accident began to take on a nostalgic glow. The streamlined interiors of the car that transformed into an iron maiden of jagged steel and glass felt like a mechanical womb that birthed me into a crystalline existence. Undead, I never felt more alive. Perhaps Rachel Garland was right. Perhaps we could live forever.

This was an epiphany worth celebrating. In the Antelope I ordered a bottle of prosecco with my double gin and tonic. I then called *The Daily Sun* from the phone behind the bar. When I couldn't reach Eleanor Wither, they put me through to the publishing director.

"I'm running a little late, two days late," I said. "Car trouble. I'll be on my way as soon as I settle my tab."

Wordlessly, the publishing director hung up the receiver.

When I eventually limped into the lobby of our office on Crucifix Lane, the receptionist (Dave) and security guard (also Dave) didn't appear to recognise me. They also said that nobody named Eleanor Wither works here. "Nobody named Eleanor Wither has *ever* worked here," they added.

"What about Leonard Lynch?" I asked. "Len will vouch for me."

"Apologies, sir, what did you say your name was?" asked the security guard, growing impatient.

"David Temple. T-E-M-P-L-E. Photojournalist."

Dave checked the log book. The other Dave picked up the phone. And then both Daves frowned.

"We're very sorry, sir, but we don't appear to have any employees named David Temple either."

"That's very interesting," I said, exiting the building.

Undiscouraged, I hobbled into The White Hart on the corner of Dolben and Great Suffolk Street, the local boozer where Eleanor Wither and I drank every evening and lunchtime. She was nowhere to be seen. I described Eleanor to the landlord: glasses, glugged house red, this tall, heavy makeup, heavy smoker. The landlord apologised. "Never seen her," he shrugged. I then used their phone to leave a message at Eleanor's flat. The number, apparently, didn't exist.

It's strange how cities swallow people whole. But it's not unknown. London tried to devour me too. The asphalt gaped open like a diseased mouth, welcoming the car and its fragile passengers. But it spat me back out again. Back into unconsciousness. Either it didn't enjoy the taste of my chemical-enriched flesh or it decided to give me a second chance. The city, I assumed, had its own motives.

Shock. Bones breaking like glass. Skulls cracking like eggshells. Ejaculations of chilly adrenaline. Trauma moves humans in strange ways. Exposure to the frailties of our mortal vessel can bring us closer together. But not Rachel Garland and I. The accident drove us to different realities, different worlds. It threw us out of our mutual destruction. But it was also the climax of a natural decline.

I'm not coming back. We're not coming back. We're moving to the Sierra Nevada. To a town called Paradise.

This is what Rachel told me in the car, in the driver's seat, before the crash, before the impact.

The first night we met, the night Rupert died, was an accident. Moving in with you, spending time with you, was not. Here's the truth–

These words, my proximity to death, Rachel Garland's departure. They gave me the motivation I needed to finish *Sick & Beautiful*. If *The Daily Sun* wouldn't accept my article (or my existence), then the world would accept my book. I decided it was destiny.

In my bathroom, I changed my bandages and dressings. I removed the stitches under my right eyebrow and across the bridge of my nose. I swabbed my pink legions with cotton wool doused in antiseptic. I watched my vivid bruises fade like a bouquet of flowers. The whole time I sweated atop Father's typewriter. Overlooking the rooftops and forecourts of Brixton, I watched the horizon shift from grey to black, black to grey, and decanted a carafe of pain. I was aware that my creative drive could dissipate at any second. Time was precious, truncated. I feverishly raced to the final chapter.

I was inspired by my body's ability to heal up and recuperate. But the doctor was right. My mind was unable to recover at the same rate. It seemed irreversibly damaged. How close did I really come to becoming another fatality in the morning tabloids? The question haunted every juncture of time. Fear waited for me in empty toilet cubicles and car parks, in-between the walls of filthy mezzanines, crouched in the cellars of abandoned high-rises and candlelit squalors. It never felt stronger, closer. But did fear also inspire me? I detested the writing process, yet I still felt compelled to finish the job.

Publishing a novel.

These words, in my mind, were weighted with mysterious esteem, like *conquering the mountain, finding the cure* or *making dreams a reality*. I needed to seize them like gilded possessions. I needed the money too. But I didn't need Rachel Garland to complete the story. Did I even need her to *start* it? I wondered. The accident vandalised my body and consciousness, but it gave me stamina, focus. Without it, I'd still be dead. In another reality, perhaps I still am. In its afterglow, it left an oblivion I never previously dared to contemplate or occupy. One that could traverse dreams and reality. One populated by a grinning spectre in a bowler hat.

Had this creature always been a projection of my neurotic imagination? Or did Rachel inaugurate its darkness?

CHAPTER
TWELVE

*S*ick & Beautiful? *I don't get it. It's a story about love, death, humanity, hope. But* Sick & Beautiful *tells me nothing. It's like your prose. Obscure and ostentatious.*

There's something I'd like to say about this critique: I disagree with Rupert Wreath.

Sick & Beautiful is the perfect title. It's elfin. Rhythmic. Juxtaposed. Suggestive of a deeper meaning. But I agree that the book's content lacks substance and clarity. This, however, isn't my fault. Rachel Garland, quite simply, refused to be a case study. She quickly fell out of love with the project when she discovered a truth I wasn't prepared to confront. Here it is – *I didn't have a clue what I was doing*. Because of my artistic ineptitudes, she only divulged the most prosaic details.

"Where were you born?" I once asked her, turning on the tape deck, pen and notepad in-hand.

"Paris."

"I've never visited Paris, but I can picture it. The Eiffel Tower. People sitting outside cafés under striped awnings, reading papers and drinking espressos. Music in the night. It seems so– *romantic*."

"That part of the city, the images you see in movies and magazines, is just dramaturgy. It's far from romantic when you grow up in the banlieues."

"What are the *banlieues*?"

"The suburbs. There are gangs. Gun crime. It's where people are forced to go when they don't live up to your romantic ideals. My only escape was the local cinema."

"What is your favourite memory in that cinema?"

"Sneaking through a fire escape to watch *The Lost Boys*. I sat in the back row, smoking cigarettes, mesmerised by Jami Gertz."

"Did this moment inspire you to become an actor?"

"Perhaps. I'd say Virginia Madsen, Jodie Foster and Sigourney Weaver's respective roles in *Candyman*, *The Silence of the Lambs* and *Alien* had a more profound effect on me."

"What else has a profound effect on you?"

"The sensation of raindrops and snowflakes on my skin. Skies filled with stars. Swimming naked. Visiting different countries, experiencing different cultures. And walking through commons at night, barefoot, utterly alone."

"What has the opposite effect? What's your worst nightmare?"

"I used to have recurring dreams about being buried alive. Being consumed by billions of maggots and spiders in a coffin, in darkness, in a hole in the ground."

"No. I mean, what's your worst nightmare in *reality*?"

"Delayed trains and buses. Crowded airports. Being recognised, being stared at, in a public space. The feeling of wet sand and seaweed between my toes."

"On a beach?"

"Sand. Seaweed." Rachel smiled. "Isn't it obvious?"

"Tell me more about the beach. Where is the beach? When did you visit it? Who were you with?"

"That, David, is not your concern."

This is how it went, our interviews. I'd ask questions. Rachel Garland would offer vague answers, but then her responses would grow bolder, more confident, only to stagnate again as she retreated into herself, leading me through her labyrinth of dead ends and blind alleys. Her behaviour suggests an obvious theory – she has nothing interesting or horrific to hide. Rachel Garland is pursuing movie stardom, but it doesn't necessarily mean that she eked out a past any less ordinary than every other human dragging their heels across the planet. Birth, growth, love, spiritual loss, professional failure, driving lessons, car crashes, inadequate pay checks, reproduction, redundancy or forced retirement, sickness, bereavement, death, cremation or burial. By telling me nothing, she wanted me to believe that she is following the script of normal life. But I wasn't buying it. It was scribbled in her anatomy, her observations, her misanthropic charisma. I knew there was something there, hiding inside her. I could *feel* it.

When Rachel Garland refused to open up, I started to conduct my own research. I read through my notes, searching for clues, leads, shreds of information that could reveal her secrets. First, I rang the casting agencies that sourced the talent for the movies she said she acted in. I asked if they had anyone named Rachel Garland on their books. Four came up positive, but get this: none could verify if they ever invited her to an audition. And they all had her registered at different addresses. I wrote these down and hung up the phone. It turns out that she lived in a wave of dingy flats in Bow Road, Hammersmith and Gypsy Hill before she moved into Rupert Wreath's riverside apartment on Canary Wharf. One of her ex-flatmates, another struggling actor named Earnest Norrie, told me that Rachel made her movie industry contacts waitressing at coke-fuelled wrap parties in-between taking acting classes at the National Theatre in Lambeth. But when I interviewed the coaches there, they couldn't confirm is she ever attended any of their seminars. This was the problem. These characters knew as much about Rachel Garland as I did – almost nothing. After a promising start, the trail had ran cold.

My only other lead was Rachel Garland's drug dealer, Docklands Dave. When I picked up a gram of coke off him back in February, I asked if we could talk about Rachel Garland. "Never heard of her," he said, receding back into the jaws of Stockwell tube station. When I picked up another gram two days later, he gave me the same answer. He wouldn't talk. Not even for money. Not even when I offered to change his name to a clever pseudonym, something like Dalston Dave or Docklands Daryl. He had an integrity my other interviewees lacked. Perhaps Docklands Dave adheres to an anomalous set of ideals that are more principled. Or, perhaps, he possessed all the knowledge on Rachel I was seeking. Dealers, after all, know what makes you tick, what keeps you up (and down) at night. They know your body. They hold the keys to your soul.

The next time I picked up off Docklands Dave (two more grams, just three days later), I decided, quite impulsively, to follow him into the underground. I learnt that he lives in

Bermondsey, in a canal boat on the Tower Bridge Moorings. Flanked with thriving, brightly-painted flower boxes, his floating home has a name: *Paradise*. Sat inconspicuously by the riverbank, I listened to him use the pronouns *she* and *her* when referring to Paradise with an accent somewhere between Cockney and Caribbean. By all accounts, he is a creature of habit, fine-tuned to the palpitations of the city. In the morning he eats breakfast and reads the papers in a greasy spoon on Wolseley Street, two roads from the docks. Fried eggs (sunny side down), bubble and squeak, buttery triangles of burnt toast. He then rolls a fag and follows the river to the Market Porter in Borough. That's where he spends the rest of his day, in the boozer's embrace, working through the ales, fingers gliding over the fruit machine, conducting his business diligently.

Docklands Dave: a *fascinating* character. Surreptitious. And somehow more well-rounded than Rachel Garland. But my knowledge of him didn't bring me any closer to knowing my protagonist. It was another cold trail. Another dead end.

I haven't stalked or contacted Docklands Dave since. But my nightmare of the Market Porter feels like a fresh lead, an ambiguous clue.

We're only beginning to understand the true purpose of our roles. I have a feeling things are going to get weird, but I have devout faith in the script.

Rupert Wreath's words keep playing through my mind too. What is Docklands Dave's role in this story? I wonder. If I approached him tonight, would he finally reveal something significant that could progress my own narrative?

Stood in my sitting room, I listen to the rainfall.

"Probably nothing," I mutter, talking myself out of it.

I pace around the flat, seesawing between nausea and apprehension, unable to temper my excitement. As instructed by Rupert Wreath, I attempt to get some shuteye. I put on two movies (*Piranha II: Flying Killers* followed by *Cujo*) and repose into the sofa. Arms folded, head propped up, eyes closed, I drink a large gin and tonic with a diazepam. I get stoned. I drop another pill into an even larger gin and tonic. I try everything, but I can't sleep. I can barely sit still. Consumed with simmering trepidation, I concede that relaxation under the circumstances, even with the support of sedatives, would be impossible. There is another problem. I can't reach my regular dealers either. I try ringing them three times each before finally placing the receiver back on its hook. I realise that I won't have the strength or valour to confront Richard Hayes and seize the photo album without the ministration of drugs. I *have* to step into the Market Porter tonight. I *have* to find Docklands Dave. It doesn't matter if it's preordained, if it's part of the script. I have no choice.

Also as instructed by Rupert Wreath, I slither into something with more *panache* – a mustard corduroy three-piece with a paisley shirt, floral socks and ruby bowtie. For the first time since our university days, I feel obliged to counter or, inconceivably, trump Richard Hayes's pageantry. The colour of the bowtie, by no coincidence, matches the wrapping paper of the gift on the breakfast table, a small surprise for my old friend. I pull on my overcoat, pick up the gift and briefcase, forget my brolly, exit the flat. I then ride the tube six stops from Brixton to London Bridge, surface into the rain on Borough High Street, turn right onto Stoney Street and step through the heavy doors of the Market Porter.

The boozer is packed with women and men in soaked

suits and raincoats, hunched across sticky tables cluttered with ashtrays and pint glasses. Tangles of fairy lights and iridescent tinsel are roped behind the bar and over the windows. I feel relief, safety, invisible in the throng of limbs, the clouds of cigarette smoke. But there's no sign of Docklands Dave. I shoulder to the bar. The bald landlord nods earnestly when I order a double gin and tonic. I thank him, find an empty table, knock back my drink, unfold a deserted paper. I skim the headlines (murders, fatal drink-driving accidents, delayed trains, a plane crash in India). I start the crossword. I give up on the crossword. I look at my pocket watch. I return to the bar to order another gin. And then I smile.

There he is. Cradled in the glow of the fruit machine, broad shoulders bulge inside his tracksuit. One hand clutches a pint glass. The other is cocked over the buttons. His rings and crucifix necklace reflect in the light like distant stars. Underneath the brim of his flat cap, piercing blue eyes watch the wheels of the bonus revolve with promise. He twirls his cornrows around his index finger, watching, anxiously waiting. The trainers, remarkably, are flawlessly white. They're practically celestial. How does he keep them so immaculate in this perpetually deluged city? I wonder.

I lean over the bar and say to the landlord: "Tell me what you know about Docklands Dave."

"If you want to do business with Dave, you need to speak to his spirit," he replies.

We fall silent, watching Docklands Dave confidently navigate the constellation of twinkling buttons, as if he's mastered the controls of an extraterrestrial spacecraft. There is a hypnotic beauty in these proficient movements. They're music, like birdsong and traffic.

"Dave can't trust you until he understands the abyss of your pain," he adds.

"I got the impression that Dave isn't the talking type."

"He isn't, per se. He's more of a listener. But if you *give* him something, a piece of yourself, he'll give something back. He'll give you his everything. He has this ability for bringing it out of people."

"Bringing what out?"

"The truth. The plot."

"That's good to know," I say, unsure how to interpret this advice. When Docklands Dave hits the jackpot and the shrapnel cascades into his cupped palms, I walk up behind him and lean against the fruity. I rope my arm around it. Docklands Dave narrows his eyes, examining my face, my obtrusive attire, with vague curiosity.

"It's good to see you, Dave," I say, holding out my other hand.

He tips his winnings into his tracksuit trousers and sips his pint.

"I don't want to talk about Rachel Garland," he says.

I slide my hand back into my pocket.

"Me either," I reply, surprised that he remembers our conversation several months ago. "Here's the truth, Dave. I had a dream about the Market Porter last night. A bad dream. I can't explain why, but I feel like I'm supposed to be here. Forces are driving me to this place. Forces I cannot decrypt."

"In that case, let's continue this conversation somewhere more private. Right this way, David."

The landlord nods solemnly as Docklands Dave leads me behind the jump and through a door that reads *STAFF ONLY*. We scale a narrow staircase and enter a disused function room. When he flicks the light switch, a single bulb fizzes to life in the cobwebbed chandelier. The room is filled with ragged furniture, broken bar stools, pool tables draped with dust sheets. Rusted springs moan as we sink into the armchairs by the window. Docklands Dave and I sit opposite each other, listening to the soundtrack of rainfall, human traffic bottlenecking the market, the hum of life in the pub below. The dilapidated interior of the function room reminds me of the Market Porter from my nightmare. I peer out of the window, checking the sky for interstellar fire.

"What would you like to talk about, David?" he asks, rolling a cigarette.

It's interesting how you can share your life story, your darkest secrets, with a complete stranger. It takes almost nothing to break down and spill your soul. Head cradled in my hands, I tell Docklands Dave everything. My authorial ambitions. Getting sacked from *The Daily Sun*. My neighbour's talking cat. The cloud. The accident. The nightmare. My bizarre meeting with Rupert Wreath and the plan to steal the photo album from Richard Hayes. The overcrowded tube on the way here. But most of all? I tell him about Rachel Garland. While I unload my meandering backstory, the landlord dutifully brings up fresh drinks in 20-minute intervals, taking the empties back down with him. Halfway through the fourth round, I stand up and embrace Docklands Dave, gently weeping.

"Don't cry, David. Everything will work out in the end. For better or worse, it usually always does. I can *feel* it."

I slump back into my armchair in a billow of dust, exhausted by my confession. Did he expect this? I wonder, studying his face. Blue sky-eyed, serenely spoken, Docklands Dave isn't even mildly tipsy. His expression is ruminative, aesthetically pleasing. He stares into his half-empty pint glass, immersed in quiet reflection.

"Thank you for your honesty," he says. "Your vulnerability. Today I'm your guardian angel, David. I'm here for you. To help you realise your dream. To guide you safely towards the gates of Paradise."

Docklands Dave slaps two baggies in my palm. One contains a white powder, the other six blue pills pressed with the silhouette of a TV set. He closes my fingers around them with an unexpected tenderness, giving my hand a forgiving squeeze.

"You believe that your role is to publish your book," he says, "but what if it's bigger? I believe that we serve a broader purpose. Something we can't yet understand. I have faith that we'll both be enlightened soon. Until then, you're following the clues, David. You're taking opportunities as they present themselves. You're driving the plot. I'm excited to see how this thing plays out. I'm thrilled to be a part of the process. I really am. I'm sure Rupert feels the same way. Even Rachel. Like I said. We're all part of something bigger. Bigger than publishing a novel. Bigger than anything we could ever fathom."

I pull a copy of *Sick & Beautiful* out of my briefcase and place it on his lap. We stare at the manuscript wordlessly.

"What could be bigger than publishing a novel?" I finally ask.

I blink and feel fresh tears trickle down my cheeks. We both sense that reality is on the verge of evolving, deforming, *moulting*.

"The answer is nothing is bigger," I say. "Absolutely nothing."

CHAPTER
THIRTEEN

I enter London Bridge tube station and, in one fluid movement, trip on the escalator, summersault down the bottom four steps and smash my gin and tonic on the platform. I squeeze my briefcase to my chest, feeling the world spin uncontrollably around me. In a puddle of shattered glass – cackling, sobbing, shaking, sweating, struggling to unravel the components of my body – I'm drunk, delirious, reminiscing about Richard Hayes.

Clean shaven, immaculately dressed, Richard Hayes always fits in. It's effortless. I don't know what to say. He just connects with people. He's cordial, approachable, dripping with charisma. And once you get him talking? He has a broad understanding of the arts, an eclectic knowledge. Greek philosophy. Ancient Egypt. The Roman Empire. Cinema. Stocks. Current affairs. Global politics. High fashion. Serial Killers. Football (premiership and club level literacy). Astrology. Pornography. His comprehension is endless.

He has jokes too. Timeless gags. Highbrow quips. Poignant anecdotes. Yeah. This guy has it all. "It's all in the timing, David," he always explains. I hate to admit it, but his timing is meticulous. The guffaws and backslaps that follow are entirely justified. The punchlines? Merely an afterthought.

Most remarkable of all? He doesn't wait to speak. Richard *listens* – body language responsive, eyes dewy with attentive sincerity. He knows what it takes to converse, to communicate. Nobody ever asks Richard if the tales he conjures are true. They don't care. They simply want to believe in him. It's difficult to blame them. His hope is contagious.

I always felt left out of Richard's carefully engineered circles. A spirit floating on the periphery. I have what you might call *weird energy*. Whenever I talk, it's like listening to an orchestra of untuned instruments. Something is off. I shuffle, grind my teeth. I stall and stammer, punctuating excruciating silences with rude interruptions and nervous laughter. I shovel drugs and hors d'oeuvres into every unobstructed orifice, desperately searching for something meaningful to say.

Rachel Garland stopped inviting me to parties because of these eccentricities. The last event we attended together was in July. It was the night of the accident. An afterparty on St George's Square following the premiere of *The Passion of Darkly Noon*. At this point, Rachel Garland decided she was finished with horror movies, horror people. She was ready for serious roles, connecting with serious people. Richard Hayes, who hobnobbed with said serious people, asked Rachel Garland and myself to come along. He invited Rachel to advance the trajectory of her career. He invited me because he knew it wouldn't take me long to publicly implode. He was right. In fact, it took less than 30 minutes.

"*The Passion of Darkly Noon* isn't even realistic," I muttered to Rachel. We stood near the buffet table, my mouth stuffed with shellfish and stale bread. "Hardly anyone dies in the whole movie. I've already seen two bodies today and heard about an accident on the Blackfriars Underpass killing five more. This movie isn't *art*. It doesn't imitate reality. It's cheap trash, Rachel. You're better than this."

"Why don't you get a cab back to the flat?" she suggested, embarrassed by my volume. "Nobody will talk to me when you're hovering over my shoulder. Everybody's on edge. They know you're a journalist. They're probably worried you might write up some ruinous quote about them. They've been burned by your kind before."

I slipped my pen and notepad into my pocket, feeling self-conscious. In the background, by the bar, I could see Richard Hayes, smiling, quaffing champagne, watching our acrimony blossom. This detail irritated me.

"What the fuck am I supposed to do, Rachel? Isn't it my role to record the scene, to capture you in motion?"

"I don't know what your role is, David," she screamed. "Perhaps you don't have a role anymore. Perhaps you never did."

"Perhaps," I whispered.

I looked at the small but anxious crowd gathering around us (they seemed to be hoping for a violent confrontation) and decided to exit the party with a false sense of dignity. I barged through the murmuring spectators, plucked my overcoat off the hat stand and slammed the front door behind me.

Alone, smoking in the rainfall, I waded across the puddled pavements of Pimlico and Vauxhall Bridge, meandering south-west towards Brixton. I was coked-up, eyes inundated with tears. Richard Hayes would already be embracing Rachel Garland, consoling her with astonishing compassion. *He doesn't understand you, Rachel*, he would say. *David doesn't get it.* But a darkness lies behind his tenderness. A creature wearing a mask, desperate to confess its secrets.

Like Rachel Garland, my relationship with Richard Hayes was born through the lens of violence. We boarded in the same halls during our first year at King's College, his room directly above my own. One night I heard frantic pacing through the floorboards above, drawers slamming, extended pauses punctuated by sporadic bursts from the bedroom to the bathroom. When I heard a knock on my door, I wasn't surprised to find Richard stood in the hallway, sweating profusely, dressing gown parted at his hairless chest. He smelt like vermouth and cigarettes.

"It's my roommate," he said. "There's been an accident."

Although I'd seen Richard Hayes around our halls, awkward and apparently friendless, this was the first time we had spoken. His voice was notably delicate, playfully curious. I felt instantly drawn.

"Bring your camera too, David," he added, pointing to the Praktica Super TL2 around my neck.

How does he know my name? I wondered. At this point, I didn't even know his. But the detail felt insignificant.

In his bathroom – identical to my own, so small the tiny basin protruded over the back of the toilet – a naked man was slumped in the shower. Round flesh flattened against the tiles. His hands covered his face, as if he was hiding from the living world. The mouth gaped open, frozen in a silent scream. Both wrists were slashed from the base of the palms to the inside of the elbows. We studied the ruffles of tissue,

How they metamorphosised into something compelling, something beautiful. This human, from the same planet, the same city, filled with unrealised aspirations and memories, just like us. The scene moved me, its undiluted sorrow.

"What was his name?" I asked.

"I don't know. He was a solitary chap. Quiet. Studied Physics, judging by the books on his bedside table. But honestly, David. Who cares what his name was? He wasn't even famous."

"Perhaps he never wanted to be."

Suddenly noticing the sickly aroma of dried blood, I opened the bathroom window, welcoming the smells and sounds of the weather and traffic, breaking the serenity of this claustrophobic space. Richard Hayes tilted his head sideways, trying to comprehend the body from a unique perspective.

"When did you find him?" I asked.

"Last night."

"You've been in here with a dead body since yesterday?"

"I guess I wanted to preserve the moment," he shrugged unapologetically. "Get cushty with the notion of death. Have you ever seen a dead body before tonight?"

"I was barely 10 years old when Mother collapsed in the kitchen," I said. "An asthma attack and cardiac arrest in fatal succession. I remember all the small details. The chessboard linoleum. Father arched over her limp body, pressing his fists into her chest, tears in his eyes. Their teacups on the worktop, still producing little palls of steam. Our neighbours banging on the front door, telling us to keep the noise down. It was dark outside. And raining. Inside this memory, the only thing that I can't recall is Mother's face. She's an androgynous mannequin in a floral dress, without eyes, without a nose or a mouth. No shape. No contours. When the ambulance finally arrived, I asked Father if I could watch the paramedics save her. He nodded with his forehead cradled in his hands. I remember Father had already removed his wedding ring and placed it in the centre of the dining table. He just stared at it. This heirloom from a reality that would soon be inaccessible. Before the paramedics rolled her into the back of the ambulance, Father leant over her body and took a photograph. He never let me see this photo or any others of Mother. Perhaps he thought this would help us heal, so we could move forward into the past."

Why did I feel inclined to share this information? I wondered. I was surprised by my desire to impart these intimate details so openly, so explicitly. Richard Hayes looked pleased. In fact, he looked *delighted*.

"Death does that to us," he said. "Have you ever noticed how traffic slows down to look at an accident? Or how crowds always flock around a casualty in the centre of the street? You and I are experiencing a similar sensation, David. The violent collision of fear and fascination. What do you think it means?"

"I think it means we need to call an ambulance."

"What's the rush? He's already in Paradise."

"Indeed," I whispered. Although I was disgusted by this suggestion, I was more appalled by my own actions as I felt my hands creep down to the camera. I looked through the lens, aiming at the deceased's expression of pain, and took a photograph, unaware that this act would be a precursor for my journalistic future, unaware that my ambitions of reporting from the national affairs desk of an acclaimed newspaper were already manufactured for failure. I took another photograph. And another. Richard Hayes attempted to conceal the erection bulging underneath his dressing gown.

"When you get those negatives developed," he said, "I'll pay you for them. It would be a shame not to capture this memory. The mind is like a photo album in many ways. We need to fill it with our experiences, our evocations of the present and the past. Who are we without memories, David?"

The paramedics took the body away the next morning, Richard moved into a new flat and, inside a few weeks, everybody forgot about the dead boy in the shower. But Richard Hayes and I continued our friendship. Sultan Gillespie, my other friend who sat next to me in my English Lit. lectures, sensed a simmering threat.

"Who knows what he did with that body before you showed up," he whispered in the back of a seminar on dystopian fiction (Atwood, Orwell, Ballard). "Richard is sick. Perhaps even infectious."

I probably should have listened. Sultan Gillespie had intuition and foresight beyond his years (it was borderline telepathic), but he didn't understand the beauty Richard Hayes and I uncovered that night. The scene bonded us like a vulgar sex act that we were unable to resist or consent to. It was as if a lightbulb fizzed to life before exploding inside the darkest alcoves of our consciousness. Like the effects of an eternal acid trip, we opened the gateway to an inescapable reality. In-between lectures, exams and slasher marathons in the Prince Charles, Richard and I lurked in the A&E waiting rooms of St Bartholomew's and St George's, or on crash-prone blind bends and junctions, late at night, hoping for flurries of violence. I wanted to get lost in his world. I followed death with Richard because I was terrified of it. I wanted to test my endurance. I wanted to learn what compelled him. If he felt fear. Back then, I felt the same way about Richard as I did about Rachel Garland when I met her a decade later, in the rain, in front of the corpse of Rupert Wreath: a vocation, a perverse reverence. Even now, I believe that their words, their aberrant perspectives, have the power to heal me. Richard Hayes and Rachel Garland. They seduce me like Sirens.

While Sultan Gillespie soared towards a 1st degree and I struggled to a palpatory 2:2, Richard slowly disappeared from his Film Studies lectures to rubberneck traffic accidents, watch horror and porno movies and bribe cash-strapped medics at the Royal College of Surgeons to flog bits of their apathetic cadavers. His apartment is still adorned with these grisly souvenirs. Formaldehyde-pickled eyeballs. Deformed foetuses. Male and female genitalia. And so on. His collection is always growing. Just last Christmas he flaunted a leather wallet he claimed was handcrafted from bona fide human hide. His affluent parents didn't care how he spent his time or their bottomless pit of money. Their son was frighteningly happy in the umbra of their derelict marriage, in the gulf of his sullied fantasies.

I admit it. I despise my friend, Richard Hayes. I really do. But I still refuse to judge him. I won't. It's hypocritical to cast conclusions about his character without acknowledging the genetic, generational defects which disease us all.

After Mother died, I started to exhibit symptoms of the same sickness. It always flourished on stormy afternoons. In my yellow waterproofs, I scouted Streatham Common to pluck spiders from their raindrop-jewelled cobwebs and trap them inside glass jam jars. I'd then watch these creatures fight to the death, clambering over each other's twitching bodies, before piercing the metal lid with my pocketknife and drowning them with rainwater. I even displayed these jars on the windowsill of my childhood bedroom. But why? Did I want to be death's dealer instead of its helpless victim, just like Mother? Or did I want to remind myself, even as a child, of humanity's congenital cruelty? The cruelty that defines the universe and its tenants.

That's why I can't condemn Richard Hayes. He's one of us. Richard made the team. He's just so painfully predictable, so hopelessly human, *so us*. We all incubate this terminal sickness. We should nurture it, embrace it, just like Richard Hayes.

There is no known cure for the human condition.

CHAPTER
FOURTEEN

I sniff a bump of coke off the tip of my front door key as I exit South Kensington tube station, into the underpass of Exhibition Road. The memories of Richard Hayes and Mother's death blur, fade, evaporate.

Sheltered from the storm in this brick and concrete trachea, eight buskers honk and wheeze on trombones, horns and trumpets, stood behind a row of upturned bowler hats. Their cracked notes harmonise with the drum of distant traffic, the audio of tyres on flooded tarmac above us. I check Father's pocket watch. It's 10:56PM. After my emotional exchange with Docklands Dave, I'm almost an hour late. I swallow two of the ecstasy pills, scale the staircase to street level and emerge in the emphatic downpour.

I squint into the black abyss of the overcast night. "I'm not scared of you," I whisper. The cloud responds with a violent clap of thunder. It's laughing at me, mocking my resolve. It wants to remind me, remind all of us, of its looming presence, its undeniable power. I hold my briefcase over my head to shield myself from the rain and circumnavigate the arched façade of the Natural History Museum, towards the East Entrance. When I hammer on the doorknocker, I hear heavy footsteps grow nearer, louder, the sound of keys turning inside the lock. The door groans open a few inches. Sapphire eyes examine me through the gap. Ballroom music, from somewhere inside, drifts into the night.

"No visitors," says the voice on the other side. "This is a private party."

"Wait," I shout as the door starts to close. "I'm a special guest of Richard."

I pull the iridescent invite out of my breast pocket and hold it in front of me. *ONE ADMISSION TO PARADISE* glitters in the lamplight. The eyes narrow with suspicion, tilt, blink twice, and then soften.

"Apologies, sir," says the voice. "I'm sure you can appreciate I'm just doing my job."

When the door fully opens, I'm speechless, hung in time, heart juddering frantically.

The body of a hulking bouncer in a black double-breasted topcoat and bowler hat fills the width of the doorway. He's so tall, *so gigantic*, he has to crouch down to inspect me: the soggy attire, the bowtie drooping in my collar like a wilting flower, the gift tucked beneath my arm, the dilated pupils. He frowns, unimpressed by my shrinking presence. I stare back at the mosaic of scars across his face, the huge hand curled around the doorknob. He could cup my skull inside his palm and crush it like an eggshell, pluck my limbs from their sockets like an insect. He could do anything he wanted to this frail body.

"Follow me," he says, closing the door behind us, turning the key, locking us inside.

I trail a few paces behind him in the dimly-lit gallery. I can now see that the bouncer towers over seven feet tall. *Jesus*, I think. Every object and piece of furniture he passes appear dwarfed, crooked, off-kilter. It's like watching a behemoth walk through a human doll house. It's unsettling. It's trippy.

"How are you and Mr Hayes acquainted?" he asks, syllables and footsteps reverberating through the empty corridor.

"We went to university together," I say vaguely.

As we walk through the anthropology department, I study the human remains and artefacts softly illuminated inside the glass display cases. Every crude tool and split skull reminds me of a familiar fairytale – the rise and fall of our species, the recurring hiccups of humankind. They also remind me of Father. This place. These halls. It's as if I'm rambling through my own memories.

When I was a child – when I wasn't scribbling inside colouring books on the floor of the bookies while Father heckled television sets projecting images of galloping horses and sprinting greyhounds – I remember our fortnightly father-son junkets to the museum. The Hornium Museum & Gardens. The Huntarian Museum. The V&A. The Science Museum. The National Portrait Gallery. The Grant Museum of Zoology & Comparative Anatomy. And here. Father admired the building's architecture and the truths it protects.

"It's crucial to understand how far we haven't come," he once told me as I sat on his shoulders, eating ice cream, trying to be a child. "Humanity is gripped in an endless spiral. Loops within loops within loops within loops. You and I, David, are just another iteration of that inescapable cycle."

Then, I didn't understand him. But now? I'm not so sure. After all the things I've seen through the camera lens, in my depraved nightmares, I've gradually lost faith in the human race. Just like Father.

"I assume you studied evolutionary anthropology with Mr Hayes?" asks the bouncer.

I smile. I wonder again why Richard Hayes would lie about his education or profession to a complete stranger. Whether he is a famed director or an esteemed anthropologist, does he dream about being anybody but himself? Will any role or reality suffice, as long as it isn't his own? He is a shapeshifter, an urban chameleon, capable of effortlessly adapting to his drab surroundings.

"I'm a digger and dabbler in ancient texts, actually," I reply, deciding to engage in this unusual game. "Philology and archaeology, to be precise. In many ways, I suppose I'm like a time traveller."

"That's very interesting," he says, but he doesn't sound convinced (or interested). I can only assume he doesn't believe Richard's fabricated backstory either.

I follow him to the top of a spiral staircase, across a buckled atrium, under an arched doorway and into a vast library. The walls are lined with bookcases and vitrines filled with stuffed primates that snarl with inane, glassy-eyed hostility. Vacant dining tables are arranged in the centre of the room. They are covered with furrowed napkins, dirty plates, flickering candelabrums, empty flutes and champagne bottles. At the far end of the library there is a stage and lectern. The banner hung above it says *PARADISE AUCTION*. Behind the stage, over the balustrades, ballroom music floats up from the ground floor of the Hintze Hall below us. I let out a crushed sigh. I've missed the auction. *I've blown it.* What am I going to tell Rupert

Wreath? Would he still publish *Sick & Beautiful* if I couldn't obtain the photo album? Hope, expedited by the coke, evacuates my body, leaving a vacuous numbness.

The bouncer clears his throat.

"Someone to see you, sir," he says.

I hear a strained giggle and spot a scarecrow-like silhouette sat behind one of the dining tables. How long has he been here, waiting alone in the darkness? He rises unsteadily like a reanimated corpse, gripping his seat to steady himself. I force a smile.

It's him. It's Richard Hayes.

"Is that David Temple surfacing under the bowed rafters?" he asks jovially, trying to seem sober as he approaches us. He cups his hands around mine. His eyes glow in the candlelight behind horn-rimmed spectacles. The tang of champagne and cigarettes sours his breath. "Late as usual, but it's always splendid to share the floor with an old academic," he continues. "You must tell me, though, what in God's name are you *wearing*? I can't decide whether you're dressed for a wedding or your funeral."

Here he goes, I think. Richard Hayes is performing, striving to look and sound compelling.

"I'm dressed with panache," I reply quietly, pretending that his comment hasn't antagonised me.

"Who cares how the invisible man is dressed? He can wear anything, pretend to be anybody and no-one."

Richard Hayes: in the dancing candlelight, what is supposed to be a pert smile looks more like a tormented grimace. At one time, he was excellent at concealing his grief and insecurities behind an irreverent, cheerful veneer – enough for people to say things like, *Isn't Richard just outrageous?* Or, *Richard is quite a character, isn't he?* – but those corrosive emotions seem to have taken a physical toll. The skin looks papery, dried out, pulling the eyes deeper into their sockets, causing the scarlet lips to recede, exposing the grey gums and yellow teeth underneath. Slowly, cracks have started to emerge on his mask. It's on the verge of breaking apart, disintegrating, sliding off with moist relief.

Richard Hayes notices the bouncer is still standing in the doorway (very still, very enormous).

"Thank you," he says, waving him off. "Please disappear. David and I have much to discuss."

"Very good, sir," nods the bouncer. Without question, he turns around and exits the library. I can hear his slow, heavy footsteps echo and vanish into the darkness of the museum's endless corridors.

"Your towering watchman says you're an anthropologist," I remark, deliberately flippant. "Does he know you're a university dropout? Couldn't even pass one year of *Film Studies*, for Christ's sake."

Richard Hayes stumbles to one of the empty dining tables, cackling with laughter. He picks up a half-empty champagne bottle and fills two flutes to the brim. He hands one to me. We both drink.

"We're actors who like to disappear into the fissures of our bizarre reality, David," he says. "Don't pretend you don't manipulate your surroundings too." He lets this statement resonate as he sinks the rest of his champagne. I follow suit. He tops up both our flutes again. "Are you well?"

"Very well," I reply. "In fact, I feel fantastic."

"You don't look it."

I smile with strained insincerity.

"How about you?" I ask, more out of conventional politeness than genuine interest.

"I've been a busy bee. Just last month I hosted two world premieres at the Prince Charles, the afterparties in Soho. One for *The Howling: New Moon Rising*. The other for *The Mangler*. I met Tobe Hooper. A wonderful man, David. We have photos together. The executive producer even invited me to spend the summer with him in Miami. I may just join him. Apologies for not extending an RSVP. You never were much of a hit at parties."

"So why tonight?" I ask quickly, struggling to conceal my irritation, already bored with his thinly-veiled rodomontade. Tension seems to be filling this huge space, creeping into every vacant crevice. Perhaps sensing this, *enjoying it*, Richard Hayes smiles before yawning dramatically (another small performance).

"I invited you tonight so I could congratulate you in person," he says.

"On what?"

"On *Sick & Beautiful*. I received your copy in the post. It was very thoughtful, David. Apologies for not ringing sooner. Like I said, it's been a busy six months since I last had the pleasure of your unique company. You certainly made that night more– *interesting*."

The way he says that last word. It sounds strange, unnatural, as if he cannot find the correct vocabulary to truly express himself. *That night*, of course, was the night of the accident. Richard Hayes closes his eyes, perhaps lost in these memories. But he isn't. He's firmly inside the present, listening to the rain hammering the rooftiles above. He shudders.

"My God, David," he says. "Old friend, have we ever witnessed such dismal drizzle? The cloud. It knows something we don't. It has secrets, just like us. I've been watching it all day. Studying it. What do you think it's planning up there? I've never seen it so swollen and septic. It terrifies me. We need to make first contact before it's too late. We've peacefully coexisted for so long. Us down here, that cloud up there. But now? It feels like it's preparing to wrest back control. Maybe it always has been. Once, you could see its edges. The head chef downstairs told me you still can in places as far as High Barnet and West Wickham. Now it seems to sprawl beyond the horizon, dilating into the blackness of outer space."

"Perhaps it's just a cloud," I suggest.

"Perhaps."

After an uncomfortable silence, listening to the chatter and ballroom music off-screen, I say: "I brought you a gift." I pick up the box between us and hand it to him. "Happy Christmas, Richard."

He removes his spectacles and slips them into the pocket of his waistcoat. He lifts the gift. And then he smiles. It's a real one this time (an ingenuous, toothy grin). The shape of the object, its stiff corners, the pleasant weight of it. He already knows what's inside. I do my best not to smile too, not to give into the simple happiness of this moment, but I can't resist. He peels the wrapping paper off like burnt skin. Inside are three videotapes: *Fright Night II*, *Return of the Living Dead 3* and *Children of the Corn*. Trading horror movies is a tradition we've followed every Christmas since we first met. Yeah, I know what I said earlier. That bit about hating my best friend, Richard Hayes. But, again, I couldn't resist. As one horror fanatic to another, I just couldn't.

"Thank you," he says, perhaps surprised by his own sincerity. "What a fantastic stack. Has there ever been a better cinematic adaptation of a short story than *Children of the Corn*? John Franklin is sensational too."

"He is," I agree. "A remarkable performance."

Suspended in this moment, it feels like old times. A pre-Rachel Garland epoch where there was less odium, strange love. A time when the term *friend* felt pertinent. I open my briefcase and hand Richard Hayes a copy of *Sick & Beautiful*. He takes it, silent, lips slightly parted.

"The final draft," I say. "I've made a few edits since I last sent you a copy. I think they've really elevated the text."

Richard Hayes seems lost on the front page. Not reading, but staring through it. Internally, the smile seems to falter, but it's impossible to gauge the authenticity of his expression.

"You must be delighted to finally secure a publisher. It's an extraordinary achievement, David."

"How do you know about the book deal?" I suddenly feel cold, dislocated from this scene. Is it possible he knows about the plot to steal the photo album too?

"I didn't," he shrugs. "I just naturally assumed you would have one. Jesus, David. I've read it. How can they *not* publish it?"

I nod, trying not to let this compliment dull my focus, my purpose, my tepid scorn. But my vanity can't resist the opportunity for acclamation.

"What did you think of it?" I ask.

"*Sick & Beautiful*?"

"*Sick & Beautiful*."

"It's– *interesting*."

That word again. And that's all it is. A word masking his true opinions.

Richard Hayes tilts his head back to chin another flute of lifeless fizz. The dregs trickle down his chin and inside the sleeve of his crushed velvet suit jacket. He doesn't appear to care or notice. His face is convulsed with excitement and iniquity. I can't decipher which emotions he's attempting to suppress. And then he laughs, mostly to himself.

"I brought you a present too, David," he says, changing the subject. "Something a little different." The grin returns, but this time it looks staged, almost sinister. "A gift that screams, *Bloody well done on publishing a novel, old friend.* I'm breaking our little tradition, but I believe the occasion warrants it."

Richard Hayes rises, teeters through the dining tables to the stage at the far end of the library and removes something hidden inside the lectern. He totters back, clears the smeared glasses and dinnerware and places my gift on the table. It's wrapped in a dirty cloth. I can't determine whether I'm imagining this sensation or if the ecstasy is beginning to waterlog my synapses, but I can feel a gravitational pull in its presence. It's like a magnetic field, the tide that slowly pulls you out to sea. I bite my bottom lip, desperate to create the illusion of self-control. Can Richard feel it too? Perhaps sensing this complex energy, he carefully unwraps the cloth.

"Happy Christmas, David."

It's an old book, bound in beaten red leather. One word is printed on its spine in gold-leaf italics: *PARADIS*. The letters twitch like flames in the candlelight. The front cover is embossed with a strange symbol. It looks like– it looks like a smiley face. I laugh. And then I shiver, recalling the finger-painting the man in the bowler hat left in my flat last night. Only one emotion ripples through my body in the presence of this object – sickness. It's abhorrent. It's filth. Vile and contagious, like diseased flesh. An abomination that must be burned, thrown into the ocean or launched into deep space. Forever. Just get away. Get away now. Before it's too late. Before it infects your soul. Before it consumes a piece of you forever.

"Thank you," I manage to whisper. "What is it?"

"It's a photo album. A very rare, very special piece for your collection. I know how you adore this sort of thing."

It looks like a photo album. But it's so much more. You'll know it when you see it, David. They say you can almost feel it.

Rupert Wreath's words rattle in the back of my mind as Richard Hayes slips on a pair of rubber surgical gloves and opens the photo album. He taps the inscription on the inside of the cover. Three lines of imperfect loops and slashes.

Cherche ton véritable objectif. Ou un différent point de focus. Seul les anges seront exempt du Paradis.

"I'm still waiting for the translation," he says. "Who know what secrets this note may possess?"

Why doesn't Richard Hayes want to touch it? I wonder. Can he feel its hideous emanations too?

"This object is very old, very delicate," he continues, perhaps sensing my suspicions. "We don't want to impose any unnecessary damage."

But I can barely hear him. I'm absorbed in the faces staring back at me as he turns the pages of the photo album.

Sealed behind cloudy walls of glassine, every photo is a portrait of agony. Angels with feathered wings plucked from their shoulders, careening from a clouded sky. Mayan sacrifices. Crucified slaves. Burning houses. Motorway pileups. Flayed corpses in a field of sunflowers. Soldiers executing civilians with bayonets. Humans disembowelled, decapitated, dismembered, hung, drawn, quartered, broken on the wheel. Were these atrocities staged by a sick shutterbug? Or is this something else, something inexplicable? Rupert Wreath's motivations for obtaining this artefact are almost as ineffable as the photo album itself. I can't metabolise its content for another second. I can't believe it exists. I can't believe it's here. I can't believe *I'm* here, we're here. I can't–

"That's enough," I say, gripping Richard Hayes's wrist before he can turn another page. He smiles before closing the photo album. "How did you acquire such a peculiar anthology, Richard?"

"That doesn't concern you, David. All you need to know is that we were supposed to auction it tonight, but I bought the piece myself at the last moment. I had this overwhelming feeling that you and this object *belong* together. I just couldn't shake it. It has an inscrutable beauty, doesn't it?"

"It's undeniable," I agree, but these are just words. Words to veil the unreality environing me. If Rachel Garland was with us, she would have recognised the photo album's awful beauty. She would have roped her arms around Richard Hayes's waist and rested her chin on his shoulder as he turned its pages. She would have bitten his neck, loosened his tie, unbuttoned his shirt, caressed him and the photo album with an abandoned affection. She would have understood him unconditionally.

Richard Hayes removes his gloves to rack up two lines of coke on the table. He rolls up a score and snorts the first line. I take the note and huff the second. The coke (which is, without doubt, of superior quality to my own) elevates me almost instantly, conversing seamlessly with the ecstasy. Richard stands up, only to collapse into his chair again. He drops his head into his palms and then, from out of nowhere, says: "I'm not certain what's real and what isn't anymore, David. My dreams and my reality seem to be merging, copulating."

Does he want me to cradle his trembling skeleton and softly whisper – *Don't worry, Richard. It will all be hunky dory in the end*? I can't bring myself to do it. Even the surging feelings of love from these potent drugs can't override my disdain for Richard Hayes. I feel empowered by his dull pain.

"You're being paranoid," I suggest feebly. "A psychologist on the TV suggested that excessive consumption of pornography and violent horror movies can inspire everything from sexual deviancy and suicide to inflation and mass murder. The only cure is eight hours of sleep a night and four litres of water per day. My editor, Ellie, told me it's vital to find a work-life balance that respects reality without submitting to its dreariness." I pat his shoulder with contrived reassurance. Then I shrug. "Perhaps you're just letting the city get the better of you, Richard."

"I haven't been sleeping well," he concedes. "Bad dreams."

This admission sends a blunt jolt of panic through my spine.

"What kind of bad dreams?" I ask.

"I can't remember." Richard Hayes awkwardly rises again and staggers towards the balcony behind the stage. "It's true what they say," he sighs, slumped over the balustrades. "Bad things really do happen to good people. Bad dreams and bad things."

I join him, gazing at the immaculately dressed guests dancing in the Hintze Hall below. They spin, step, weave and pivot to the music while waitresses swim between them, filling their gobs and glasses.

"Who are these people?" I ask.

"MPs. CEOs. TV and movie producers. Hedge fund managers. Actors. Wealthy people who aren't famous. Famous people who aren't wealthy. Not as wealthy as the *exceptionally* wealthy people, at least."

"You mean like your parents?"

"Precisely," he says, deciding not to engage with this provocative question.

And then I see her. My heart swells, tremors. In the middle of the dancefloor, I can see Rachel Garland. Abstract, weightless, she twirls in her floral dress, scattering raindrops in her wake like a halo of tears. She looks up. I wave, smiling. She doesn't smile. She doesn't wave back. Behind her, under the doorway of an empty gallery, I spot somebody else that deluges my body with dread.

His suit and overcoat look tattered, derelict. How did he get past the bouncer in this appalling attire? I wonder. He awkwardly imitates the motions of the guests, waltzing alone in a sick lullaby. I'm hypnotised, unable to move or look away. He's staring directly at us (sneering, sniggering). His eyes are black. They're oblivion. The dead space in-between realities. I sneer back, unable to stifle the bubbles of laughter clawing out of my throat.

"What's that pisshead been drinking?" I chuckle, nudging Richard Hayes with my elbow.

I clap, applauding this unsettling display.

He doffs his bowler hat and bows cordially.

I can now see his brain pulsating under his scalp, throbbing like a nest of eggs ready to hatch. He brushes aside the threads of long hair on his crown and gores his fingers into his skull. When he tears the soft flesh and bone apart like an envelope, butterflies swarm out of the wound and flutter upwards, all around us, flooding the hall's grand ceiling.

The other guests walk past this vulgar display linking arms, joyfully tipsy, sipping judiciously from flutes and tumblers. They can't see him or, conceivably, have chosen to ignore him. He grins as flies and spiders crawl out of his mouth, over his skin. He bites into his bottom lip, ejaculating a spurt of black blood across the floor.

"Interesting," I say. Richard Hayes, on the other hand, doesn't say anything. His face is drained of its sparse colour. If he sees the man in the bowler hat too, he isn't prepared to admit it, terrified what it would mean for both of us if this apparition isn't a mirage.

"You look like you've seen a ghost," I tell him, still fishing for a reaction.

When I look back towards the dancefloor, Rachel Garland and the man in the bowler hat have vanished. I gaze up at the ceiling. The swarm of butterflies has vanished too. "Did I just imagine that whole scene?" I ask. But Richard Hayes is already stumbling back into the darkness of the library, visibly shaken.

"I didn't know you invited Rachel," I say, maintaining a tone of casual disinterest. "I assume she stayed at yours last night? She didn't even stick around for the end of *Candyman*. And you know how much Rachel adores Virginia

Madsen. I'd be lying if I said I wasn't jealous. In fact, I was distraught."

Richard Hayes freezes mid-step, pivots sharply and marches back. He squares up to me, pressing his perspiring forehead against mine.

"Is that supposed to be a joke?" he asks.

Richard Hayes drops his flute. Knives of glass skate across the library's stone tiles.

"You're sick," he whispers, jabbing two fingers into my chest. "I know what really happened that night. I know what you did, David. And I know it wasn't an accident."

Time slows. I hear the gaps between each raindrop elongate, ticking on the slate rooftiles like a metronome. My heartbeat thuds in my eardrums like subterranean music. I examine the contracted frame of Richard Hayes, scanning from the twitching tenons in his neck down to the restless motion of his feet. Both hands are knots of white knuckles. I resume my cool stare, locked into the tempest of his moist eyes. I try not to let the corners of my mouth curl up into a giddy smirk. *Poor, butterfly-bellied Richard*, I tut. I feel a sense of pity, borderline guilt, for what is coming next.

"You think you've got what it takes, Richard?" I ask, arching a curious eyebrow. "Go on then, old friend. What are you waiting for? Throw your best shot. But be warned. I'll only give you one chance to land it."

I step back two paces and raise my fists, relaxed and ready. My shoulders are loose, chest puffed out like a breeze-bloated sail. I have already calculated several avenues for countering his orthodox attacks.

Scenario one. If Richard Hayes opens with a jab, I'll slip the left hand and launch the uppercut like a ballistic missile, sending him to the floor, likely unconscious.

Scenario two. If a comically telegraphed overhand right comes crashing from above, I'll sidestep the shot, taking my head off the centreline but staying in range to answer with a knee to the solar plexus. Before he meets the floor, winded, I can, if necessary, follow up this debilitating blow by ripping a hook to his jawbone or the woefully vulnerable liver. I might even do it for fun.

Scenario three. If (somehow) he closes the distance to clinch or link his fingers behind my neck to kiss the bridge of my nose with his forehead, I'll drop my centre of gravity, drive my shoulder into his hips and, with my hands cupped behind both knees, topple him into the tiles. From here, pinning him down with my knee on his stomach, I'll unleash a hailstorm of devastating elbows and punches.

Scenario four. I doubt Richard has any kicks in his arsenal to strike from distance. But if he does? It's obvious. I'll lift my leg on either side, turning the shin outwards to protect the meat of the calves and thighs, ready to replant my front foot and blitz a left-right-hook combo with the alacrity of an–

And just like that, all quite suddenly, I'm on the library floor, crawling with diffident limpness. How long have I been here? I wonder. I try to stand, but I can't. "I didn't see it coming," I mumble. Dazed, on my hands and knees, I look up at Richard Hayes. He is standing over me, trembling. I feel my swollen cheek, the blood trickling out of my numb mouth. My other hand feels boneless as it searches for stability. It's like I'm sinking in quicksand. "How could you do this to me, Richard?"

Richard Hayes catapults a shoe into my ribs with such enthusiasm his fringe and coattails spin like the frills of a twirling ballgown. He shakes the hand he threw to land the opening punch. He flexes his fingers, wincing as if the precious bones inside might be broken. Split skin weeps blood over raw knuckles.

"You ruined my life!" he screams. "You ruined *our* lives. Did you even know if it was a boy or a girl?"

When I fail to answer, Richard Hayes stampedes through the tables, flipping chairs and hurling plates as he emphatically exits the library.

"You can't judge me!" I scream back. "You don't know what it's like being me. *You don't know what it's like.*"

I pull myself up the balustrades and lean over the balcony, gasping for breath, dripping blood onto the hall three storeys below. The drunk guests are apparently oblivious to the melee that just occurred in the shadows above them.

I lurch back to the tables and, attempting to compose myself, drink from one of the champagne bottles until the tepid liquid inside foams from the corners of my mouth. Fighting back an onslaught of tears, I look at the photo album on the dining table. I stroke the leather cover. It feels like human skin, perspiring like living tissue. My peripheral vision widens. My equilibrium stabilises. I'm back in the scene, back in reality. The book deal, the plan, the fight, the fact that Richard Hayes may return with the bouncer at any moment, eager to escalate the violence. It all comes back to me. Who I am. Why I'm here.

Sensing the need to act with urgency, I snort another line of Richard Hayes's coke, wrap the photo album in its rag and lock it inside my briefcase. Rejuvenated by the drugs and bubbles, I race up and down staircases, through unlit passages, across empty rooms. I run until I spot an *EXIT* sign smouldering at the end of a long corridor, like a beacon cutting through the darkness. I take a deep breath and push open the fire escape. "*God*," I hiss. I've never been so relieved to feel the wet snog of rainfall. I dart down Exhibition Road, plunge into South Kensington tube station and hop on the last service back to Victoria and Brixton.

I open the briefcase on my lap and stare at the photo album. How was it so *easy*? I wonder. It almost feels like cheating. No galloping doormen. No alarms. No police cars with their screeching sirens and fluorescent pyrotechnics. Just a chasmic silence that leaves me feeling cold and undone. I pray getting published isn't as anticlimactic. A pathetic puff of smoke, like a firework in the squall. Rupert Wreath won't believe a word of it.

I pick up a discarded newspaper on the empty seat next to me, attempting to look normal. A young couple sat opposite me (wonderfully dressed, holding hands, apparently sober) assess my appearance with unconcealed shock. The bloody face and shirt, the lopsided bowtie, the briefcase across my thighs. I have the approachability of a serial killer, with all of the physical attributes and none of the lethal charisma.

I laugh, perhaps more manically than intended.

"It's been one of *those* days," I say apologetically. I laugh again, rubbing my swollen jaw. "But it's going to be OK. In the end, it always is. This time next week, I'll be a famous author. You'll see me on the television. Remember this face." I point at it and smile broadly. "Soon, everybody will know me."

They look away, visibly disturbed, alighting at Sloane Square only to re-board the same train in the next carriage. But I get it. I do. They don't want to expose themselves to my incurable sickness.

It's strange. I thought I'd be relieved that another human other than Rachel Garland could see the man in the bowler hat. But I'm not. Until now, I never seriously contemplated that he might be more than a hallucination. A hologram of communal guilt. I never wanted to believe that he was *material*.

A distressing question haunts me as I exit Brixton tube station.

Was the man in the bowler hat performing for me, or was he performing for Richard Hayes?

I hate to admit it, but I'm starting to like the guy.

He's growing on me. He's becoming a part of me.

CHAPTER
FIFTEEN

I examine my front teeth in the bathroom mirror, loosened by the right hand of Richard Hayes.

With little effort, I pull two incisors and one canine free from the gum and lay them in a neat pile on the lip of the basin. How can one shot inflict so much damage? I touch my jaw with my fingertips, probing the purple swelling. And then I smile at my toothless reflection. *That broken grin.* You know who it reminds me of? It reminds me of her. Everything, it seems, reminds me of Rachel Garland.

I exit the bathroom and pour a large gin and tonic, looking over my shoulder at the photo album on the coffee table. Just as I suspect, it's still there, sat on top of a stack of ragged movie magazines, mute and unassuming like a bored house guest. I take an arduous swig, enjoying the sting of alcohol inside my wounded mug. I'm relieved to feel something other than obtuse numbness, the looming horizon of the coke and ecstasy comedown.

I emigrate to the sofa, edging closer to the photo album. I want to touch it. I have the desire to explore the anatomy of its glassine ruffles, to caress its skin-like bindings, but I abandon this notion, terrified that opening it again might summon the man in the bowler hat. I imagine the painful smirk, the soulless eyes, appearing in the tall shadows of the bedroom or the hallway. *And what if he has friends?* I shudder.

Until next time, David.

I pick up the remote and turn on the television set. *The Silence of the Lambs* is on one of the terrestrial channels. It's the scene in which Hannibal Lecter escapes his cell, beating a guard to death with a baton. He hangs his body on the wall, disembowelled, arms spread like a beautiful butterfly. I feel like that murdered guard – gutted, draped, decontextualised, hung in public like a piece of conceptual artwork, a prop to progress someone else's plotline.

Wrapped in the warmth of the television screen, I relight the joint I started last night. I quickly forget about the photo album. I forget about the weather, the unreality of my interview, the violent altercation with Richard Hayes. I forget about everything. Even the dull ache along my jaw and the sharp throb between my ribs fades like a distant memory. In days, I will be a published author. Famous, augmented with money. Every ambition resuscitated with hope.

Stoned, exhausted, my eyes slowly shut, unable to resist the relief of sleep. Behind my eyelids, I see holographic pyramids, geometric shapes, a 100-storey lighthouse in the centre of a fallen utopia, red sunshine bleeding over an ocean of cloud cover, a derelict chapel strangled with wisteria, Rupert Wreath slithering towards me, organs trailing behind him, Father's skeleton in a soiled hospital bed, Rachel Garland without a face, the smashed windscreen of a crashed car, a burning house, a burning city, an upturned bowler hat overflowing with dead spiders and rainwater, a prophet having an orgy with his disciples, a white beach of human bones, a sea of blood, a screaming cadaver, bottomless darkness.

I open my eyes, gasping for air, chilly, uncontrollably sweating. How long was I asleep? The ice cubes in my gin and tonic are still angular. The end of the joint still burns with orange light. I check Father's pocket watch. A lifetime of hellish abominations, witnessed in seconds. Is it even possible? I glare accusingly at the photo album, still feeling its invisible fingers boring into the cerebrum of my brain, manipulating my abstractions, editing my memories. Too frightened to go back to sleep, I finish my drink and exit the flat, taking the joint with me.

Sealed inside the telephone box outside the estate, I tip the shrapnel inside my pockets into the coin slot and dial the number for Paradise Publishing. I pull on the joint greedily, unable to organise the chaos of my thoughts. Is this the next scene of the same nightmare? Am I still on my sofa, in my flat, witnessing a carousel of violence as my mind attempts to grip reality? In this phone box, it feels like I'm marooned on an artificial island, cornered by the incessant weather, adrift, striving to make contact with another dimension. Rupert Wreath instructed me to deliver the photo album by 9AM Friday, but that's – I consult Father's pocket watch again – almost 31 hours away. Newsflash: I can't wait that long. I don't want this object in my possession for another hour, never mind another day. But I'm confident that Rupert and his team will be delighted to receive it early. They might even be impressed with my efficiency.

I like you, David. You're passionate with an endearing anti-charisma. A risk-taker with soaring ambition. And true grit. Someone willing to bend the rules of reality for his aspirations.

When the front desk of Paradise Publishing doesn't pick up (there isn't even an answer machine to leave a voice message), I rest my head against the keypad, flushed with panic. I take a long breath and, reformulating a new plan, make another call – my other old uni friend, Sultan Gillespie.

No one answers at his second-hand bookshop on Mitcham Road, so I ring his local, the Antelope off Bickley Street. When I get through to the landlord, he says that the Sultan is scoping the betting lines in the sports pages. "Can't be disturbed, I'm afraid." The landlord is right. If Sultan Gillespie has one weakness, one human flaw, it's his gambling habit. It's the reason he never achieved anything with his esteemed university accolades. He could have been anybody. He chose to be a low roller.

"Tell the Sultan it's an old friend in desperate need of a favour," I insist. "Please. I *need* this."

Down the line there is inaudible chatter, an arduously long pause, a brief commotion. I hear Sultan Gillespie exhale down the receiver, his black London lungs deflating like scarred balloons.

"What is it, David?" he sighs.

"It's good to hear your voice, Sultan. I know we haven't spoken in some time."

"Not since the accident."

"I'm sorry for not being in touch, but you'll be pleased to know that I've been productive. I've got big news. *Sick & Beautiful* has a publisher. My agent is confident it can be a bestseller. Enough about me, though. How are *you* keeping, Sultan? Any big races on tomorrow?"

"I'm happy for you, David. And there are always big races. But I know you haven't rang for the first time in six months to talk about what's going on in my life. I'll say it again. What is it, David?"

"Can you meet me tonight? It's urgent. I need your insight. Your knowledge."

Sultan Gillespie liberates another protracted sigh, a begrudging grunt, an empathetic tut. I can almost hear the cogs in his punter's brain whirr as he calculates the odds and consequences of my question. I listen to his dwarfed bookie's pencil frantically scribble digits, tallies, fractions, human errors. He's deciding my fate in real-time.

"Meet me in the launderette in an hour. Upper Tooting Road. Don't be late, David. And make sure you're not followed."

He hangs up the phone.

Sultan Gillespie's characteristic disinclination can always be interpreted as friendly affirmation, but he sounds nervous. I can hear it in his voice, its lifeless intonation. He sounds like he's rattled.

From across the city, can he also feel the photo album, pulling us into its inescapable orbit?

CHAPTER
SIXTEEN

I *hate the book. It's like bad porn.*
That thing Rachel Garland said in the cab on the way to the Prince Charles last night. I feel like I need to address it. I feel like I need to clear this up. If *Sick & Beautiful* is *like bad porn*, it's because she steered the narrative in this direction.

I asked her everything you'd expect to find in a biography. Inspirations, fears, childhood trauma, aspirations, nightmares. All the details that add definition to the peaks and nadirs of every life story. I wanted her to reveal these exquisite secrets, but she seemed unwilling or unable to trust me. Even my ruthless invasiveness, my journalistic intuition, couldn't expose the truth. She forced me to fill in the blank spaces of her past and present, to believe what I wanted to believe about Rachel Garland.

She only exercised an extemporary openness under the leverage of coke and double measures, but these moments were rare. In fact, they were *exceptional*. The majority of our interviews were a car crash. When I turned on the tape recorder and reeled off my questions, Rachel either fell silent, refusing to engage in dialogue, or strived to flesh out every page with her sexual conquests.

Here's an example of her talented evasiveness.

"You never talk about your parents," I once said, thumbing through my notes. "What were their names? What did they do? How did they raise you? How do *any* parents raise a child in the poorest suburbs of Paris?"

"My grand-mère raised me," she replied. "My mother was in the hospital. And I never knew my father."

"This is good, Rachel," I nodded, trying to sound reassuring. "Your mother. Why was she in the hospital? What hospital? And for how long? What did the ward look like? What did *she* look like?"

"It's really not important. And I'm not sure I want to discuss it." Rachel bent forward to do a line of coke. I followed suit. "But I'll give you something else," she continued. "I first met Rupert Wreath on the set of *Puppet Master 4* in LA. One night, we went for shots on Santa Monica Boulevard, near the studios. We ended up in a motel. Just me and him. We were drinking by the outside pool, in the heat of summer, talking about movies. And then he told me about his childhood. He grew up in the UK, on the south coast. A town called Broadstairs. When he was six, or maybe seven, he was on the beach making sandcastles with a plastic bucket and spade. He was with his mother, who often left him playing on the beach while she swam in the sea. Rupert told me he watched her paddle out, as always, into the waves, and then he returned to his kingdom of sand and seashells. He doesn't know how much time passed, but when he looked up again, the sun was setting, the tide had crept in, and his mother had vanished. They never found her body. Rupert remembered something else from that day too. Something strange."

Rachel Garland lit a cigarette. I was into the story now. I was gripped. I sat watching her, waiting.

"Rupert said there was a man standing on the surface of the water, at least 100 metres out from the shore," she said. "And he wasn't dressed like someone who would visit the beach on a sunny afternoon. He wore a black hat, an overcoat. And he smiled and waved at Rupert as he sat in the sand, crying, screaming for his mother. Creepy, right?"

"What kind of hat?" I asked.

"Rupert didn't specify. And I never asked. Besides, how would a child know? A hat's a hat, right?"

"Right," I agreed, disappointed with this lack of clarity.

"I was so moved by his story, David," she said emphatically. "Rupert was so candid, so forthcoming, I'd never felt so attracted to a person in that moment. I felt almost outside of my body as I removed my dress and underwear in front of Rupert on the edge of the pool. I sat on his lap, bit his earlobe. He ran his hands over my ribcage, my hips, the inside of my thigh–"

And so on. This is where Rachel Garland's stories always led. Haunting romances. Primeval passions. Existential crisis-inducing orgasms. Unprotected sex acts orchestrated on beds, beaches, benches, by the pools of seedy motels, in penthouse apartments, bungalows, B&Bs, villas, wooden chalets nestled in coke-white mountain ranges. In these sex scenes, nature was in tune with every thrust, with every whimper. I frowned attempting to visualise scenery beyond my comprehension. Topography I've only ever seen in movies. I shut my eyes and cast myself onto these androgynous nobodies performing explicit sex acts with Rachel, attempting to immerse myself in their motion.

But there's an issue with these sex scenes. They're too perfect, too shamelessly polished, like a plastic reality created for my detriment. When Rachel Garland and I mixed mutual despondency with sedatives and amphetamines, sex looked more like real life.

We had sex in strangers' beds, the back seats of abandoned cars, cathedrals deserted by their faithful flocks. We snuck into terminal wards at midnight to have sex on unchanged hospital beds, sullied by the recently deceased. We had sex on the mossy graves populating Lambeth Cemetery, inside the upmarket mausoleums of Golders Green Crematorium. We had sex on the towpaths of Victoria Park and Haggerston.

We crushed codeines into hubcap cleaner and cough syrup when we had sex. I recall distorted flashes of naked flesh like an overexposed roll film, monochrome images exploding into psychedelic colours. Wet hair, caesarean scars, the shared relief from the burden of our animalistic afflictions. I rue over the aroma of lubricated latex, sweat-soaked bedsheets, bad breath, developing chemicals, stale cigarette smoke. The satisfying pain of glossy, spit-soaked skin stretched beyond recognition. Minds turned inside-out like used condoms. Sperm-soaked sex dreams slotting together like an X-rated fairytale.

Rachel Garland admitted that nearly every orgasm was either faked or exaggerated, but she told me, with unconcealed pleasure, not to take it personally. It was a rehearsal for a higher purpose – a movie role with a sex scene or, perhaps, a future relationship. She would even debrief me in bed or at the breakfast table, cataloguing my various sexual errors (some areas had space to grow, others were an unequivocal disaster, quite possibly beyond redemption). Rachel Garland was determined to maintain an emotional distance while indulging in these sexual screen tests. She said she simply didn't feel inspired.

"Then let me inspire you," I said, misinterpreting her boundaries as a challenge.

I adorned the walls of the flat with my photographs of women and men oozing their vital fluids across the city's floorboards and pavements. Rigged to a circulatory system of extension leads and power cables, humming with the cold heat of electricity, I stacked four televisions and video players on top of the chest of drawers at the foot of the bed. One TV played hardcore pornography sourced from sex shops on Green's Court. The second and third spliced flesh-heavy classics like *Shivers, The Howling, Ilsa, She Wolf of the SS* and *Cannibal Holocaust*. The fourth projected images of the 24-hour news cycle: car crashes, high-rise infernos, floods, famines, war, terrorism, plutonic violence searing the cities and suburbs. Rachel and I repurposed these torn limbs and lives into broken instruments. During sex – before and after it – the chorus of wails always harmonised into twisted porno scores.

We'd pass out, only to awake in the black and white hiss of television static, the downpour spitting on the window (all night, the cloud watched our sex acts from the back row of its celestial porno theatre). I sometimes prayed for those televisions to suck me into their oceans of galvanic distortion, locking me behind the screen. How long would it be until I'm an image of agony on the other side of the glass? I wondered. This is how I often visualised my death:

reflected on the TV, reclined on my sofa, like a cadaver on an autopsy table, deceased from middle age or an overdose, waiting for technology to cannibalise my flesh and upload my spirit.

For Rachel Garland and I, it soon became impossible to summon sexual arousal without these visual stimulants. The passion and the success of these sex scenes stagnated at an exponential rate that drugs and alcohol couldn't remedy. Each sex act drove us further apart. And the distance that grew between us, between the times that we had sex, became a physical presence. I struggled to accept that I wasn't enough for Rachel (that perhaps I never was). I was enraged and tearful, but unsurprised when she started a sexual relationship with Richard Hayes.

They first met in February, when Richard visited the flat to buy my gruesome snapshots of Rupert Wreath. Since the night we photographed the dead boy in the shower, Richard has been a fan of my grimmest work. Rachel Garland poured our drinks and then proceeded to flirt with Richard Hayes on the balcony, giving him Rupert's backstory. Profession, physical appearance, sexual ability. The story about his drowning mother, the man in the hat and overcoat who stood on the water. He listened to her, nodding earnestly, absorbed in her implicit beauty (he saw it too).

"I must admit," he said to Rachel, "these details make the images even more extraordinary, even more *lifelike*. What was the victim's name?"

"Rupert Wreath," she said.

"*Rupert Wreath*," he grinned. "I like that name. I'll remember that. *Rupert Wreath*. It's perfect."

Candid laughter. A touching of hands (just for a second).

The instant attraction was undeniable. I took my gin and tonic to the sofa and watched television, quietly ignoring this blossoming romcom.

It was then that Richard Hayes, intent on provoking a reaction, told Rachel Garland that my article about her was growing into a book. She just smiled, performing with rehearsed sincerity.

"You're writing a book about me?" she said, running her hands over Richard Hayes's lean torso, twirling his tie around her index finger. "That's *very* sweet, David. I'm flattered. I really am. What's it called?"

"*Sick & Beautiful*," I replied quietly.

"*Sick & Beautiful*? What does that even mean?"

"It's something you said to me once. I thought it was brilliant, profound. I still do, even if I'm still unsure what it means. Perhaps that's the beauty of it, its ambiguity."

"I don't remember saying that. Perhaps you made it up in one of your dreams?"

"Perhaps," I conceded.

Whenever Rachel Garland didn't return to the flat, I accepted that she was with Richard Hayes, bemused by his affluent, alternative approach to reality, inside his exorbitant apartment in Arcadia Gardens. With its private indoor swimming pool and squash courts, state-of-the-art gym equipment, closed courtyard and renovated Victorian features, I felt emasculated by the sanctuary he was able to provide. A bespoke Paradise, sheltered from the cloud and the violence of the city, even more high-tech and luxurious than the one God commissioned for Adam and Eve.

When I confronted Rachel Garland about it (drunk, stoned, deprived of sleep and unable to work through a tricky middle chapter of the book), she countered my shrill anger with an irrefutable truth.

"We're not in a relationship, David."

Although we lived together and I wasn't having sex with anyone else, it didn't necessarily mean that we were in a mutually monogamous romance, even if I ceaselessly hoped for it. I knew that my outburst was nothing more than a sexually-starved tantrum. So did Rachel Garland. Naturally, Rachel took a sick delight in it. I didn't own her (nobody does). She was content to coexist, revolving around each other like two distant planets orbiting the same burning star. We passed at high speed, always inches away from an increasingly rare collision.

Desperate to reclaim control of the situation, I said that I was comfortable with her and Richard Hayes. I didn't care. But I had one condition if she wanted to continue living with me rent-free – that they filmed their sex scenes for research for the book. It was a ludicrous suggestion, completely off the cuff. I thought Rachel Garland would pack her meagre possessions and leave that night. Instead, she presented the first sex tape to me the next morning, filmed using Richard's cutting-edge camera equipment. It signified my official relegation to the role of passive observer, exiled to the margins of their merging compatibilities.

I insisted on pretending that the whole thing was my idea. I assured myself that the three of us were conducting broader sexual experiments. Rachel Garland and Richard Hayes were happy to give me this simulacrum of agency, treating the sex tapes like a consolation prize, a small window into an alternative sexual reality. If this was what Rachel wanted, it was, reluctantly, what I wanted too. To say I was crushed by this arrangement would be a grotesque understatement, but happiness was a small price to pay. In fact, the subsequent humiliation and heartache felt more like a gift, a gratis monthly membership to the city's most exclusive skin flick rental shop.

I slid the cassette into the video player, determined to extract meaning from the sex scenes I was progressively omitted from. I examined the unique arcs and angles of Rachel Garland's body. Aspects I would have never been able to capture from my one-dimensional, first-person perspective.

Take, for instance, the thrust of her narrow pelvis. The alleviation and tension in her calves, thighs, triceps and hamstrings as she works through a dizzying carousel of sex positions. The head tilted in numb ecstasy. The angular shoulder blades and small breasts. The toes curling and relaxing. The drops of sweat that manifest on her forehead, cascading in glistening streams down the arched spine and in-between her buttocks. The anus yawning and contracting with the lunge of Richard's hips, like a mouth moaning with pleasure, drinking her perspiration like a thirsty, crucified messiah praying and pleading for penetration.

Richard Hayes, wearing Rachel Garland's wig, stares into the camera, completely expressionless. Is he attempting to embody another character? And is Rachel acting here too? It's almost impossible to distinguish between performance and reality in these passionate sex scenes.

I've obsessively watched this sex tape and the countless others that followed, analysing the panting actors with false detachment, desperate to suppress my pangs of suffocating envy. Rachel Garland scrutinised these sex scenes with the same clinical eye she would study her cameos on film or her rejected casting tapes. They motivated her to make small adjustments to what she perceived as shortcomings in her own sexual performances, piloting new methods with me in preparation for her next encounter with Richard Hayes. Her surgical amends made me feel even more inadequate. I couldn't match her talent for personal betterment, whether I was addressing my deficiencies as her biographer or my fallacies as her sexual understudy. I conceded that Richard's interventions saved (or at least protracted) mine and Rachel's own sexual prerogative.

Over time, I learnt to appreciate these sharply-focussed pornos. After multiple views, subtle beauty emerged from their subtext. An unstaged and unexpected truth. I realised that I didn't solely fantasise about Rachel Garland when I examined these sex scenes. I fantasised about Richard Hayes too. What it would feel like to be inside him. What it would feel like to have Richard inside me, while inside her. Would their orifices feel the same? Or would there be discrepancies in depth, flex, texture? Watching him have sex with the person I love taught me more about myself than unmediated sexual intercourse ever could.

Rachel Garland applauded these sexual revelations. And the prospect of a mutual love interest – the ensuring jealousy, the neverending arguments, cheating behind each other's backs, tangled in a web of lies and limbs – excited her. She encouraged me to have sex with Richard Hayes so she could see if she would feel any pain or envy. She wanted to watch. She wanted to direct, touching herself behind the camera. In a characteristic display of one-upmanship, Richard told Rachel that he was willing to test these sexual possibilities. I knew he was being serious, but my feelings of betrayal and loathing for him overpowered any hope for exploring these curiosities. It wasn't just that, though. I feared that I wouldn't be good enough for him either. Based on hours of video footage, it was evident that Richard and Rachel operate with a sexual competency I'd never be able to master or emulate.

When Rachel Garland left in March, all that remained were the echoes of our sex scenes. Black, frightening and clammy, they soaked into the flat's porous walls like mould. But she didn't just leave because of Richard Hayes. Against the laws of nature, despite all of the toxins we smoked, spooned, sniffed or swallowed, she became pregnant. It felt like an awful revelation, incomprehensible in its prodigious chemistry set conception.

I remember her emerging from the bathroom, wielding the plastic pregnancy test like a shiv. She walked into my arms. We held each other tightly.

"I'm keeping it," she said with conviction. "I want to know how childbirth can alter my body, my soul."

We sobbed and tremored beneath the weight of apprehension, the reluctance of indefinite responsibilities. It was too much. With the phantom of an unrealised biological blueprint already manifesting into a physical barrier between us, it felt like we had become irreversibly divided. It was a new chapter for the book. A new chapter for us. What a twist. I shut my eyes, determined to get used to the concept, and decided – even though it could be Richard's, even though, conceivably, it could be Rupert Wreath's – that the baby was mine. It felt like the right role to conjure. The foetus, I suspected, had already began to absorb our flaws and strengths, incubating them for its future existence.

Rachel Garland whispered a secret to me on the night before she left, the same night we learnt about our little miracle. She was wrapped inside the duvet like a silk cocoon, squinting drowsily at the bedroom's ceiling rose, the cobwebbed light fixture.

"Richard knows that you hate him, that you think you're better than him," she said. "He always has."

"So what if I do?" I replied (feeling confrontational, feeling facetious). "What exactly do you see in Richard that makes him so special?"

Rachel smiled. "His self-belief. His fearless imagination. His body. His delusion. All those little things you always seem to miss, David. In the living *and* the dead."

"And what about me? What makes me special?" Silence. "Do you love him, Rachel?"

More silence. The preceding comments, it seemed, were all she felt obligated to say.

The next morning I discovered a note on my desk, on top of my early chapters of *Sick & Beautiful*.

David,

I'm boarding the lifeboat to LA. Richard and I will wave from the shores of Paradise, but we can't save you from drowning.

The ocean is your reality. The book is the ship. You are the captain. But it doesn't have to be this way. You can be anybody. The ocean can be anything.

Tell Abraham and Osiris I'll be thinking about them.

Love,
Rachel.

Whatever this meant, Rachel had vanished like a ghost. The shrine of bedsheets, with the spectral silhouette of her head and body etched into the pillows and duvet, is the only piece of evidence that suggests she was ever really here.

But something troubled me about these vague remains.

Could I have planted them myself to create a false memory of her existence?

It's entirely possible. Now, it seems, anything is possible.

CHAPTER
SEVENTEEN

I reel through these sex dreams on the top deck of the 355. I'm riding the night bus to Tooting, edging closer to Sultan Gillespie. I caress the photo album in the open briefcase on my lap. Through its tattered cloth I feel the gnarled spine, the raised gold-leaf letters, the cover scarred like septic skin. I acknowledge its awful sex appeal. And I hate to admit it (to myself, to anybody): I'm growing fond of this object. I really am. I need to get rid of it, before it convinces me to keep it.

I close the briefcase, press the stop button, jump off the bus and jog across Upper Tooting Road, towards the launderette. *FREE SOAP* is printed on its window in rotund hieroglyphs. I push open the door and step inside.

Sultan Gillespie is already here, sat on a bench in the centre of the laundrette. He is reading a battered paperback (*The Drowned World*) opposite a rumbling tumble dryer. It occurs to me that I haven't read anything since university. Not since the disheartening, leviathan *Moby Dick*. (Aren't all writers, at the very least, required to write *and* read other pieces of writing?) When I sit next to him, he declines to acknowledge my arrival, licking his thumb to turn another dogeared page. I analyse the launderette, deciding to give the Sultan his time.

The canary yellow wallpaper – probably attractive and bolder in a past reality – has faded like an overexposed photograph. The owner behind the counter holds a cigarette, watching a television set fixed into the far corner of the room. Her eyes are glassy, somehow both thoughtful and vacant. It's the forecast. The temperatures are dropping. And the cloud, as predicted, is going nowhere anytime soon. I look outside. Rain splashes against the glass, bleeding across the concrete. The owner stares at me, blinks, squints at the television again. We are the only three souls in the 24-hour launderette. Only the lost and forsaken can be found here at such an antisocial hour. It's where we congregate when Sultan Gillespie senses trouble.

He clears his throat, rummages in the pocket of his polyester tracksuit and pulls out a handful of shrapnel. He circles the lustreless coins in the creases of his chubby palm (deliberately, methodically) before dropping them back into his pocket. His lungs wheeze inside their hulking frame. He dabs the beads of sweat on his waxy forehead. His presence, *his aura*, captivates me. It always captivates me.

Sultan Gillespie. Real name: Soner Gillespie. A second-generation British-Cypriot. A native of reality, carrying his physical and ancestral weight. He's not known as the Sultan solely for his size. It's the princely presence he exudes from every armchair, from every vantage point. His Mediterranean mannerisms have been slowly ebbed away by the rain and patois of the city, but he still commands a powerful sense of theatre in his orbit. With his sullied trainers, fluorescent tracksuit and black specs, you've probably seen Sultan Gillespie's type before, clenching his betting slip in bookies, sports bars, snooker halls and mutt track boxes, eyes wet with hope. But this guy has a 1st in Eng. Lit. He's fluent in Greek, Turkish, Cockney, French. He has a 1,300+ chess rating. He shot down countless job offers at national newspapers and government think tanks. He did it all to dedicate himself to the boozer, the betting dives, his second-hand bookshop. There's no denying it. Sultan is an unorthodox package in a heterodox world, but he fits in. He fits in unnaturally well. You feel like a background character in his personal screenplay.

Sultan Gillespie finally releases a deflated sigh, signalling that he's ready to talk. This is all part of his unique performance. When he turns to look at me, the bench's slats groan under his weight. All 300 pounds of it. He scans me head-to-toe (silently, impassively), eyeing me like an animal clipped by oncoming traffic. At first, I assume it's disdain for losing touch, for replacing his friendship with the numb affections of Rachel Garland. Perhaps it's pity. But it's none of the above. It's fear. As if he's scared to touch me, to catch my illness. When I place my hand on his back to test this theory, I feel the flesh recoil beneath. When I take my hand away again, it softens back into its natural shape.

"What happened to you, David?" he asks.

"I've been busy with the book, Sultan."

"No. I mean, what *happened* to you?" He sighs, shaking his head sadly. "Why didn't you call to tell me that you needed help?"

"I didn't until tonight."

"Look at you, David. You needed my help a long time ago."

I glare at my blurry reflection in the window. Do I really look that unrecognisable? A mirage, a deconstructed image Sultan Gillespie is struggling to identify. He seems sombre. Suddenly lost for platitudes. He looks away, staring into the smudge of colours turning bonelessly inside the tumble dryer. His eyes are heavy, milked of emotion. This, I imagine, is how Sultan will look at my funeral.

To break the silence, I open my briefcase and hand him a copy of *Sick & Beautiful*.

"The final draft," I say, feeling an earnest sense of pride. "It's going to make me famous, Sultan."

He forces a smile and drops it into the empty laundry bag between his legs.

"I assume you haven't called me in the middle of the night to talk about your book?" he says.

"Worse," I assure him.

When I pull the photo album out of the briefcase and unwrap it in my lap, Sultan Gillespie frowns, returning his gaze to the unobtrusive bliss of his spinning laundry.

"Richard gave this to me as a gift," I say. "This morning, I had a meeting with a literary agent who wants to publish *Sick & Beautiful*. There was one condition for the book deal: that I needed to steal a photo album from Richard tonight. This *exact* album. But get this: Richard just gave it to me, Sultan. And now I have it, I feel paralysed. I feel defenceless. Doesn't it all just seem so– *unbelievable*?"

"Richard came into my bookshop with that photo album on Christmas Eve," he says. "I haven't even seen the guy since university. He asked me what it is, what it's worth. I told him photography isn't my expertise, but it looks hundreds of years old. Photography wasn't invented until the 19th Century, so I'm aware something doesn't add up. And who knows what it's worth? I'm a bookseller, not an antiquarian. Richard also asked me to translate the writing on the inside cover. I did it, but not because I wanted to help him. It's because I didn't want to be in the same room as him, in the same room as that *thing*. It makes me feel nauseous, David. It's poison. Jesus. Can't you *feel* it?"

Sultan Gillespie looks relieved when I lock the photo album back inside the briefcase, where it can't be seen or acknowledged.

"And how was Richard?" I ask. "When I saw him last night he seemed a little- *irritable*."

"Richard was performing," he says. "Just like he always does. But I knew it was an act. I could see it in his movements. He looked stiff, anxious, unconvincing. His usual arrogance seemed off. He tried to hide it all behind this awful grin, muttering endlessly about you, about Rachel, about bad dreams. I can't explain why, but I think he wanted me to see the photo album, David. It's spooky. It's as if he knew that you'd call me, that you'd bring it back to me. It's as if Richard predicted this whole scene."

"What kind of bad dreams?" I ask. "Did Richard elaborate?"

"The real question is why do *you* have the photo album? And what does a literary agent want with it?"

It's a good question (a *great* question). I look at the floor, unable to articulate a credible answer.

"Did Richard do this to you?" he asks, nodding at my face.

I touch the swelling, the cut on my cheek, remembering the dull pain colonising my jawline.

"Richard landed the first shot, but I finished the job."

"If you say so, David."

Slowly, the drum of the tumble dryer chugs to a lethargic stop. The bench exhales with relief as Sultan Gillespie rises to his feet. He scoops his laundry into his bag, on top of the fresh copy of *Sick & Beautiful*. It's a soft bundle of white tube socks, cotton joggers and knock-off polo shirts, exuding the warm aromas of washing powder and overheated machinery. He slings the bag over his shoulder.

"I wish I could help you," he says. "I wish I *did* help you, but I can't get involved with this plot. It might be too late for you, David, but I still have a chance of evading Paradise. The odds are still in my favour."

He raises his arm to pat me affectionately on the shoulder, but he pauses, hovering inches away, before deciding against it. He slides his hand into his pocket, rummaging with the loose coins inside.

"What is the translation of the text inside the photo album?" I ask.

Sultan Gillespie pulls a small piece of paper out his pocket and hands it to me. It's lined, folded.

"When you called," he says, "I knew it would be you. I knew what it would be about. Last night, I had a dream about us, in this launderette, in this moment. But in my dream, your cheeks were sliced open, from the corners of your mouth to your ears. When you spoke, spiders and butterflies crawled out of your wounds, over your hands, your overcoat, your bowler hat. And your smile. Christ, David. I woke up screaming."

A sensation passes through me like a cold draught. It stays there.

"That's very interesting," I admit. "What did I say in my dream?"

"You told me that you were sorry for what was going to happen to me. But you said to have faith in the script. You promised that it would all work out in the end. For both of us."

Sultan Gillespie opens the door, pivoting his titanic frame sideways so he can squeeze through the relatively narrow gap. He gazes sullenly through the steamed glass, like a mourner staring into an open grave. And then he's gone. When I turn back around, the woman behind the launderette counter has disappeared too. It's just us now – me and the photo album in our deserted universe.

I step outside. The street is empty, but I notice an idling van parked across the road. *PARADISE FLOWERS* is printed in vinyl letters across its side panel. As I walk towards it, trying to peer through its tinted windows, the van speeds off, worn tread shrieking on wet tarmac. The driver is heading north, into the storm, into the heart of the city.

"Probably nothing," I mutter.

I sit in the shelter of the bus stop, waiting for the 355 back to Brixton. It's in 28 minutes.

In the downpour I realise an irrefutable truth – I can't spend one more hour with the photo album. It feels like it's forcing dreams and reality, the past and present, to collide, amalgamate.

I decide to take the 155 night bus to London Bridge instead.

I hug my briefcase to my chest.

I can feel the photo album pulsating within. Or perhaps I imagine it.

The 155 is in four minutes.

I decide it's a good omen.

CHAPTER
EIGHTEEN

I check Father's pocket watch.

It's almost 4AM when I arrive at the Market Porter. All the shopfronts are locked and shuttered, the gates of Borough Market chained until sunrise. When I push on the heavy doors of the pub, I'm surprised to feel them gently open.

Illuminated under the fairy lights draped across the empty bar, Docklands Dave has his back to me, pint of bitter in one hand, yesterday's paper in the other. Behind the jump, the landlord is drying glasses with a tea towel. He studies my mauled face, the rainwater pooling around my feet.

"Come inside, David," says Docklands Dave, without taking his peepers off the page. "We've been expecting you. You've missed last orders by almost four hours, but we can always make an exception for a friend. Let's discuss your progress."

I follow Docklands Dave to the fruit machine. He tips a handful of shrapnel into the coin slot. I sink into the armchair next to it, head hung like a sinner inside a church confessional. The landlord places a gin and tonic in my trembling hand. Thirstily, I sip.

"How did it go?" he asks, eyes lost in the electric smoulder of the fruity. "With Richard."

"We had a scrap," I say, pointing to my face, trying a simper. "But I got it, Dave. I got it."

I pull the photo album out of my briefcase and unwrap its cloth. Docklands Dave looks at it, smiles, returns his gaze to the fruit machine. He almost looks saintly in its polychromatic twinkle.

"This object, Dave," I continue. "It's having an appalling effect on me. I'm seeing *him*. And I feel this constant dread. I can't quite explain it. It's like burning." I pause. "I just need a place to keep this thing until 9AM Friday morning. A place where it can't *reach* me. Does that sound utterly insane?"

"When I was a boy," he says, "my father told me a tale from the war. He was stationed in a rural village in France. In a chapel they found a photo album. Days later, a soldier in his unit wiped out the village. Prisoners. Women. Babies. My father said the photo album drove him to it. Infected him. My father felt it too – this undertow. But I digress. I haven't seen my old man since I was a little nipper."

Docklands Dave sips his pint, the other hand fluidly traverses the galaxy of effulgent buttons. I wish I could write with the aptitude Docklands Dave operates the fruity. His shoulders are relaxed. The posture is erect. His dexterous fingers elegantly soar. He looks like a natural. Docklands Dave is having fun out there. It's more than I can say about myself in front of Father's electric typewriter – hunchbacked, face contorted, platen jammed, hands balled into arthritic talons, muscles knotted with lactic dissent.

"Do you think anyone else could be looking for it?" he asks.

"No," I say, after an unconvincing pause.

"Dave," says Docklands Dave over his shoulder.

"Yes, Dave," says the landlord, still behind the bar.

"David needs to stash something upstairs. He'll pick it up by 9AM Friday morning. Isn't that right, David?"

"Yes, Dave," I nod.

The landlord nods back gravely.

"How can I repay you?" I ask them.

"That doesn't concern you, David. At this moment in time, that information is immaterial."

I nod again, walk behind the bar, climb the stairs and enter the function room. I flick the light switch next to the doorframe, illuminating the lone lightbulb in the chandelier. When I step underneath it, crossing the creaking floorboards, the lightbulb intensifies, as if it's about to detonate into a ball of fire. When I reach the opposite end of the room, it subsides again, reverting back to its soft glow. I place the photo album in the drawer of an antique sideboard, close it and rest my head on its dusty surface. Desperately, I attempt to haul myself together.

"Be unafraid," I whisper. "Be too fucking cool. This is your character, David. This is you now."

And then the lightbulb explodes with a violent pop.

I spin around, staring into darkness. Streetlight sags through the window, slicing across the centre of the room.

In the corner, in the shadows, I can see a shape. Motionless, it looks like a person. On the head I can make out the outline of something. It's a– *of course*. It's a bowler hat. The figure smiles. Pointed teeth catch the streetlight spilling into the function room, creeping around his face in a sadistic grin.

I close my eyes and listen to the sound of the rain. Within the sideboard I feel the photo album emit a heartbeat. Fierce, high-pitched pulses that reverberate like a tortured glass harp. The function room suddenly feels like it's haunted, the stale air groaning with phantom agony. I hear the man in the bowler hat limp towards me until I feel his hot breath on my face. The sick tang of rancid flesh. I hear flies swarm around us. I feel them crawling over my hands, my face, under the cuffs of my shirt, under the collar of my overcoat. They're attracted to my sweat, my wounds, the sticky sweetness of fear.

"You're not real," I say.

"We're the chosen few," he sighs. "Somehow, our family always has been, David. We're destined for Paradise. Don't worry. You won't have to wait much longer to find the truth. To understand who you really are."

"I'm David Temple. I'm going to be a bestselling novelist. I'm going to be famous."

"That's right. Soon, everyone will know the name *David Temple*. I'm going to drag you inside the television with me, through the glass, where we'll live forever. You, me and Rachel. We're part of an endless spiral, David. It's inescapable, just like Father told us. Loops within loops within loops within loops within loops within loops–"

I open my eyes, screaming. The room is empty, the lightbulb hums warmly, the rain spits on the windowpanes. Opposite me, on the far side of the room, a full-length mirror leans against the wall. I look at my reflection: laughing painfully, tears cascading down both cheeks, I look more like the man in the bowler hat than myself. "Jesus," I mutter. How did it happen? This regression. It's incredible.

When I reach the bottom of the staircase, the landlord is propped against the bar. He looks me over impassively.

"I have another favour to ask," I say. "Can I order another round and use your landline?"

"We're here to serve," he says reluctantly. "Dave says we need to play our parts."

Drink in-hand, I dial the number for Richard Hayes's apartment, hoping that Rachel Garland will answer the phone. I feel an uncontrollable urge to confess everything to her. After just a few rings, I abandon the idea and slam down the receiver. What if Richard picked up? And what would I say to either of them? Would Rachel believe my implausible story? Would she even recognise my voice?

I sigh and unfold the piece of paper in my pocket. It's Sultan Gillespie's translation of the words inside the photo album.

Seek your true purpose. Or seek the camera lens. Only angels will be spared Paradise.

I finish my gin and tonic. Its bitter flavours reassure me with reality's tangibility.

The landlord picks up my empty tumbler. He stands there for a long time, studying my bruised anatomy.

"Dave told me something about you," he says.

"And what did Dave tell you about me, Dave?"

"Dave told me about your talking cat."

CHAPTER
NINETEEN

Osiris started talking two months after Father's funeral. Following a nightshift on the paper, I entered my flat to find his ashes strewn across the carpet like a tipped over ashtray, the ceramic urn smashed into several pieces. Father's gold teeth twinkled in his remains like starlight. To my horror, Osiris was crouched over them, licking up the grey dust like powdered milk.

I shooed him onto the balcony – almost launching him over the railings – and slammed the back door behind me. I dug out the dustpan and brush underneath the sink, swept up Father and tipped him into an empty jam jar. I screwed on the lid, wrote *DAD* on the label with a magic marker and placed him on top of the television set (where he could watch his son sleep, devolve, age, deplete). The whole scene, the experience of mopping up my dead maker, left me feeling mildly traumatised. This, however, was merely a taste of what was to come.

The next time I fed Osiris, he decided to make first contact.

"Tuna," he blurted, deep and unholy.

"What?" I replied.

"Television."

"I don't understand."

"Paradise."

"This isn't happening."

"Cloud."

At first I refused to acknowledge it. I put it down to the sleep deprivation, a bad reaction to Abraham Maher's pills, the stress of living and working in the city. But it became impossible to ignore.

By the time Rupert Wreath died outside the Mandarin Oriental and Rachel Garland moved into the flat, Osiris had transformed these barely audible words into fully-articulated sentences, eloquent anecdotes, complaints about the weather.

"Who is this fair lady? Aren't you going to formally introduce us?" he purred as Rachel Garland stroked him on the balcony for the first time. Back then, Osiris still spoke like he'd been watching too many period dramas on daytime television. "Don't be so uncouth, David. I know you can hear me."

It was frightening to witness this rapid evolution. I assumed Osiris learnt our language watching movies or listening to Abraham Maher and I talk in strained, inebriated flurries from his throne on the arm of the sofa. From our conversations, he learned my name, age, DOB. In fact, he memorised almost everything about me. Sensitive data like my tainted credit rating, my addictions, unresolved issues with my employers at *The Daily Sun*, my struggles writing *Sick & Beautiful*. I hoped he didn't take mine and Abraham's discussions too seriously. Not everything humans tell one another is true (often almost none of it). I hoped he learnt this too.

When I asked Abraham Maher if Osiris had ever spoke to him (if any animal had), he dropped his teacup and saucer on the kitchen linoleum. It exploded on impact, shards of bone china erupting like shrapnel. I almost had a cardiac arrest. Osiris? He didn't even flinch. If anything, he looked amused.

"Don't be so ridiculous," Abraham Maher reproached, painfully kneeling down to help me pick up the pieces. "Jesus, David. What would your old man think? Pull it together. You're losing your mind."

Osiris watched us drunkenly attempt to clean up the small mess.

"If you won't talk, David," said Osiris, "perhaps Rachel Garland will."

"This isn't real," I laughed.

"You want to risk finding out?"

The threat was loud and clear.

I approached Osiris while he watched the rainfall from the windowsill.

"The cloud. It's quite beautiful, isn't it, David? Why is it so sad? Does it ever stop weeping?"

"What are your conditions?" I asked, unsure what line I just crossed forever. "What will it take for you to leave me and Rachel alone?"

"They're simple, David. Feed me. Pet me. Talk to me. And don't interfere with me and my human. Capeesh?"

Another new word, I thought. Is it Italian-American? He probably learnt it from a gangster movie. Something with tommy guns, mafiosos in pinstriped suits. I didn't like his insubordinate tone.

"We're the humans," I said, prodding Osiris on his moist, pink nose. "We call the shots. Capeesh, pussy cat?"

In retaliation, he swiftly displayed his capabilities. Within a fortnight, I noticed a prompt overthrow of leadership inside Abraham Maher's flat.

Osiris started sleeping on the bed while Abraham was relegated to restless nights in his tattered reading chair (legs crossed, fingers linked, fully clothed). He repurposed the bathtub into a kitty litter tray. He clawed the furniture, regurgitated hairballs in the hallway, did whatever the fuck he fancied. I realised Abraham had stopped showering or leaving the flat, even for the boozer or the bookies. He ignored the cat shit and everything else. He simply lost hope (in the universe, in himself). It was quite remarkable. In two weeks, Osiris had lulled Abraham within an inch of his own death, dispossessing him of his dignity and human rights. He did it all with a gleeful sadism that was scarily anthropoid.

As long as Osiris limited his depraved acts to flat 35, I decided I was happy to meet his terms and ignore these subtle atrocities (we're all dying, after all). But even this concession wasn't enough. He quickly built a rapport with Rachel Garland I couldn't occlude. She left my balcony door ajar so Osiris could come and go as he pleased (which he did), but he soon began to take liberties and emphasise his unsettling presence. He shed gummy hanks of hair over the carpet, disgraced every surface with muddy pawprints, ate the leftover food on the breakfast table and worktop. He really went to town. Several times I even found him sat on the closed toilet seat, watching Rachel Garland in the shower, soaking up the gratuitous nudity. Rachel didn't mind. But I did.

"I know your game, Osiris," I said, rolled up newspaper in-hand, ready to take a swing. "Why are you doing this to me? Why are you doing this to Abraham?"

Osiris narrowed his eyes, arched his spine and hissed, loud enough for Rachel Garland to hear it.

"Jesus, David," she said, peering around the pellucid shower curtain. "What's wrong with you? He's just a cat."

"But he isn't," I protested, unable to offer an honest explanation.

Osiris looked on, pretending he had no interest in our tedious human melodrama.

After Rachel left, I briskly revoked his privileges. Osiris was officially barred from the premises. Still, that abomination prowls my balcony in her wake. Every morning, I find him on the windowsill, pink paws pressed against the window. Who knows what he's planning next? That's why I continue to feed him – *protection*. You can't buy cats with money, but you can buy them with tin coffins of tuna and oil-drowned anchovies. It feels like a small price for the delusion of normality.

Don't forget to feed Osiris. He's a very special kitty.

This may sound inconceivable, utterly bonkers, but I'm going to put it out there, for the record, for the sake of transparency. Secretly I believe that Father (*somehow*) is inside Osiris's body, testing and taunting me, piloting the animal's furry frame like a flesh-mantled spacecraft. That's why I can't summon the courage to kill Osiris. I choose to believe that, soon, Father will drop the act to tell me that he loves me, that he loves Abraham. To tell us both that everything, in the end, will be alright.

Like Abraham Maher, Father was always disinclined to reveal his true emotions.

Perhaps he is holding back for the perfect moment to express himself.

Watching.

Waiting.

CHAPTER
TWENTY

Do I believe this implausible theory, even now?
Or am I still coming to terms with Father's death and the sentiments we couldn't share in life?

I contemplate its credibility as I walk up Loughborough Road, approaching Eden Estate. It's dawn. Eclipsed by the cloud, the black-eyed sky breaks into an iridescent grey.

As I cross the forecourt I spot Abraham Maher on his balcony, clinging to the wet railings, squinting into the rainfall. He is watching a plastic shopping bag, which gyrates in the wind like a synthetic jellyfish. Hypnotised by its implicit grace, he doesn't notice me as I shimmy onto his balcony five minutes later.

He's mumbling something, over and over, like an unheard prayer.

It sounds like *pyre dies*.

But it isn't that. It's something else.

It's one word.

Paradise.

"Abe?" I say.

I place my hand on the shoulder of his soaked dressing gown. How long has he been out here, staring into the horizon? When Abraham Maher looks up (eyes as placid as dead oceans, raindrops secreted across his cheeks like diamonds), he doesn't seem to recognise me. He lets me guide him back inside, back into the safety of his armchair. I pull off his soggy slippers and turn on the electric heater next to his footrest. The orange glow of the coils, the aroma of searing dust, reminds me of the crematorium at Father's funeral.

"Are you hungry?" I ask.

"Whisky."

"Let's get you a drink," I agree.

I move to the spirits cabinet. As predicted there is no gin, so I fix myself a black Russian with vodka and coffee liqueur and the usual whisky (no ice) for Abraham Maher. I help him with his first sip, holding his quaking hands as he tips the tumbler towards his lips. His cheeks flush with colour. The network of burst capillaries on his nose emanates like forks of crimson lightening. He blinks, as if waking from a deep sleep, and looks at me with revived focus. He seems irritated to find himself shivering, feeling frighteningly sober. This, judging by his agitated expression, is entirely my fault.

"David?" he says, massaging his temples, taking another sip. "David, what are you doing here? Did you refine the core theme of your final chapter? My God. It's almost as important as your first. I assume your agent echoed the same view?"

This is where we left off three days ago (mid-sentence) when I told Abraham Maher about my meeting with Paradise Publishing. Rachel Garland, Richard Hayes and Sultan Gillespie all detested updates on the book's slow progress. Character development. Plot twists. Plotholes. New chapters.

Expansions and rewrites of old ones. None of them pretended to be vaguely interested (*especially* Rachel). Abraham, though, was content to follow the book's evolution. As far as I know, he's the only person who actually read it (*all* of it). But his feedback doesn't come without acrimonious honesty. Overcomplicated prose. Flat passages that drive little or no action. A complete lack of purpose. He sees defects in every sentence, every syllable, aspects of the craft I wish I had the natural talent to recognise. I stare at the copy of *Sick & Beautiful* on his coffee table, tattooed with his annotations. My words are almost illegible, as if the prose can only be understood in the context of its errors.

I refill Abraham Maher's tumbler with another generous dram.

"I'm working on the final chapter," I assure him. "I'm working on a lot of things."

"It all comes down to dedication, David. You did an English Literature degree, but you don't like reading. You wanted to be a journalist, you aspire to be a *novelist*, but you don't like writing. I don't get it, David." Abraham lights a cigarette. "In my lifetime, I've been a paper boy, a cleaner, a forklift driver, a courtroom stenographer, a soldier, and I've read more books than I can remember, but I've never been a writer. What I'm trying to say is, I'm not an expert. But *this*, David." Abraham nods at *Sick & Beautiful*. "This isn't like anything I've ever encountered. It seems to ignore the basics. The fundamental demands of storytelling."

I pull out my pen and notepad.

"What *fundamental demands*?" I ask.

"The resolution, David. The central question to your narrative – *Who is Rachel Garland?* – isn't answered because you don't know your protagonist. You don't understand her motives. This is why it's impossible to create conflict or forge conclusions. But that's the issue with writing a book about a ghost. Phantoms don't want you to know who they are. They don't want you to know why they're here. This has been the problem from the start, David. I'm not sure how many times I need to repeat it."

I write this down. *Fundamental demand = resolution. Central question = Who is RG? A ghost?*

"He's got you there, David."

That's when I notice Osiris perched on the armrest of the sofa, watching the television on mute. It's a news report about violent clashes in Bahrain. I look at Abraham, who looks at the glowing tip of his cigarette, resolutely impassive. Did he hear Osiris speak too? Or is he choosing to ignore him?

"What would you know, Osiris?" I reply. "All you know are these four walls, the trash you watch on TV. Your knowledge and experiences equate to nothing. You have no idea what it's like being us. You don't know the pain humankind suffers, the pain authors suffer. You can't even hold a fucking pen."

"What did you say, David?" asks Abraham Maher.

"Nothing. I said nothing."

Satisfied he's irritated me, Osiris stretches like a rusty box spring, dismounts the armrest with a heavy thud and retreats into his bedroom. I feel relief wash over me in a cool, sobering wave as he waddles out of sight. There's even a small chance that I might have irritated *him*, that I might have won this short exchange.

"What were you saying outside?" I ask Abraham, my voice practically a whisper. "On the balcony, you kept repeating the word *Paradise*. Over and over again."

Abraham Maher frowns, swallowing his whisky. I fill the tumbler again.

"It's nothing," he says. "Just bad dreams, bad memories. Things I haven't thought about since the war. Since we found Paradise."

"What did you find in Paradise?"

"Your father was no angel," he says, evading the question. "When we were teenagers, he dredged the Thames for shellfish with your grandfather – also named David. They leaded stained-glass windows in derelict cathedrals. They painted the ceilings of canal lock chapels. But your father robbed churches and moorings too. He made money scrapping sedans and chevrons jacked from airport car parks. He really enjoyed the crime, but he paid for these transgressions inside Feltham, Wandsworth, Brixton. Small stretches. Even the army couldn't straighten him out. Did I ever tell you that during the war he sold antiques stolen from the towns we occupied? Paintings. Jewellery. Family heirlooms. Some of them were probably priceless."

Abraham Maher knows that I know nearly nothing about my father. Father taught me about human nature, the human sickness, but, just like Rachel Garland, he never revealed anything about himself. For Father, the war was strictly off limits, even the word itself. This morning, though, it sounds like Abraham wants to talk. I decide that this might be a rare opportunity to press the topic that haunts him.

"What did you find in Paradise?" I ask again.

"We found French countryside. Stone cottages with terracotta rooftiles. There was also a one-screen cinema, a hotel, a chapel. Christ knows why there was such a big hotel in such a small village. There was nothing for miles.

Just endless fields of sunflowers, as far as the horizon. This meant that there were practically no soldiers stationed in Paradise, so we captured the village with only a few fatalities. We rounded up the surrendered Wehrmacht and stored the bodies of our enemies and comrades in the chapel. Your father and some of the other men in the unit canvassed the buildings for treasure. The villagers, of course, thought they were looking for threats, snipers, artillery. That's when things started to get interesting. Reality seemed to shift."

Fatalities. Wehrmacht. Artillery. The unit. I look at these words on my notepad. I don't know much about the war, about *any* war, outside of what I have seen in movies, but these words. They sound convincing. They sound *real*, like words a veteran would say. I wanted more (more words, more information).

"*Reality seemed to shift*," I repeat. "Please elaborate."

"In the chapel, locked underneath the alter, your father found a book filled with photographs. Photos of humans dying in the most atrocious ways. And three days later, he– David lost control."

When I was a boy, my father told me a tale from the war. He was stationed in a rural village in France. In a chapel they found a photo album. Days later, a soldier in his unit wiped out the village. My father said the photo album drove him to it.

That's when it hits me. Docklands Dave's story about the photo album. The barge he christened *Paradise*. It can't possibly be true. Why would Abraham Maher never mention his own son, his own biological design? I decide to test this theory immediately.

"Your son named his boat, his *home*, after that town," I

say. "Those war stories you told him as a child must have had a profound effect on him."

To his credit, Abraham Maher remains masterfully expressionless when I drop this detail with the discretion of an atomic bomb. Does he know that his son is the Docklands Dave in *Sick & Beautiful*, a character he eulogised as the narrative's most well-rounded? Or is he concealing this knowledge for an unknown advantage?

"And how would you know about that, David?"

"Because I have the photo album."

This time Abraham Maher does react, but only slightly – a minute jolt in the arm that causes the ash to fall off the tip of his cigarette.

"Here?" he asks.

"Not here."

"Did you look inside it?"

"Yes."

"Did you touch it?"

I don't answer. Abraham Maher nods.

"Your father claimed he never touched it either," he continues. "But it still altered him. The day after he found it, he staggered through the village, under the punishing sunlight, screaming for rain. He looked sick. Gripped in a trance. That night, someone saw him walk into the sunflowers. He didn't return the next morning." Abraham pauses, perhaps to conjure dramatic effect. "Fast forward three days. David was still MIA. And I'm on the night patrol. It was quiet, almost serene, and then I spotted a shape slip into the chapel. Those corpses had been in there for days now, in that heat. Who would want to go inside? I wondered. Someone delirious. Someone suffering from shock and dehydration. Someone like your father. But I was wrong. It was something else entirely. Please, David."

Abraham Maher jiggles his tumbler, signalling for a refill. I oblige. Three drinks in, he really starts to come to life. It's beautiful to watch, to listen.

"As I crept up to the chapel," he ruminates, "I remember the intolerable stench of death, the sound of the blowflies and hornets swarming inside. When I peeked through the gap in the door, a figure was stood before the alter, under the moonlight spilling through the stained glass window. It was knelt over the remains of a dead soldier, removing his organs." Abraham giggles. "It looked like it was stuffing them inside its overcoat, but it wasn't, David. It fed them into a cavity in its chest. A mouth filled with teeth, slurping around the flesh like a pair of lips. And the whole time it whistled, like a man strolling to work on a sunny August morning. When it looked at me, when it looked *into* me, grinning, its eyes were infinite blackness. An abyss. Pure oblivion. It doffed its bowler hat as if it were an old friend. And then it spoke."

Abraham Maher clears his throat and rolls his eyes into the back of his head.

"What are you doing up so late, Abe? Very naughty. Sufficient sleep is crucial for body and soul."

That voice. *Jesus*. Abraham sounds like he's possessed.

"Johanna misses you, Abe. So very, very dearly. Your boy, David, will be in her arms. One day, I'll come back to tell you your role, your purpose. And then I can take you to them, Abe, to the city in the cloud where you can hold hands forever. I promise. Until then, we'll be watching over you. Waiting."

"*Watching over you,*" I whisper, scribbling on my notepad,

trying to capture the detail. Abraham is on fire this morning. He's soaring.

"It knew my name, David," he says, in his normal voice again. "It knew my late wife's name. My son wasn't even born yet, for Christ's sake. How could it know? How could *I* know? I convinced myself it was an awful nightmare. The next morning, your father returned. He told us he heard voices coming from the sunflowers, but when he ran into the field to investigate, he said he got lost, disorientated, swimming through the rows for days before he found his way back. Do you know what he did when I told him about the chapel? *He smiled.* And then he said the strangest thing: *You see him too.* I've never seen a man look so relieved and horrified. When he walked away, he whistled the same tune as that thing in the chapel. I wanted to scream. I still don't know what I saw or why it elected me to be its witness."

Abraham Mather doesn't believe this entity was my father, but what if it was? I wonder. Could Father be the man in the bowler hat, haunting us in past and present realities? There is no denying that he was an oddball. He didn't even enjoy horror movies. Slashers. Vampires. Exploitation. Body horror. Creature features. None of the niches got him going. When I attempted to introduce Father to the classics (the pictures that supersede the shackles of subgenre and personal taste), he scarcely twitched an eyebrow in tepid interest. *Basket Case. Day of the Dead. The Gate. Waxwork. Class of 1999. Halloween. Phantasm. The Thing. The Fly. The People Under the Stairs.* I got nothing. Just stoic silence behind a billow of cigarette smoke. Now, the reason for his disinterest is painfully obvious: Father was desensitised, unmoved by violent imagery that paled to the atrocities of real life.

"How long did you stay in Paradise?" I ask. "After the scene in the chapel, Father hearing voices in the fields, surely you wanted to escape before something awful happened?"

"We left the day after David returned. Nobody believed his story about the talking sunflowers. I wouldn't have either if I hadn't seen what I did in the chapel. The unit thought he was losing his grip on reality, so we put him on night patrol. If your father was on the cusp of a nervous breakdown, at least it would be *out there*, as far away from us as possible. But I should have helped David. If I was braver, perhaps I could have stopped him."

Abraham Maher takes a swig, a drag, a sharp breath. I let him do his thing. "This is great, Abe. Take all the time you need." But will that be enough time for me too? I feel underprepared for this moment – to meet my father, my *real* father, for the very first time. Abraham doesn't look at me when he says this next bit. He says it into the muted television set.

"While we slept, your father rounded up the villagers and POWs at gunpoint and locked them inside the chapel. And then he burnt it to the ground, the living with the dead. I remember screams. A horizon of black smoke and sunshine. And then the rain, the way it turned the ashes into mud. But it was too late to save them. The war was over three months later. We came home heroes and never spoke about Paradise again. But the cloud that formed over the smouldering steeple of that chapel." Abraham points to the window, the storm gobbing on the glass. "It followed us over the ocean. And it's haunted the city ever since. It feeds on our sin and sewage like a levitating parasite. It inundates the grass, melts the leaves off the trees, washes away the daylight. It saw what we did in Paradise. And it's still up there, watching me. Waiting."

When the cloud responds with a whump of thunder over the rooftops, Abraham Maher jumps to his feet with surprising speed, almost losing his balance. As I put my hands on his shoulders to steady him, he collapses into my arms, trembling, gently sobbing. He feels weightless, like he's made out of cardboard and old newspapers.

"I haven't made contact with my son, with *David*," he says (pronouncing his name as if it causes him physical pain), "to protect him from the cloud, from the curse of the photo album. I didn't want him to catch our sickness. But I was a fool to believe that creature wouldn't follow us back too."

"It's not too late to speak to him," I say. "To David."

"I won't do it," he says very quietly. "I won't let that cloud win. I won't let *them* win."

Abraham Maher, agitated by these painful regrets and memories, quickly descends into familiar territory, incoherently ranting, pacing up and down the rug, spilling whisky and cigarette ash in his wake.

"The cloud is just part of a broader conspiracy, David," he explains, drawing the curtains. "Our government spikes the water supplies and pumps buses, tube carriages and aeroplane cabins with mind-altering gasses that keep us crashing cars, overdosing on cheap drugs and falling off platforms and balconies so they can harvest our corpses and sell our organs to hospitals, secret laboratories, supermarkets and curry houses. Even our precious credit ratings, number plates, road tax discs, TV licenses, telephone numbers, lottery tickets, video shop subscriptions, criminal records, postcards, postcodes, pub quizzes, 24-hour surveillance cameras and sex chat lines are just channels for *them* to collate our date. They monitor every movement and habit, either to measure societal evolution, or to upload our memories into androids that can outperform our roles after our death. But who's controlling *them*, David? The cloud? That's the really scary part. Even the cloud might not be an *it*. What if it's a *them*? What if there's another metropolis up there, controlling everything down here? Maybe *they* are the hydrogen-based beings humans have been painting, sculpting and worshipping for millennia. Are they our creators or our destroyers? Are we their prototypes? London might be an elaborate stage set for our overseers in the cloud to test our durability for an unknown purpose. Or perhaps it's entertainment. Perhaps they enjoy watching us discover spectacular new methods to maim and execute each other. Everybody is filming everybody. Reality? It's just another TV show."

"It's just a cloud," I counter, barely audible.

"You're addicted to the cult of the human race, David. It's time to wake up to reality."

Abraham Maher's behaviour makes me want to disbelieve his stories about the war, about my father, but a knowing smile lingers on his lips that suggests it might all be true. Every word. He holds my gaze, reminiscence grappling with despair in his wet, lethargic eyes. Are a cursed photo album or a shapeshifting spirit in a bowler hat any less plausible than his theories about government control and sentient rainclouds?

"Did any of the other soldiers see the photo album?" I ask, eager to steer our conversation back to the war, the burning chapel. "Did they touch it?"

"Your father showed it to two people. Iain Bassi and Alan Parkin. Nice lads. Both from Wakefield. Young. Friends since childhood, just like me and your father."

"What happened to them?"

Abraham Maher settles back into his chair and lights another cigarette. He picks up the remote control on the armrest.

"We found them nearby, laying down in a field of sunflowers," he says, unmuting the television. "Without their skin."

I look at the television screen, trying to metabolise this information. It's another news story. A double-decker bus careened through the barrier of the Hammersmith flyover and flattened a limo driving on the road beneath it. Nine people died. The newsreader claims that the crash was caused by the weather. If feels like the cloud wanted to exercise its power with this fatal accident. A small sacrifice to remind Abraham and I that it's always watching us, always listening.

"You can convince yourself I'm insane," he says, "but I know the real reason why you refuse to believe me – you're scared. We all are, David, believe me, but don't be so naive. That cloud *feels*. It's smart and patient. Insatiable and sinister. As callous as humanity itself. But who knows? Perhaps it'll hang around, feeding from above until the end of days, until the fall of London. Or maybe it'll shrivel and perish with the rest of us. I wonder if I'll live to see the sun shine again? I haven't felt it kiss my skin since Paradise."

A single tear spills down Abraham Maher's cheek and vanishes in the collar of his dressing gown.

"You wouldn't understand," he says. "You're that cloud's child, David. You were born in the rain."

"What if I told you I've seen the man in the bowler hat," I say. "What if I told you I saw him in my flat two nights ago."

Abraham Maher smiles.

"It visited me in a dream last night too," he says. "For the first time in decades. It came back, just like it promised."

"What did he tell you?"

"It told me my purpose. Can you guess what it is? To hide my car keys." Abraham Maher laughs bitterly (not a real laugh, just the effect of one). "Can you believe it, David? My purpose in this life, on this planet, is to hide a set of *fucking* car keys. It's like a sick joke, but it promised it would all work out, that it would all be over soon."

"Where did he tell you to hide your keys?"

"It told me not to tell you, David. And stop calling it a *he*. It's something far more complex. We don't have the pronouns to define it."

"Why would *it* give these instructions? Think about it, Abe. It's ludicrous. It's just so *insignificant*."

Abraham Maher shrugs. "We grow up assuming we're ordained for great things," he says. "But more often than not, we're destined to play a smaller role in somebody else's story. We don't have to understand it, but it's important to accept it, to embrace it. We need to keep faith in the script."

I flinch when the telephone on top of the spirits cabinet starts to ring, rattling the skyline of bottles like a small earthquake. I take a deep breath and (on the fifth ring) pick up the receiver.

"Hello?"

"David, there's been an accident involving your friend Richard. Sounds like it could be big news."

The words sound breathless, splintered with static, like a phantom making contact from a distant realm. But the voice is unmistakable. It's my former editor, Eleanor Wither.

"Ellie?" I stutter. "Ellie, where have you been? I thought you were dead. Jesus. I wasn't even sure if you existed."

"I haven't got time to explain everything, David. You need to trust me. And you need to move fast."

"I don't work on the paper anymore. They told me that you don't work there either. That you never did. What's going on, Ellie?"

"If you're not the man for the role," she says sharply, "I'll ring Leonard Lynch instead. Perhaps he'll be better suited to the task in hand."

"That won't be necessary."

"Good. Get to Richard's apartment pronto. You'll find the answers you're looking for there. Until next time, David."

When the line goes dead, I put the receiver back into its cradle. My hand shakes as I raise my glass to my lips. Abraham Maher, transfixed on the television set, doesn't ask me who I was speaking with. Perhaps he assumed I already left, like a spectre passing through the walls of a haunted high-rise.

"How did Eleanor Wither get your number?" I ask.

"Number?" he laughs. "I haven't paid for a landline since the 1980s. You don't really need one when all your friends are dead."

I look at the telephone. The receiver and keypad are coated in a thick layer of dust. I kneel on the floor and pick up the cable attached to it – it has been torn out of the wall, dislocating the jack from its socket.

"You want to know the strangest part about that story?" says Abraham Maher over his shoulder. "Your father told me he didn't just burn those people alive in the chapel. He said he burnt the photo album in there too."

CHAPTER
TWENTY-ONE

I'm going to kill him. And I'm going to enjoy myself.
These are the words I whispered into my half-empty tumbler when I realised an unbreakable, venereal relationship had blossomed between Richard Hayes and Rachel Garland. A relationship beyond my control, beyond the previously implied boundaries.

I fantasised about drawing a knife out of the wooden block on my kitchen worktop and stabbing Richard Hayes to death in the back of the Prince Charles during a scream drowned slasher like *Driller Killer* or *Maniac Cop*. I envisaged garrotting him on an unlit common with the power cord of my VCR. I imagined what it may feel like to cut him down with Abraham Maher's car in the narrow alleyways of Soho or Whitechapel. I daydreamed about shoving him over the railings of Vauxhall, Westminster or Lambeth Bridge into the river's black undertow. I wanted Rachel Garland to hear him cower, beg for mercy. I wanted her to understand that Richard isn't special. That he's just like everybody else – frightened to death, obsessed with self-preservation. Even now, I feel this ingrained rage, the desire to commit violence to bring Rachel and I together.

In the end, of course, I did none of these things. I simply wept into my hands, shielding my face from the cruel world that had abandoned me. I apparently didn't want to murder Richard as much as I thought I did. In the end, it turns out I didn't have to. As the taxi stutters up the tailbacks of Brixton Hill and Cavendish Road, I didn't expect to experience any sensation of loss or sadness, but I do. I've felt it since I got the call.

Eleanor Wither didn't need to tell me that Richard Hayes is dead.

Like I said, I could already feel it, his material absence, like a change in air pressure, a refraction of light.

I check a roll film is loaded in my camera as I smoke a cigarette, readying myself for the death scene. I can see it now. The fleet of emergency vehicles lined on the forecourt of Arcadia Gardens, Richard Hayes's luxurious apartment complex. The TV crews and tourists elbowing for dominance, pressing their faces between the bars of the front gates like netted fish. But when the cabbie pulls over on Clapham Common North Side, there is no mob. No teeming throng of limbs and umbrellas jutting towards the cloud. Just a single police car parked outside the lobby, the thrum of the traffic behind me, the odour of exhaust fumes, the rain. I type in the code for the gate (3434, memorised by heart), cross the forecourt and enter the lobby, feeling detached from reality, from myself, as if I'm stepping through somebody else's reverie.

In the centre of the lobby, the concierge is talking to a policewoman. She nods earnestly and scribbles over her notepad as he sweats profusely, speaking with pace. Whenever I visited Richard Hayes, when we were still friends, I always found the concierge positioned behind his desk with an acute aura of control – vertical spine, clean suit, clean shaven, eager to assist – but tonight he looks stunned, exhausted, his hospitality on autopilot. We briefly make eye contact as I walk towards the elevator, but he is too flustered to recognise me. Perhaps he doesn't remember me. Perhaps he can't even see me.

"There you are," says a voice behind me. "You should have been here nearly an hour ago."

I freeze mid-step, turn around, smile. The policewoman studies my abstract frame, the way I clash with the polished floor, the grand chandelier overhead, the opulent brass and marble décor. She smiles back (eventually), but it's more of a simper, a reaction to the car crash in front of her.

"Forensics, right?" she says, pointing at the camera around my neck.

"You've got it," I say, picking it up, jiggling it, confirming it's a real object, confirming I'm a real object.

"I can tell. You guys in forensics– you always have that haunted look."

"It comes with the job, ma'am," I say, trying to sound convincing, trying to get into the role. Where have I heard this line before? A police drama? A neo-noir crime film?

"Go to floor 5. Apartment 27. Detective Constable Scythe will be waiting."

"You've got it."

I salute (too much?) and call the elevator. The concierge appears to be on the precipice of tears. The policewoman puts her hand on his shoulder, giving it a consoling squeeze.

She gives me that sad smile again, as if she feels sorry for him, for me, for all of us.

"That scene upstairs," she says as the elevator doors open. "My God. It took my breath away."

She wasn't being hyperbolic.

The apartment is a horror show. Overturned furniture. Shattered mirrors. Videotapes and paperwork thrown across the carpets and floorboards. Cupboards emptied, drawers hauled off their runners. A life turned upside-down, inside-out. It's a shame to find the gaff in such bad shape.

Richard Hayes furnished and decorated his apartment with a pathological eye to detail. You can see it everywhere, his pretentious, hyper-stylised bluster. The writing desk overlooking the balcony was handcrafted with reclaimed driftwood in Highbury & Islington. The Persian rugs that dignify the floorboards were purchased on Albemarle Street. The settees in the living room were upholstered in Chelsea. The jars of foetuses and wet specimens filling the display cases in the bedroom and study were purchased from his university-days contacts at the Royal College of Surgeons.

How do I know all this? Because Richard Hayes made a point of cataloguing these details every time I visited him. With a flute of fizz in one hand and a cigarette in the other, he would recite these scripted soliloquies like a drugged up tour guide as he roamed in and out of palatial rooms, speaking with rehearsed confidence as he described the possessions he adored, enjoying the resonance of his voice as it filled the high ceilings. He even itemised the tabletops, alcoves and chaise lounges where he had sex with Rachel Garland and countless other women and men, running his fingers over these surfaces as if they resonated with a sexual afterglow.

Even before our fallout, he never made me feel like a guest in this apartment. I was an interloper, trespassing in the universe he joylessly created.

Glass crunches under my feet. I look down. It's a framed photograph of Richard Hayes. I pick it up. His arm is snaked around the waist of a quasi-famous actor. Richard smiles broadly, eyes void, expressionless. I smile back. Now it's my turn to photograph him, finally freed from the weight of his own self-importance. I always knew (and hoped) I would photograph his dead body, likely within the walls of his apartment complex – floating face-down in the private swimming pool or his claw-footed bathtub, or crumpled on the cobblestones of the private courtyard, five storeys below the railings of his balcony – but I never thought I'd find him like *this*: tethered by his wrists and ankles to a dining chair in the centre of his sitting room, a camcorder mounted on a tripod in front of him, the rug soupy with blood.

Three detectives stare at the corpse like tourists lost in a gallery of conceptual artwork, unsure how to interpret this violent, abstract jigsaw puzzle. The woman knelt at the feet of the body must be Detective Constable Scythe. Her eyes (intelligent, somehow both sharp and exhausted) examine the victim, the objects that surround him, searching for hidden meaning. Her yellow anorak reminds me of the polyester raincoat I wore when I was a child, skipping across the common with my jar of dead spiders. Her lipstick is bright red, the colour of an open wound. Absorbed in the chaos of the apartment, the detectives have apparently not noticed me.

"There doesn't appear to be any signs of breaking and entering," she says. "Whoever did this knew the victim. But what was their purpose? That's the question. Did they turn the place topsy-turvy looking for something? Or were they here to make a statement?"

"The tape is missing from the camcorder too, ma'am," adds one of the detectives. "Who *was* this person?"

"A director, perhaps," suggests the other, picking up one of the screenplays on the desk.

"Or just another human with another litany of perfunctory, half-hearted obsessions," she counters.

I walk through the rooms in a daze, objectively trying to come to terms with the brutality around me through my camera. Instead of the answers that Eleanor Wither promised, I can only find deeply disturbing questions. Five instantly come to mind.

> Q1: *Who ransacked the apartment?*
> Q2: *Who smashed the mirrors in every room, as if they couldn't bear to look at their own reflection?*
> Q3: *Who mounted the camcorder on its tripod with the lens pointed at the victim's face (the same cutting-edge equipment Rachel and Richard used to film their visceral, drug-fuelled sex scenes)?*
> Q4: *Who created an orifice in the centre of the victim's abdomen, a cavity wide enough to fit a fist?*
> Q5: *Most disturbingly of all, where is the victim's skin?*

Once upon a time, Richard Hayes was really attached to it (his skin). Now, playing the role of the victim, he is flayed head-to-toe, exposing the pornographic detail of the musculature underneath.

Staring at this vulgar scene from the hallway, I listen to DC Scythe postulate with her colleagues.

"Judging by the ligature marks around the wrists and Achilles tendons," she continues, "the victim squirmed when he was bound, which leads me to the hypothesis that he was still alive when the skin was removed. He didn't just struggle. *He suffered.* More than one could imagine. An average human body holds a dozen pints of blood. How many do you think the victim shed before passing out or dying first?"

One of the detectives releases a long, high-pitched whistle, like steam escaping a boiling kettle.

"Awful way to go, ma'am."

"Awful," agrees the other.

But I can hardly hear them. This information, like a distorted signal from a distant planet, fails to resonate.

Lost in the pandemonium of Richard Hayes's apartment, the most mundane props of his reality become apparent. The half-finished crossword from yesterday's newspaper on the coffee table. The unopened utility bills stacked on the davenport. The bedsheets still imprinted with the silhouette of his body. The holiday snaps of his parents holding the smiling child he used to be, on a beach they used to visit. These subtle cues are everywhere, all around us, bursting through every fissure of the apartment. In death, Richard suddenly appears more interesting, *more put together*, defined with human complexities. Not just sick, but heartbreakingly beautiful. Maybe Rachel Garland saw these poignant banalities too. Perhaps she adored them.

When I turn around, DC Scythe is stood right there in front of me. She's so close I can smell the perfume on her neck, the aroma of endless cigarettes. Her eyes dart frantically between my dilated pupils. Her stare feels like a million tiny fingers digging into my brain, sifting for unspeakable secrets. The silence drills through my skull like a police siren, a hypodermic needle of white noise. I have the sudden urge to cup my ears and scream. I want to wake up from this nightmare.

"Forensics?" she asks, pointing to my camera.

"You've got it," I reply.

"Jesus. You look terrible. When's the last time you slept?" She smells my breath and winces. "Have you been drinking?"

"It comes with the job, ma'am."

"I can imagine. So, what are you waiting for? Get over there and photograph the body. We haven't got all day."

Dutifully, I shuffle back down the hallway, towards the victim. I kneel on the blood-soaked rug and twist the lens into focus. Through my camera, I gaze into the victim's eyes. His dying expression is fixed with that familiar question (the question I've seen a thousand times).

I'm a good person, so why me? And why like this?

No one in this room is more stunned with the way things have turned out than the victim. I wait for him to pose for the camera, flashing that sham grin he has crowbarred into every photograph in the apartment. I hold back the hysterical laughter bubbling behind this notion. If he moves (even the twitch of an eyebrow, one final breath), I'll launch myself off the balcony, just like Rupert Wreath did on the night I met Rachel Garland. I'll either do that, or give into the bliss of insanity. Both have their appeal.

I take the photograph. And then I spot something over the victim's shoulder. It's a smiley face, finger-painted into the condensation on the inside of the balcony window. Just like the one the man in the bowler hat left in my own flat two nights ago. Flies crawl over the glass, searching for an exit.

DC Scythe places her hand on my shoulder.

"Do you have everything you need?" she asks impatiently. "Or are you just admiring your work?"

"It comes with the job, ma'am," I repeat unimaginatively, unable to improvise fresh dialogue.

"You said. Now give us some space to do *our* job."

"You've got it."

Obediently, I step back and continue my directionless tour of the apartment. I photograph the smiley face on the balcony doors, my reflection in a splintered mirror, the display cases of abscised body parts, the bookcases of horror movies that stretch across the sitting room and disappear down the hallway. The breadth of Richard Hayes's collection always moves me. There must be over 3,000 titles here, all alphabetised, from classics to rare foreign and grindhouse movies I've never seen or heard of. It's painful to see so many of these videos pulled from the shelves, stamped into the floor, disembowelled of their magnetic tape. I shake my head sadly. And then I lower my camera. I spot something in-between *The Shining* and *The Silence of the Lambs*.

"Interesting," I whisper.

It's a videotape with *Sick & Beautiful* scrawled on its label in jagged hieroglyphs.

"Yes," I nod. "That's very interesting."

An agonising coldness envelops me. I know what I have to do. I try to resist it, but it's impossible to ignore. I look over my shoulder. DC Scythe and her detectives are still distracted with the corpse. With a grimace, I pluck the tape off of the shelf and slide it inside my overcoat. I shudder, imagining the fingers that gripped this object, the hand that penned *Sick & Beautiful*. I can almost smell it, the fetid odour the man in the bowler hat leaves in his wake. Something inside me, something terrified, screams for intervention. But the detectives don't see me take it. They don't see a thing. They don't acknowledge my existence in this room, in this time or space. They're preoccupied with the cadaver, the equivocal violence.

"We haven't seen anything like this in our city for a long time, gentlemen," says DC Scythe, sinking into one of Richard Hayes's wing-back chairs. The two detectives sit on the floor in front of her, cross-legged and deferentially mesmerised, like children crowding around a television set. "A long, long time." She lights a cigarette and allows the room to curdle with coarse smoke, enjoying the aura, the undivided attention. "Sometimes," she says, "something visits us from *out there*."

"Like a tourist, ma'am?"

"Precisely," she exclaims, ruffling the detective's hair. "This could be the work of gangs. British. Eastern European. Chinese. But I suspect this is something else entirely. There are unsolved murders dating back centuries with similar hallmarks. The body desecrated, skinned like caribou, the internal organs removed. Florence. Paris. Reykjavík. New Orleans. Mérida. Bengaluru. Nueva Island. London. This has recurred in settlements across the globe. One theory suggests this visitor comes to hunt us. Another that it's here to study us, watching us like television. Truthfully, we don't know its origins or purpose. We don't even know if there is more than one of them. All we are able to do is speculate." She extinguishes her cigarette on the armrest. "Gentlemen. Let's find out if this is another victim of our sinister guest."

DC Scythe removes her anorak, folds it over the arm of the chair and rolls up the sleeves of her shirt. She approaches the body and shines a small flashlight into the cavity in the abdomen. With an ungloved hand, she explores the texture of the wound's labia-like edges before inserting two fingers inside it, sliding them in and out with disturbing invasiveness. And then, quite suddenly, she plunges her whole hand inside. The tendons in her wrist flex and relax as she splays and balls her fingers. She shuts her eyes, slipping deeper inside the victim, halfway up the forearm and then past the elbow, as if she is feeling through an unlit cellar, rummaging in the darkness for a sentimental object, a mislaid memory. Finally, her arm vanishes with sickening ease, the wound puckering around her biceps like lips. Satisfied, she pulls it out again. She smells her fingers. For one moment, she looks like she might taste them. This urge appears to pass as she wipes her hand on the side of her trousers.

"Just as I suspected," she says. "He's empty."

This final detail is apparently too much.

I feel untied from my body as I cross the sitting room to extract a tumbler and a carafe of gin from the minibar. I then walk (at pace) to the kitchen to pull a bottle of tonic and a tray of ice cubes out of the fridge-freezer. I fill the tumbler to the brim, swirl the contents with my index finger, sink it in one mouthful. I slam the glass on the kitchen island and knead my eyes, waiting for the heartburn and nausea to elapse. When I open them again, the detectives are watching me. Have they clocked my familiarity with the apartment? This (surely, *mercifully*) is the end of my dark odyssey. I hold out my hands and bow my head in submission, in defeat, eager to be handcuffed, incarcerated. I've had enough, I decide. Cut the cameras. Fuck the script. I want out. I quit. Instead, DC Scythe smiles.

"Excellent choice," she says. "Three double gin and tonics, please."

The detectives nod in agreement.

"I don't think our friend here is thirsty, though," she adds, slapping the victim around his skinless face. Specks of blood splash on her cheek, her parted lips, the collar of her white shirt.

DC Scythe tries not to smile, but, quite quickly, rabid laughter starts to spill out of her painful grin.

The detectives start to laugh too.

We all laugh.

I laugh so hard my eyes flood with tears.

The laughter (noxious, inebriating) becomes uncontrollable.

It becomes unbearable.

I scream hysterically.

The victim looks on with stoic indifference.

CHAPTER
TWENTY-TWO

En route back to Brixton, I make an essential pitstop at the off license on Acre Lane. One litre of dry gin, three bottles of Indian tonic, a 20-deck of cigarettes, one large bag of microwave sweet and salt popcorn. I decide I'm going to treat tonight like any other movie night. After the interview, the fight, the crime scene, my brushes with the man in the bowler hat, I crave respite. An interlude from the turbulence.

I exit the taxi on Loughborough Road, walk across the forecourt, into the lobby, the lift, the second-floor corridor, determined to decompress, determined to anaesthetise body and mind.

Inside my flat, I stand in the hallway, staring at *Sick & Beautiful* scrawled across the label of the videotape. I place it on top of the TV set, next to Father's ashes, deciding to defer the inevitable for just a few more moments. I enter the kitchen to microwave the popcorn and make a gin and tonic. The anaemic afternoon light falters through the window, stretching my cloudy shadow across the linoleum. I sit at the breakfast table, snort a bump of coke, swallow a Valium, roll another joint, light it. When I finally collapse into the sofa, I feel myself unwind, the uncoupling of my thoughts and my anatomy. I'm *this* close to feeling pacified when I hear a knock on the door. Three innocuous taps. I look through the peephole and smile.

When I open the door, Rachel Garland is stood in the hallway. She is barefoot, dripping rainwater onto the carpet of the corridor. Her floral dress is soaked, wetly clung to the acute contours of her body.

"Can I come in?" she asks.

I nod and step aside. She walks into the middle of the sitting room, arms limp at her sides, drizzle trickling off her fingertips. We stare at one another in silence, waiting for the other to say something significant.

"Is it raining outside?" I ask.

She smiles. "It's always raining, David."

Another silence. The muffled din of exploding popcorn drifts from the kitchen.

"Richard is dead," I say, unsure why I want to punish Rachel with this knowledge. "Someone took his skin. And his insides."

"I know. Did you not see it on the news? They haven't released his name yet, but I know it's him. I know it's Richard."

"How does this make you feel?"

"The same as you, David. Abstract, desensitised."

"Did you do it?" I ask, deflated that this remarkable information hasn't affected her. "There was no evidence of breaking and entering. And you're the only person he'd trust with a set of keys to his apartment."

Rachel Garland laughs. She sits on the sofa and removes her wig, placing it in the centre of the coffee table. She scratches the stubble underneath and lights a cigarette. She looks relaxed, but this might be an act. Hidden behind her sunglasses, it's impossible to read her emotions, to gauge her pain.

"You know I didn't do it, David," she says. "You know that's impossible."

"I was afraid you might be dead too."

Rachel Garland stands up and walks towards me, leaving a trail of wet footprints on the floor.

"I'm here now, aren't I?" she says, taking hold of my hands and cupping them over her cheeks, her breasts, her hips. I feel her soft flesh through the saturated dress. It's cold, like wet stone. When I shudder, she removes my hands and returns to the sofa. I pick up the cassette of *Sick & Beautiful*.

"A lot of strange things have been happening, Rachel," I say. "And I think this videotape might have the answers. Shall we watch it?"

"Only if you make me one of those," she says, pointing to my drink. "And if it's a scary movie, you have to promise to put your arm around me. I want to feel warmth. *Human warmth.*"

Is this even Rachel Garland? I wonder. Or an altruistic manifestation of the phantom presence I have always felt haunting my flat? She seems too affectionate, too ethereal, like a hologram of the person I always wished or imagined she would be. The dialogue feels scripted, horrifically clichéd.

"Let me make you a drink," I say.

When I re-enter the sitting room (gin and tonic in one hand, bowl of popcorn in the other), I spot Osiris on the balcony windowsill, sat in the rain. He paws the glass trying to capture Rachel Garland's attention, but she ignores him, staring into the blank oblivion of the switched off television set. I put the tumbler and popcorn on the coffee table and draw the curtains, shrouding the room in darkness.

"Sorry, Osiris," I say with unconcealed satisfaction. "I haven't got time for your weird shit today."

I slide the tape into the VCR, sit next to Rachel Garland, remove my wet shoes, my wet socks, pick up the remote control and press the power button. The television set fizzes to life. It's a single image – me, in a suit, in a chair, in front of a desk, in an office, in conversation. I appear translucent, almost spectral, as if I'm a projection rather than a physical presence. I smile at this blunt portrait of myself, unsure how else to react. I can't see the face of the character sat behind the desk, but I know who it is. I recognise his voice, his suit, his immaculate haircut.

"That's Rupert," I say, pointing at the television screen. "He's my agent. I met him yesterday, on the eleventh floor of Paradise Publishing, the morning after we went to the Prince Charles. But why did he record our meeting? I don't even remember seeing a camera."

"Everybody records everybody in this city, David," she says. "Now shush. I'm trying to watch your performance."

I'd be able to steal the photo album if it was tucked inside Richard's pocket. It's just– all of this. *It doesn't make sense. It's unreal. I feel like I'm watching myself, unable to control my dialogue or my body.*

After I say this, Rupert Wreath laughs. Rachel Garland laughs too. But I wasn't trying to be funny. These words were spoken from the heart, the soul. They were an honest expression of my emotions in that office, in that moment.

Onscreen, I watch myself squirm in my seat, wincing, as if I'm in pain.

Perhaps you're not the man for the role. We overestimated you, David. You came here and seduced us with your counterfeit ambition. But it's a mask. What made us hope you would be capable of joining the publishing elite? Rachel and Richard are right. You haven't got what it takes.

And then, on the TV, I collapse to the floor, crawl towards the desk and weep into the carpet.

Richard assumes that every dream has been a tragic misfire. But he doesn't understand my ambition. He doesn't know what really happened that night.

Rupert Wreath stands up, walks around the desk, kneels beside me and strokes his fingers through my hair, holding my shuddering body. His character is complex. Compassion and disgust compete for dominance in his expressions, his idiosyncrasies. My character, in contrast, appears damaged, emotionally pliable, physically insolvent. Rachel Garland nods, gasps, tilts her head sideways.

"I love your lines," she says. "*Your ambience.* It's rich, compelling. Really *out there*. I've got to say, I'm impressed, David. I really am."

Is Rachel Garland being sincere? I wonder. Or is she enjoying my mortification, absorbing it?

"I can explain," I say, feeling my cheeks flush. "This is all out of context, Rachel. Here, *I'm* out of context."

But, thankfully, I don't need to explain anything. The video cuts to another scene. It's Richard Hayes, naked, tethered to a dining room chair in the centre of his apartment, realising his role as the victim. Notably, he still has his skin. He looks into the camera. Behind him is a stretched image of his petrified face, projected on his enormous television set. I tap my hands on my knees. I gently sweat, feeling seasick. I know what's coming next. I've already seen the ending. Rachel Garland squeezes my hand, just like she used to when we watched her sex tapes.

"Don't feel sadness," she says. "Richard always dreamed about starring in his own horror movie. He would have wanted us to watch."

The victim's words drone in and out like a hovering wasp. He's whimpering, pleading, praying incoherently. He begs the director on the other side of the camera to show mercy. He says he can take whatever he wants. The artefacts, the videotapes, the vintage wines and continental spirits in the cellaret. Anything. He even gives him the code to the safe hidden inside his desk. He promises not to tell a soul, not even the law, if he'll just cut him loose and let him live. The director giggles. And then he speaks.

I'm afraid it's too late for that, Richard. This is your role. It always has been. And it always will be. How many more times will you die in that chair? And how many times will you beg for your freedom? Look at yourself, old friend. Imagine what Rachel will think when she sees you snivelling, grovelling?

When the director finally moves into view, the victim tenses. His eyes are feral with terror. Rachel Garland's grip tightens. I can only see the director from behind. He's wearing a black overcoat. And a bowler hat. He holds a scalpel in his right hand.

"There he is," says Rachel Garland. "Our antagonist."

I don't answer. *It isn't necessarily the apparition*, I think. Everyone wears a bowler hat in London (do they not?). I take a long sip of my gin and tonic. It transforms my stomach into an acerbic tundra. The muscles in my shoulders knot together like shoestrings. It feels like a headstone is balanced on my chest. I feel like I can't breathe.

Why are you doing this? asks the victim.

Because you summoned us, Richard. You sought the photo album. You set this plot in motion. Now, I'm afraid, it cannot be stopped. Believe me. I've tried. Thousands and thousands of times.

The victim screams as the director sinks the scalpel into his forehead, slicing across the hairline, along the jaw, around the eyes. His screams ascend into a sickening falsetto as the director peels the skin away from the victim's face. He kisses the victim on the cheek, stroking his hair, attempting to pacify him.

It's OK, Richard. You're doing great. Let it out. We haven't got long left together.

Rachel Garland bites her bottom lip as she runs her hands over her face, around the areolae of her erect nipples, in-between her thighs, perhaps imagining that her fingertips are the edge of the scalpel. She removes her sunglasses. Her eyes are focussed, groping for the sensuality buried in the violence.

A series of loud bangs can be heard off-screen. The director turns, staring into the camera lens. Black eyes sparkle inside deep sockets. The lips are stretched over serrated teeth, distorted into a perverse smile. Spiders and flies crawl over his shoulders, his skin, creeping under the collar of his filthy shirt.

"I knew it would be him," says Rachel Garland, imitating the director's smirk. "It was obvious."

Hayes? shouts a muted voice (presumably an irate neighbour pressed up against the front door). *Hayes, do you have any idea what time it is? Some of us have work in the morning. Ever heard of it?*

Help me, chokes the victim. The top half of his face hangs over his mouth, so you don't see him say these words. You can just hear them. *Please help me.*

You're beyond help, Hayes. Keep the fucking noise down or I'll be making an official complaint to the concierge. Consider this your final warning.

Realising that his last chance for salvation has passed – or perhaps in a dying act of compliance with his neighbour's wishes – the victim falls silent while the director removes more tissue. The victim smiles, teeth sparkling in a mask of blood. He occasionally blinks, grappling for breath, fighting back laughter. The eyes seem to palliate with disquieting serenity, an honesty I could never recognise in Richard Hayes. He's reborn. Perhaps even improved. Slowly, the victim's head sags on his bloodied shoulders, unable to continue with the pain.

"Richard's quite brilliant, isn't he?" says Rachel Garland.

"Stop calling him that," I say. "He isn't Richard anymore. He's– *nothing*. Just another victim of the city, the universe."

"I think it's a performance worth dying for. Your scene was fantastic, David. But this is something else."

As the director starts to pull the scalp away from the skull, the victim looks up again (into the camera, into *me*) and whispers something. It's almost inaudible.

Tell David I sent you. Tell him that I did this to him.

Don't worry, Richard. David will know everything soon enough. Now keep still. Shut your eyes. Be silent. We have a lot of work to do, a lot of skin to shake. Are you ready?

The victim grins before letting his head hang limp again, as if he's bowing to an invisible audience.

I pick up the remote control and turn off the television set. I glug my gin and tonic. Rachel hasn't even touched hers (it's lost its effervescence, the ice cubes devoid of their definitive corners).

"*Tell David I sent you,*" she says. "What do you think he means by that? It's a terrific cliffhanger."

I agree. It *is* a terrific cliffhanger. But I'm more preoccupied with two other possibilities.

Will the man in the bowler hat be wearing Richard Hayes's face the next time we meet?

And could Rachel still fall in love with that face, even if she knows what lies beneath it?

She rests her head on my shoulder.

"Did I ever tell you about my mother and father?" she asks.

"You told me your mother was in the hospital," I reply. "And that you never knew your father."

"In many ways, I didn't know either of them. Two years before I was born, Mother was involved in a head-on collision in the banlieues of Paris. She woke up in a coma. When I was conceived, she was still in that coma. No-one ever found out who my father was. Investigators suspected he was either a patient or a member of the hospital's night staff. Only one detail ever emerged about him: he wore a black overcoat and a bowler hat." Rachel pauses. "Clinging to the reality she left behind, rigged with plastic tubes and beeping machinery, I imagined everything I wanted to know about my mother. Her favourite colours, favourite flowers, favourite movies. The lilt of her voice. The names she would have invented, just for me. I'd lie next to her on the hospital bed, wrap her limp arms around me and pretend she was hugging me, rocking me to sleep, humming a beautiful lullaby."

"Why did you never tell me until now?"

"I knew that you'd steal this memory for the book, twist it around, utilise it, embellish it. I didn't want you or the world to own a piece of me or my past."

I nod, absorbing this information, accepting it. *I didn't want you or the world to own a piece of me or my past.* Another great line. I resist the urge to pick up my notepad and write it down.

"Do you look like your mother?" I ask.

"I don't know. The only details I can remember about her are the ones I instituted and falsified."

"Is your mother still there, awake in the darkness?"

Rachel Garland shakes her head sadly.

"One day," she says, "my mother wasn't in her hospital bed anymore. I remember I felt– *upset*. Angry. Did she just open her eyes, walk out and leave? If she did, why did she never find me so she could hold her daughter in her arms? And then I thought – *What if she never existed?* Is it possible that I imagined her, just like I imagined everything else about her? If Mother didn't exist, it means I don't exist either. The nurse simply told me – *Ta mère a volé à travers les nuages, jusqu'au Paradis*. It means – *Your mother flew into the clouds, into Paradise.* Perhaps this is what all nurses tell little girls who lose their make believe mothers."

I feel the severity of Rachel Garland's shoulder blades, her collarbone, the damp chill of her dress, the corrugated ribcage, the goose-pimpled flesh on her forearms.

I cup her hands in-between mine.

They're as cold as trampled snow.

"You feel real to me," I say. "You exist here. Now. In this room. In this city. *We* exist, Rachel."

Rachel Garland holds my head in her hands, searching my eyes for depth, for light.

"That's funny," she says. "Because you don't feel real to me."

I'm not sure when I fall asleep or, more accurately, pass out from psychological exhaustion.

CHAPTER
TWENTY-THREE

In my flat, in my dream, I crawl into my television set and step into a field of sunflowers.

They tower over my head in neat rows, gently swaying in the wind. Barefoot, I push through them, guided by the blood moon above. My suit, still wet from the London rain, feels chilly in the silent breeze. I hug myself, trying to generate heat. The aromas of soil and pollen curdle the air.

The sunflowers are endless. The vast nothingness. It's endless.

Eventually, I step into a circular clearing. It's a cemetery dotted with wooden crucifixes. I walk up to one of the graves in its centre. The rood is crooked. A bowler hat is hung on its apex. I look around me, into the walls of sunflowers, wondering if he is close, wondering if he is watching me. I can't see him (not yet), but I can feel his presence. It's all around me.

When I turn back towards the grave, a shovel is speared into the ground, practically begging me to pick it up. The dirt here is loose. A darker tinge to the surrounding topsoil (which is carmine, like the plains of Mars). It's as if it has been recently disturbed.

I wrap my fingers around the handle of the shovel, feeling its weight, the texture of its wooden handle, and start to dig. "Yes," I agree as I sink the blade into the soft earth. This grave is fresh. I don't want to know what's buried beneath it, but what can I do? Like the world of the living, the passively awake, I'm under no illusion that I have any jurisdiction or agency in my nightmares.

I weep. I shake. I dig. I remove my suit jacket, loosen my tie, unbutton my shirt. Dark patches of sweat begin to materialise across my shoulders and underneath my armpits.

"Wake up, David," I bellow at the red moon, like it's a portal back to the reality of the sofa, the flat, the city.

I lean on the shovel, doubled over, attempting to control my breathing.

"Fine," I say. "Let's keep going. Let's dig."

Quite gradually, I'm reduced to hysterical laughter. It's so manic it disrupts the rhythm of my digging, but I persevere, playfully giggling, determined to unearth the truths buried in the cemetery of my subconscious with this imaginary shovel.

"This is thirsty work, though," I say aloud, hauling another sod over my shoulder. "I'd murder for a gin and tonic."

I peer over the edge of the deepening hole, half-expecting my mixer to magically appear on a silver tray (if this is a dream, a double measure with fresh ice and a wedge of lime would be utterly adorable). I shrug, returning to my digging. Drink or no drink, I start to enjoy myself. My shoulders loosen up. My breathing steadies. My heart rate slows. I feel invincible, smug with self-awareness, safe in the precept that, unlike real life, you can't die in your dreams. It doesn't matter if I believe this. I'm tired of living in fear. Exhausted of being reality's plaything.

Just as I start to build a workmanlike pace, the blade of the shovel sinks into something soft that isn't soil. It makes a sickening crunch, like eggshells crushed between boots and floorboards. When I pull the shovel out, the ground ejaculates a jet of black liquid.

I drop to my hands and knees, raking through the slush with my blistering fingers. I'm not even surprised when I uncover the crown of a human head. I scrape the wet dirt off the face, wiping away the oozing blood. It's leaking from a wound above the hairline, opened by the blade of my shovel.

"No," I whisper, cradling the head in my hands. "This isn't possible."

It's my own face, eyes shut in an eternal, drug-induced sleep. I sink my fingers inside the gaping wound, exploring the textures of the moist tissue within. I lick the crest of the laceration, its smooth apex, as if stimulating a clitoris. When I pull away, satisfied with this transgression, the eyes open, blinking drowsily, pupils milky like a boiled carp. My face looks at me, sobbing, quivering, searching for answers.

How could you do this to me, David?

"It'll be OK," I say, kissing myself on the forehead. "In the end it always is, David."

The head starts to scream. And then the eyeballs explode, spraying me with gore. Spiders pour out of the eyesockets. A million wasps and butterflies hatch out of the cocoon of my mind, fluttering into the night sky. My body is the jar of creepy-crawlies from my childhood. They've been incubating inside me, multiplying, waiting to escape their flesh and cartilage prison. Am I just another arachnid trapped inside a jar the size of a universe? Something is shaking it, forcing a violent reaction.

When I climb out of the grave, I spot him on the edge of the cemetery, head and bowler hat lolling above the sunflowers. He chuckles as I writhe in the dirt. I'm covered with blood, incoherently shrieking, swatting the legions of insects swarming into my mouth, crawling over my sticky skin.

"Hello, David," he says, waving warmly. "It's good to see you."

The man in the bowler hat steps into the clearing, abdomen palpitating, transforming under his overcoat. The Praktica Super TL2 camera swings around his neck like a pendulum. He is wearing the skinned face of Richard Hayes, stretched into an excruciating sneer. His arms are grotesquely long, dragging in the dirt behind him like tentacles.

"Did you know that Father got lost in these sunflowers?" he says. "By the time he found his way out, he was already changed. He left a part of himself here, in the past, in the meadows of Paradise."

"Why are you haunting me?" I scream, shielding my face from the swarm. "What the fuck do you *want*?"

"I want the same thing as you, David. To feel real. To feel *tangible*. I miss the feeling of that body, that skin. It fits me beautifully. Like a tailor-made suit. Be careful rolling around in the mud like that. You'll damage it, make it dirty."

"Who are you?"

"Do you really want to know?"

I nod.

He hooks his index fingers in the corners of his mouth and rips Richard Hayes's face apart like cheap wrapping paper. Before I can see the face underneath, the insects climbs into the sky like a tornado, blotting out the moon. It's dead blackness and dead silence now. Dead silence, except for the sound of the man in the bowler hat limping closer towards me, tittering, groping for oxygen.

I look at the stars above, oscillated with terror.

I feel like I'm falling. Like a fading star. But I faded a long time ago.

I got sucked into a black hole.

Into Paradise.

Into oblivion.

One by one, the stars disappear.

"Wake up, David," I whisper. "Please. Wake up."

I feel reality tremor as fear creeps over my skin like a million tiny spiders, flooding the darkest corners of my unravelling imagination. Reality has melted into a bottomless ocean of frozen water. I'm shivering. I'm sinking. I'm drowning.

I feel his breath on my face, the stench of dead flesh.

"Don't be afraid," he whispers from the chasmic emptiness. "There is nothing to fear. Death is below us, David. You, me and Rachel. We get our happy neverending. We get to live forever. Isn't that just wonderful?"

"Who am I?" I ask.

I feel his long arms snake around my legs, my torso.

"What am I?"

I feel his claw-like fingers curl around my shoulders.

"*When* am I?"

I scream into oblivion, into the abyss of Paradise.

CHAPTER
TWENTY-FOUR

Where is Rachel Garland?
This is my first thought when I wake up. This, always, is my inaugural thought.

The sofa is still damp from her rain-drenched template. The TV set is on, spitting static. Did Rachel follow me inside it, into my nightmare? I wonder. I surf through the channels expecting to find an image of her, of us, in this flat, on this sofa, enfolded, rehearsing real life, like real people. I crawl up to the screen and tap the convex glass, repeating her name. "Rachel? Can you hear me, Rachel?" Could I smash through it, slither back inside? What if she's really *out there*, lost in the sunflowers? I need to save her, I need to stop *him*, I need to–

"This is crazy," I mutter, rubbing my eyes, readjusting to my surroundings.

I check Father's pocket watch. It's almost 5AM. Friday. Rupert Wreath is expecting the photo album on his desk in four hours. I need to get ready to step into my new reality, my new role as the author, the bestseller, *the future*.

I sit up and finish my gin and tonic from last night. My hair is clogged with the dew of chilly sweat. My muscles scream with agony. My palms are scarred with raw blisters (the doughy writer's calluses milled and mangled). My feet are plastered with mud. It almost feels like I've been digging.

Digging a grave.

I study the bites and stings decorating my hands and forearms, the vermillion dirt underneath my cuticles and fingernails. I sniff them. They smell like putrid meat.

"Interesting," I admit, walking into the bathroom.

I contemplate taking a cold shower to wash away the physical remains of my nightmare, but I quickly abandon the idea. Some fresh air and a cigarette, perhaps, will clear my mind. I should be positive, ecstatic. In four hours, I'll be a published novelist. Contracts will be signed, hands shaken, money transferred punctually. But this optimism feels premature, like the precursor to an awful twist.

When I open the curtains Osiris is still outside, on the balcony windowsill, pawing blood down the glass.

I enter the kitchen to make another gin and tonic before I reluctantly open the balcony door. Grey snow has dusted the city like a layer of ethereal fag ash. When I step outside, it squeaks under my bare feet, biting my swollen toes.

"What happened, Osiris?"

"There's been an accident," he says. "It's Abe. He isn't working properly."

I lean over the powdered railings. A trail of bloody paw prints stains the snow. They lead all the way to Abraham Maher's ajar balcony door, as if the building itself is haemorrhaging. I sip my drink, squinting into the snowfall. I listen to the rumble of far-flung traffic, enjoying the brief interlude of serenity. This alien landscape is encumbered with an unsettling tranquillity, the kind that hangs over a place when death is close, when violence is imminent.

"Let's take a look," I say.

The tears in the corners of my eyes feel like beads of ice, chilled by the dawn zephyr.

"Let's see if we can fix him."

I finish my drink and traverse to Abraham Maher's balcony. I momentarily lose my footing on the icy ledge but snatch the guardrail just in time to recover my balance. With unexpected agility, Osiris leaps across the gap to join me.

"Abe?" I say, my heart still pounding from the near fall.

I push open the balcony door and step inside. Everything is where it should be. The television. The grandfather clock. The undusted bookcase and cluttered mantlepiece. The frayed sofa and its scuffed cushions. The stacks of yellowed newspapers, the dirty plates and cutlery. Every object, it seems, is in context. Even Abraham Maher, if we consider him an object, is where he should be – seated in his favourite armchair, facing the television, waiting for the morning news and its reel of fresh catastrophes. But something is wrong.

Abraham Maher is naked, shackled to his armchair with extension leads and fairy lights. He's wrapped head-to-toe with cling film, sealed around the edges with duct tape. Blowflies and wasps, summoned by the scent of death and the intolerable humidity of the flat, crawl across the outside of this amniotic sac, attempting to burrow into the carrion inside. I look closer. Flesh is missing from his thighs. The ears and nose have been removed. Blood drips from a rip in the plastic, perforated by the stump of splintered bone that used to be Abraham's right hand.

"Jesus," I whisper.

Was Osiris drinking this before he left his vermillion pawprints in the snow? I lean in closer. Somehow, I can still smell decades of whisky on Abraham Maher's shrink-wrapped lips, which are frozen into a defiant sneer. The fairy lights blink with joyful monotony, causing his gold-capped incisors to twinkle like stars.

I subconsciously feel for the camera around my neck. But it isn't there. I slide my quaking hands into my pockets in an attempt to occupy them. It doesn't make any sense. Abraham Maher was alive and unwell less than 24 hours ago. What could have committed such efficient savagery? Somehow, I slept through the whole thing. Did Abe scream in these dying moments? And if I had been awake to hear his cries, would I have been brave enough to save him? I look away. I already know the answer.

The whisper of car horns and bickering neighbours creeps through the open balcony door like a repressed memory. I close my eyes, attempting to retrieve that fictitious repose – five minutes in the past, on my own balcony, before I discovered the body of Abraham Maher.

"Should we call a doctor?" asks Osiris.

I press my fingers on the inside of Abraham Maher's left wrist, feeling for a pulse through the plastic. I notice the flesh has been stripped from this hand too. It's the same hand that used to hold cigarettes and tumblers, write letters, turn on televisions, rotate doorknobs, grip other warm hands. Someone (*something*) gnawed his fingers to the bone like a fairytale ogre. I shake my head sadly.

"We're too late, Osiris. Abe is dead." We stare at the corpse in silence. "Did you do this?" I finally ask.

"No," he says. "Humans. A man and woman."

"What did they look like?"

"The woman was like Abe. Old, frail, moving in slow-motion. She just watched. It was the other human that did this. He was so tall, so *colossal*, he had to crouch so his head didn't hit the ceiling."

"How was he dressed?"

"Like most humans. Suit, tie, overcoat." A contemplative pause. "Oh, yes. How could I forget?"

"What?"

"He also wore a bowler hat."

I sit on the edge of the coffee table so I don't collapse. I suddenly feel faint, as if I'm about to fade into non-existence.

"Is this the same creature you've been weeping about in your dreams, David?"

I stand up and throw my fist into the sitting room wall. I do it again. And again. And again. I do it hard. Hard enough for drops of blood to form and grow.

"Shut up, Osiris!" I scream. "Shut the fuck up! Fuck! Fuck! Fuck! Get out! Get out of my head! Get out of my fucking head! Get out! Get out! Get out!"

I freeze when I hear footsteps vaulting up the corridor. I look up and notice that the front door is slightly open, Abraham Maher's first line of defence compromised. Before I can close it and slide the chain and deadbolt into place, it explodes off of its hinges, smashing me in the nose with a volley of splintered wood. Screaming, nose gushing claret, I scramble to the back door. I barely have one foot planted on the balcony before a hand latches around my belt and hauls me back inside.

Before I can see my attacker's face, I'm beaten into semi-unconsciousness in the hallway, dragged down the corridor by my ankle and slung into the lift. I feel us begin our descent. I wheeze under the foot pinning my chest to the ground. I squint, but my eyesight is muddied. All I can make out are two silhouettes. One is thin, opaque, an angel leant on a walking stick. The other fills the carriage with its frame. The blinding, artificial light above traces sloping shoulders, an angular face, a flat nose. And a bowler hat.

"This is David Temple, the chap we've been looking for," says a voice I vaguely recognise.

"Does he have the artefact?" whispers the other voice. It's so delicate, it's almost imperceptible.

"No, Mother."

"How long does he have left?"

"Let me take a closer look."

I see a huge fist swing into the control panel, hear the hollow ding of the holding bell, feel the lift shudder to a standstill. The figure releases his shoe off my sternum, drops to the floor and clambers over my limp body. He pushes his weight into my frame as he sniffs my neck with a deep, delighted sigh. He opens the buttons on my shirt, smacking his lips, drooling from his nostrils and the corners of his mouth. He snuffles as he gropes my traumatised flesh, testing its tenderness. He's tasting me. Drinking me. Asserting dominance. As he starts to loosen my belt, his counterpart places a ghostly hand on his shoulder.

"That's enough, Piggy," she says.

"Yes, Mother," Piggy groans, returning to his hind hooves, regaining human form. He straightens his tie and hits the control panel again, resuming our slow descent.

"We need him alive," she adds gently. "And you'll spoil your dinner."

"Yes, Mother."

"Could you smell death on him?"

"Yes, Mother. He's been chosen for Paradise."

As soon as the lift doors open, Piggy hauls me through the lobby and down the stone steps, dumping me in the forecourt like human garbage. I stare up at the cloud, shivering, feeling the snowflakes disintegrate on my cheeks. Am I concussed, or can I hear it sniggering up there, freebasing my pain?

Unable to face its ridicule, I roll onto my side and watch Piggy open the back of a white van. I squint to read the vinyl letters printed across it. It says *PARADISE FLOWERS*. It's the same van that sped off outside the launderette on Upper Tooting Road last night.

"Load him in the back before somebody asks us awkward questions."

"Yes, Mother."

Piggy picks me up with frightening ease and throws me into the back of the van. It's filled with wreaths and bouquets. A rainbow of fuchsia, periwinkle, roses and posies that causes my sinuses to burn.

"Wait," I slur. "I didn't kill Abe. He was my friend."

"But you did kill him," Piggy replies. "He sacrificed himself for you, David."

Piggy smiles and slams the van doors, locking me in the redolent darkness. I can hear footsteps crunch on snow, the van's suspension sigh under Piggy's immense weight, the choke and splutter of the engine coming to life. I feel the van turn corners, round roundabouts, circumnavigate potholes and wheeze over sleeping policemen. Muted daylight trickles through the cargo barrier, dulling and brightening as we creep through a circulatory system of bridges and viaducts, electronic billboards and looming high-rises. We're on the move. But in what direction?

I sneeze blood over my shirt and gulp for oxygen, blinded and throttled with invisible mushroom clouds of pollen. I feel my eyes swell shut, my airwaves tighten. The flowers, in a coordinated act of violence, are striking me with every biological weapon in their arsenal. Is this intentional? I wonder. Has the microclimate of this van been designed to protract my suffering? Perhaps it just isn't my lucky day.

It's true what they say. Bad things really do happen to good people.

We stop. The engine idles for a few seconds before it gags and flatlines. I can hear footsteps, the clatter of hailstones on the roof.

I know who has abducted me.

And I know what drives them.

The plot, *everything*, is falling into place.

CHAPTER
TWENTY-FIVE

"Step out of the van please, David."

I step out, into the hail, onto a shoreline of binbags, shipwrecked skiffs and decaying mattresses. "Jesus," I mutter. Is this the beach from my childhood memories? It looks nothing like the brochure. It's just festering garbage and melting snow, dissolving into nothing. Perhaps everything, eventually, dissolves into nothing.

"On your knees please, David," says Piggy, pressing the muzzle of his handgun into my temple.

I kneel at the top of a concrete slipway that vanishes into the Thames. Plastic bottles and used condoms glitter on the surface of the water with insentient vigor. Across it, the sails of the Cutty Sark billow in the gathering fog. Human life is absent. It's just me and Piggy, marooned on our fly-tipped Paradise.

"There's nowhere to run, David," he adds.

"Run?" I say. "Christ. I can barely stand up. You beat the living shit out of me."

"That's just as well. Mother says I was always the fastest

sprinter at school. I have the sports day medals to prove it. No-one can outpace me."

I haven't seen Piggy since our first encounter in the Natural History Museum, when he escorted me to the library, engaging in polite conversation. But I'm beginning to wonder if this small talk was actually an inquisition. Is Piggy really a bouncer, or was he playing a role that night, just like Richard Hayes and I, pretending to be somebody else? I can't wait to find out how he fits into this narrative.

"We've been following you since the museum," says Piggy. "We followed you on the tube to Eden Estate. And we followed you to the laundrette on Upper Tooting Road. We believed that you delivered the photo album to Soner Gillespie to sell to another collector, so we followed him to his bookshop on Mitcham Road. But this was our mistake. You didn't give him the photo album. You gave him this."

Piggy holds a copy of *Sick & Beautiful* in front of me before throwing it into the water in front of us, emphasising his contempt for the work, the author.

"Soner Gillespie is a true friend," he continues. "We did terrible things to him, but he refused to give us your flat number, so we returned to Eden Estate to find you ourselves. We knocked on every door, starting from the ground floor up, asking your neighbours if they knew a David Temple, if they knew *anybody* that fits your description. Nobody has seen you. Nobody has even heard of you. It's as if you don't exist. You're either very fortunate, very intelligent, or exactly what Mother suspected – a ghost. Then Abraham Maher answered the door. When we found another copy of *Sick & Beautiful* in the flat, we knew you were close. Abraham refused to tell us where you were hiding too, so we dealt with him appropriately. Whatever you did for that old man, he was willing to perish for you, David."

"How did Abe die?" I ask. I feel the tears again, the acute shame that if our roles were reversed, I wouldn't have made the same sacrifice. "Did he die in pain?"

"Even when I sunk my teeth into his flesh, he didn't scream. It was as if he didn't feel anything at all. If it's any consolation, death was fast-approaching him. I could taste it. The booze and cigarettes, the London oxygen. It spoilt him. Made him chewy like a battery farm chicken. In the end, his valour was all for nothing. You materialised, David, from out of nowhere, like a wraith passing through the walls."

"Why do you want the photo album?" I ask.

"Do you honestly want to know? It's dark stuff, David. I don't want to give you nightmares. You probably won't believe a word of it anyway."

I smile, acting like I'm relaxed, acting like I don't have the barrel of a gun levelled at my cranium.

"Try me," I say. "I'm quite open-minded."

"We're here on behalf of our client, Father Gladioli," he says. "He's paying us a lucrative sum to find the artefact. Once we confirm its location, Father Gladioli will fly his private jet to the city to collect it. You're in God's pocket, David. We all are. But I don't believe you appreciate the deadly games you're playing here. Neither did Richard Hayes. And look how *that* turned out. Not too well."

Piggy pulls a photograph out of his pocket and holds it in front of me.

"Do you recognise this gentleman?" he asks. "One of our scouts snapped this two nights ago."

It's a grainy image of someone climbing up the balconies

of Eden Estate. It appears to be human, but the limbs are abnormally long, bent like the legs of a giant spider. And guess what? Yeah. It looks like he's wearing a bowler hat. I smile, but this is another performance. I feel my muscles stiffen, my chest contract.

"Never seen him," I say. "Probably a pisshead who lost his front door key. Happens all the time."

Piggy nods. The way he does it, though, like he's nodding in slow-motion. It suggests he doesn't believe me.

"Your friend in the bowler hat. We call it the Photographer. Father Gladioli believes it's a fallen angel that escorts you to another planet, another dimension, with promises of eternal life in biblical Paradise. The photo album, it seems, coaxes the Photographer out of its dark hiding place. It only takes one touch to summon it, to catch its disease."

"*The Photographer*," I murmur. I like it. It's pithy. Purposeful. *Concrete*. But is the camera more significant than his signature apparel? Does it really define his character? I wonder how Piggy would react if I told him that this apparition has been stalking me for months, long before I ever touched the photo album? Would it change his theories and definitions?

"What makes you think the Photographer is an *it*?" I ask.

"Father Gladioli suggested the Photographer is like an actor. It doesn't just absorb your flesh. It adopts your form, your voice, your mannerisms, to generate a distorted image of yourself. If you've already seen it, it means it's studying you. We personally believe the Photographer is an agent from Mecca or the Vatican. Maybe even an assassin hired by another investor like our client. We've even contemplated if Father Gladioli is a priest like he claims to be or if he's just another alias, conceived to mask a secret identity. Quite frankly, it doesn't concern us. The sooner we can deliver the photo album, the better. It's bad news. And we have enough violence in the city without it." Piggy pauses, tilts his head sideways, smiles. "Is something funny, David?"

"It's nothing," I say, trying to supress my laughter. "It's just– do you have any idea how ludicrous this all sounds?"

"If it's so ludicrous, why are you crying?"

When I look at the ground, unable to answer, Piggy gives my shoulder an affectionate squeeze. I feel fragile, insignificant inside this enormous hand, inside this infinite universe. He motions towards the van with his gun.

"Pull it together, David. Mother is waiting. And I wouldn't recommend lying to her like you've lied to me. She always knows when you're telling porky pies."

I nod and walk towards the van. I feel like I have left my body again as I open the door, slide onto the driver's seat and shut it behind me. The aroma of flowers drifts through the grill with suffocating invasiveness.

Mother is on the passenger seat. She's so still, *so lifeless*, I flinch when I hear the shallow breath whistle out of her nostrils. Her arms are neatly folded in her lap. Her black dress and headscarf make her look like a widow, mourning this brief recess from violence. When she removes her sunglasses, I look into her blind eyes. They are as opaque as the cloud, transfixed on the darkness that surrounds her. Is this the face of the mother I've never been able to piece together in my fragmented dreams?

"Closer, David," she whispers, moving her walking stick and patting the seat between us. "Don't be afraid."

Compliantly I edge closer to Mother, the gearstick

protruding between my knees. She drapes her arms around me like cobwebs and rocks me side-to-side. Without guidance or encouragement, I rest my head in Mother's lap and curl into a ball, the embryonic posture Father adopted on his deathbed. She then clutches my left hand with astonishing strength and snaps my index and middle fingers. As I yelp like an abused animal, she cradles me, stroking my hair with a frail claw.

"It's OK, David. Mother is here. Father too. He's out there, above the cloud, watching over us."

When I burst into tears, sobbing inside the womb of her lap, Mother surveys the lacerations on my cheeks and forehead, the wet meat of my pestled nose, just like Rachel Garland did the first time she visited my flat, the first time we touched physically. Mother tuts, shaking her head sadly. She can see me now, the creature inside her arms. I suddenly feel exposed, as if my soul has been disrobed.

"It's too late for you, David," she sighs. "Something is looking for the photo album. Something that wants to cause you unthinkable pain, just like it did to Richard. There's no stopping it now. But you can stop anyone else getting hurt if you give us the artefact. Father Gladioli can kill this devil. Help us, David. We're here to carry out God's work. We don't want to hurt you. We want to *save* you."

I hug Mother tightly. She feels like a bag of bones.

"I'm sorry, Mother, but I can't publish *Sick & Beautiful* without the photo album. I know you have your motives, but what about what *I* want? Don't you understand? I *need* this. All of this chaos can't be for nothing."

"Stop being so self-centred, David. Forget about yourself and the book for one second. Do you have any idea how much trouble you're in? You've made God angry. You've made Mother angry."

Mother points at Piggy through the windscreen, looking towards the river under his umbrella.

"If the Photographer doesn't kill you," she says, "my Piggy will. He's a good boy. And he knows that Mother knows best. Your friends know what happens when Mother doesn't get what she asks for." This time, she grabs the index and middle fingers of my right hand. "Don't make Mother ask twice, David."

I try to break her grip, but she's too strong.

"I live in flat 34. Next door to–" I pause. "Next door to where Abe used to live. You'll find the photo album there."

"Thank you, David."

Mother releases my hand and bangs on the roof of the van three times with her walking stick. Within seconds, I'm kicking and wailing as Piggy hauls me back outside, back into the hailstorm.

"You be a good boy now, David," says Mother. "We hope you find peace in Paradise."

Piggy squeezes behind the wheel and slams the door behind him. He winds down his window and hands me a bouquet of daffodils and peonies.

"Give these to your portly friend," he says, starting the engine. "He'll need cheering up on a gruesome morning like this."

"Sultan is still alive?" I gasp.

"Just about. He gutted it out longer than most. You rarely witness altruism of that ilk these days, especially in the city. It's a pity we had to do what we did."

"If Sultan didn't give you the information you needed,

why did you let him live but not Abe?"

"It wasn't Soner's time. And I wasn't particularly peckish yesterday anyway. This morning, though? I was *ravenous*."

The way Piggy smiles when he rasps this last word. It makes me think of the pain I've caused. It makes me want to regurgitate, cave in, scream.

"You didn't need to do any of this," I whisper. "You could have stolen the photo album in the museum, in the launderette, anytime you wanted, but you chose to wait. Why did my friends have to suffer when you could have taken it at any moment? So you could satisfy your sick appetite?"

"It wasn't just my appetite," he says, still smiling. "We needed to be patient because we didn't want to touch that godforsaken object. Don't you understand? Once you touch it, for as long as it's in your care, the Photographer sees you. It believes that you've chosen it. Perhaps it thinks that it's saving you in its own twisted way, ferrying you to its kingdom. Abraham and Soner suffered, but our methods pale compared to the Photographer. The things it does to you– it's for eternity."

Death is below us, David. You, me and Rachel. We get our happy neverending. We get to live forever. Isn't that just wonderful?

"What about your client," I say. "Isn't he afraid of suffering too?"

"Father Gladioli?" Piggy shrugs. "He has his faith. Although I'm more sceptical than Mother, I want to believe in him. You know why? If he's telling the truth, it means we're the good guys. We're batting for God. You know what that also means? You're playing for the wrong side, David. Your role in this story might not be what you thought it was."

"How can you be so sure I'm not one of the good guys?"

"Because the good guys never seek the photo album. Darkness attracts darkness, David. It makes me wonder – Why are you so irresistible to this insidious creature? What secrets are *you* hiding?"

Piggy waves out of his window as the van vanishes into the fog. Apparently he wasn't interested in a response (perhaps his questions were rhetorical).

I watch the hailstones dissolve the petals off my bouquet until it's a fist of naked stalks. A note is tied around the stems (blue ink bleeding).

David. Pain is fleeting. Paradise is endless.

"Mother!" I scream, one arm stretched out in front of me with theatrical sincerity.

I sink to my knees in a puddle of icy rainwater. I tremble, holding my broken fingers.

"Mother, please," I cry. "Please don't go, Mother. Please help me. Mother?"

I look up to the cloud, tasting its cold precipitation on the tip of my tongue. It's coppery, like blood.

"Please," I whimper. "Don't leave me again. Don't go to the beach without me."

Wandering the streets of Millwall (shoeless, shivering), I enter The Ship on Westferry Road to order a gin and tonic and call the front desk of St George's. I ask the receptionist if a Soner Gillespie was admitted yesterday morning or afternoon. She puts me on hold before transferring me to the Gunning Ward, the hospital's trauma and orthopaedics centre.

Piggy wasn't joking about the Sultan. They really roughed him up.

"They gave me the works," he growls down the line. Mother broke all his fingers before Piggy gnawed away the flesh on both hands, starting with the digits, then the meat of the palms. That, apparently, is when Mother instructed him to stop. The surgeons had to amputate what was left of Sultan's hands, all the way down to the wrists. I imagine Sultan Gillespie in a gown, in a wheelchair, in a hospital corridor, pinching the receiver between his shoulder and cheek, without his hands.

"What did you tell the police?" I ask.

"I didn't tell them anything."

"Why? Jesus, Sultan. He ate your fucking hands."

"Don't you get it, David? They *are* the police. They control this city." There is a short pause. "I'm ashamed to admit it, but I felt relieved when they stopped, when they said they were coming after you instead." Another pause. "David, am I a coward?"

I almost do it. I almost tell Sultan Gillespie that I cracked after just two busted fingers. I almost admit that after all my experiences with death and violence, I'm still unable to embrace it. I almost confess that *I'm* the coward. I'm *this* close. Instead, I ask him: "Did you read *Sick & Beautiful*?"

Sultan Gillespie laughs. I can hear him snivelling, wheezing, retching on fright and high fever.

"I'm sorry, David. I tried, but I just couldn't. I could never finish it. *That* would've been torture."

When the line goes dead, I suddenly feel adrift, disorientated.

Who am I? What is my purpose? Is my character still relevant?

It's too late for you, David. There's no stopping it now.

It won't take Piggy and Mother long to discover that I lied about where I hid the photo album. It will take them even less time to find me again. I need to escape, dematerialise. With every passing minute, death inches closer, so why can't I bring myself to flee the city? I wonder. It isn't indecision. It isn't Rachel. It isn't even the impending book deal. It's the photo album itself. It's the overwhelming feeling that I'm following the script, that I'm one of the good guys.

Sultan Gillespie. Abraham Maher. Docklands Dave. Eleanor Wither. Rachel Garland.

I'm surrounded by guardian angels. I watch them flutter, rise and circle all around me.

Their wings cool the sweat on my skin like the breeze on the beach in my memories.

CHAPTER
TWENTY-SIX

When I reach the Market Porter, I suck on Docklands Dave's cigarette like a hideously overgrown baby slurping milk from its bottle.

"You can keep hold of that," he says, grimacing when I try to return it.

The landlord puts a gin and tonic in front of me. I pick it up and sip. After my two-hour, barefoot hobble through Deptford and Bermondsey, I needed a moment to gather my thoughts and my body.

"Dave hasn't got a wink of sleep all night, you know," he adds, nodding to the landlord, turning the page of his newspaper. "Bad dreams, he says. Nightmares. He thinks it has something to do with that thing you've hidden upstairs."

I look at Dave, the landlord, and notice his drained complexion, how his eyes have retreated into their sockets. He looks like trash. Christ, I'd kill to look like that kind of trash. Docklands Dave, on the other hand, looks fresh, ready for a new day. Searching for purchase in this spinning room,

I lean on the bar and clasp my head in my hands, frightened it might disconnect.

"You won't need to worry about bad dreams anymore," I say to both of them. "I've just popped in to pick it up. Rupert Wreath, my agent, is expecting me to deliver the artefact by 9AM. We're then going to sign a contract for *Sick & Beautiful*." I finish my gin and tonic and smile. It hurts to smile. It's close to agony. "The next time you see me, I'll be inside the television."

Docklands Dave turns another page of his paper. The landlord polishes another wine glass and hangs it on the rack above the bar. In their communal silence, it occurs to me that neither Dave has unglued themselves from their positions since I saw them yesterday. They're always on point, always in character. But when are they going to ask me what happened and who did this to me? When are they going to vow to wage violence upon those responsible for my dilapidated body, my complete loss of confidence?

"That's exciting news, David," Docklands Dave finally admits. He looks at the clock behind the bar. "You better grab it now if you want to get to Cannon Street before nine. In that state, it'll take you at least 20 minutes to get across the river."

I nod, stagger behind the jump and limp up the staircase to the first floor, feeling dull pain judder through my bones with every step. When I enter the function room, the photo album is on top of the sideboard, on top of its dirty cloth, open. Did they touch it? I wonder. Slowly, I approach it. And then I gasp in terror at the open page. It's a photograph of a car crash. The bonnet is crumpled, wrapped around a steel pillar. The windscreen is shattered. Rachel Garland is behind the wheel, bleeding from a gash in her forehead. I'm in the passenger seat next to her, staring into the camera, mouth curled with horrified laugher. I touch her wound with my fingertips. In the recesses of my mind, I can hear her voice. I can hear Rachel mouth the same words over and over and over again.

Don't go to Paradise.

I hear the syllables so clearly. A rising whisper of a thousand tortured voices. Would I join them soon? Immortalised in my own portrait of agony, wriggling like a maggot in the rancid carrion of the photo album.

Don't go to Paradise.

I snap the book shut and lumber back down the staircase. Docklands Dave is now sat behind the table in front of the unlit fireplace. He's made it to the sports section of his newspaper. He looks up and smiles.

"Did you do this?" I ask, trying not to let his equanimity derail me. I slap the photo album on the table and thumb through its pages, searching for the image of myself and Rachel Garland, but I can't find it. I can't find it anywhere. Docklands Dave has recoiled, but only slightly. And not from me – it's from the object itself. He sips his stout, studying the moisture pooling in the corners of my eyes, the anger flushing my cheeks and forehead. If he knows violent conflict is looming, he doesn't show it. In fact, he doesn't show me anything. He sits his pint on its cork beer mat. He does this so carefully, with such precision, it feels like a provocation.

"Is this your idea of a sick joke?" I ask, struggling to control the volume of my voice. Some of the early-morning drinkers on the tables near us have started to watch this confrontation with a medley of concern and apathy. "Where the fuck did you get that photograph, Dave? Or are you working for *them* now? Tell me." Silence. "Fucking tell me!"

I swipe an empty beer bottle off the bar and smash it over the corner of the table. When the landlord moves around the jump to diffuse our standoff, Docklands Dave waves a dismissive hand at him, not taking his eyes off of me. The landlord nods and obediently takes two steps backwards.

"Are you sure you want to do this, David?" asks Docklands Dave.

I look at the jagged bottle in my trembling hand. I feel my bottom lip spasm with simmering fear. My vision splinters with tears. I nod earnestly.

"Let's go," I say, siphoning every reservoir of adrenaline in my traumatised body.

"So be it," he sighs.

As soon as I raise the bottleneck above my head and lunge towards Docklands Dave on a heavy front foot (telegraphed, poorly timed), he flips the table and springs out of his seat with petrifying speed. Objects spill and shatter across the floor. Gripping the wrist of my hand holding the weapon, he plunges his forehead into the bridge of my already broken nose. I shriek and drop to the deck in agony, disarmed, cupping tatters of bone and cartilage. Our altercation: it's over in seconds. He stands over my shuddering frame, evaluating his swift and accurate handiwork.

"Let me see," he says, moving my hands away.

He inspects the wound with unexpected tenderness. Satisfied (not with himself or his ability to inflict damage, but with the conclusiveness of our confrontation), he steps over me and walks to the bar.

"Same again please, Dave," he says to the landlord, who has already instinctively pulled a fresh pint.

I groan, rising to my feet in a puddle of splintered glass and fag ash. I pick up the photo album. Is it feeding off my pain like a parasite? I wonder. Docklands Dave helps me balance on the apex of my bar stool. I teeter this way. I totter the other. The landlord passes me a beer towel and a first aid kit before standing the table back onto its legs and sweeping up the mess with a dustpan and brush. He seems completely unmoved by our cursory descent into chaos. His face is a picture of passivity.

"No hard feelings," says Docklands Dave, raising his glass. "Cheers."

"Cheers," I echo nasally, pinching my bloody nostrils with the towel.

Wrapping my broken fingers with the bandages in the first aid kit, I follow Docklands Dave to the fruit machine. When he feeds it a fist of tenners, it titters with mechanical joy.

"You seem on edge, David," he says. "Would you like to talk about it?"

"It's nothing," I insist. "Except–"

"Except what?"

"Except I can't tell what's real and what isn't anymore." I slump into a frayed armchair, a scrap-heap of bruised tissue, blackened dreams. "Richard has been flayed alive on camera," I continue. "Sultan savagely beaten. My neighbour, Abe Maher, brutally murdered. I keep seeing *him*. I keep seeing *her*. I feel like ghosts are gathering around me, screaming for me to stop. Am I going barmy, Dave? Or Is the universe trying to tell me that I'm not one of the good guys?"

When I mention Abraham Maher, Docklands Dave jerks like a glitching robot, lifts his hands off the buttons of the fruit machine, pauses, flexes his fingers, returns them to their position. He looks troubled, speechless. I don't blame him. He's just found out he lost his father. Will he finally admit this connection? Clearing his throat, his voice uncharacteristically wobbly, he croaks: "Your friends must have thought of you as a brother, as a son. My old man wouldn't have made that sacrifice for me."

I couldn't tell whether this was a universal observation or a deliberate understatement. It forces me to question if Abraham really was Docklands Dave's father. Is my hypothesis all wrong? Perhaps he is beyond, or not quite within reach, of the concept of grief for a patriarch who surrendered more for me than he ever did for his own chemical conception.

"There's another theory," he finally adds. "Perhaps they were following the script. Perhaps they were meant to die so you could get to Paradise Publishing this morning. If that's the case, then they performed their roles. That means you need to perform yours too, David. We all do, or their deaths will be for nothing."

He studies my naked, bleeding feet and unlaces his impeccably white trainers.

"Take these," he says, handing them to me. "You'll need them to continue your journey."

"You'll need this too," says the landlord, handing me a dusty black overcoat. "It was my father's, God rest his soul. He won't be using it anytime soon."

I unfold it, noticing its length, rubbing my fingers over its dull buttons. I read the label inside the collar. *Kensal Green Cemetery.*

"What did you father do?" I ask, slipping it on, buttoning it up.

"He was a pallbearer," he replies proudly. "It suits you, David."

Who pushed him?

A man in a bowler hat.

What did he look like?

Black suit. Black overcoat. Hair like cobwebs. He was dressed like a pallbearer, except he was smiling. But it wasn't a warm smile. It was a grimace. It was pain. His mouth was like a wound filled with barbed teeth. He had a camera too, just like yours.

That's how Rachel Garland described the phantom who shoved Rupert Wreath off the eleventh floor of the Mandarin Oriental. It only just comes back to me as I exit the Market Porter, hobble up Borough High Street and stare at the skyline across the river. The cranes and high-rises that jut and vanish into the crevices of the cloud have an uninviting presence that intimidates me. The horizon vomits acid rain, sniggers fog, thunder, lightning. I try to ignore it. I try to remind myself – *It's just a cloud*.

Overcome with nausea, I lean over the parapets of London Bridge. That's when I see them. Christmas trees – hundreds of them, trailed by their tinsel and fairy light tentacles – float down the Thames in silence. Some are marooned in the silt beaches like stranding whales, but most will continue upstream, east, towards the North Sea.

I envy their resilience and buoyancy. I want to be inspired by their gallantry.

When I look at my feet, Docklands Dave's trainers are already caked in mud.

CHAPTER
TWENTY-SEVEN

Scaffolding now masks the façade of 34 Cannon Street, the building's unclad brickwork exposed like a silky, see-through negligee.

When I step through the revolving doors and enter the lobby, I'm met again with the same gust of tropical oxygen, the same sweating receptionist cemented in his seat. But everything else looks different. No. Not different. *Hollow*. It looks more hollow than it did two days ago. The striking ferns have wilted into a lifeless auburn. The paint has peeled off the walls like burnt skin. Even the leather sofa is peeling. And where's the whistling janitor? The floor is *filthy*. The letters above the reception desk have changed too. It doesn't say PARADISE PUBLISHING anymore. It says PARADISE PRODUCTIONS. Is it possible I misread it on the morning of my meeting? It's impossible to know. The receptionist looks up from his newspaper.

"Can I help you, sir?" he asks.

He's leaning forward now. Paper down, hands on kneecaps, I have his attention. I stare at the sign, mute and unresponsive. He stands up, walks around the desk and cautiously approaches me. He looks at the strange object clutched to my chest. And then he forces a smile.

"I'm sorry, sir," he says. He digs into his pocket and drops a handful of coins into my palm. He closes my fingers around them. "I'm afraid we can't have homeless in here, sir." He starts to guide me towards the door. "Get yourself a whisky and some heat by the fire in Ye Olde Watling. Out of this awful weather."

He settles back into his seat and returns to the back-page crossword. I return to the desk and pull down the top of his newspaper with my index finger.

"I'm- I've- I'll- I'd- I don't think I made myself clear," I manage to say with vague authority. "My name is David Temple. I have a 9AM with my agent, your director, Rupert Wreath."

The receptionist leans back and nods, but something is wrong. His face is creased with confusion. His skin is glossy from the humidity of the lobby. He consults his clipboard. He tuts. He flicks through the pages of his logbook. He tuts again. I decide to help the guy out.

"David Temple," I repeat. "T-E-M-P-L-E. Novelist. Author of *Sick & Beautiful*?"

The receptionist looks up apologetically.

"It's OK," I say. My smile is on the cusp of degenerating into a sneer, but I hold it back. "Listen, I've had a turbulent 48 hours," I admit, pointing at my hideous face with a bandaged hand. I laugh nervously. The receptionist laughs nervously too. "If you could please just buzz me up to Rupert's office on floor 34, it would be much appreciated." I point to the sofa. "I don't mind waiting here if he's in a meeting that's overrun. I get it. I do. Rupert's a busy, busy bee."

"I'm sorry, sir," says the receptionist. "We don't appear to have either of those names on our books."

"Interesting. What about Eve, Rupert's PA?"

"I'm afraid we don't have any clients named David Temple. And we don't have any employees named Rupert Wreath or Eve. I'm afraid, sir, that we don't even have 34 floors in this building." He stands up again. Concern is etched in his expression, his posture, the way the air escapes his chest. "Sir, please. Please don't cry. Are you absolutely certain you're at the correct address?"

"Paradise Publishing, 34 Cannon Street, London," I recite, eyes sealed shut. When I open them again, the receptionist is stood in front of me. When I look into his eyes, I don't see empathy. I don't see a desire for connection. I see fear. (Fear and I. We go way back. Fear has more friends than I do, billions more, but it's kept in touch after all these years. Who stands by your side for a lifetime, in unhappiness and ill health? Fear. That's why I recognise its feral stare a mile away.) The receptionist places his hand on my shoulder and takes a deep breath. He looks like he's tormented by an awful secret.

"We're not a publishing house, sir," he says, very gently. "We're a production studio." He points to the gilded letters behind the reception desk. "It says it on the wall too, sir. But listen. If you'd like to leave a message or a memo, I'd be more than obliged to relay it to the right people. I'm honestly not sure how else I can be of any assistance."

I pinch the bridge of my nose.

"Don't you recognise me?" I ask, perhaps louder than intended.

The receptionist flinches, removing the hand on my

shoulder. He rubs it shamefully, like he just touched something dirty. Making the decision to physically reconnect, I latch onto his wrist and haul him back towards me. Our faces are inches apart, the photo album thrust between us. He looks terrified. Absolutely terrified.

"If Rupert Wreath and floor 34 don't exist, then let me see it for myself," I say. "This is going to sound strange, but I need to know where reality ends and where it begins again. Am I making sense? This is very important to me."

The receptionist attempts to pull away, but I won't let him escape. I pull him closer, towards me, *into me*.

"*Please*," I hiss. "I *need* this."

When I finally release him, he steps backwards, still facing me, hands held defensively in front of him, until his back is flat against the wall.

"As you wish, sir," he says, gesturing to the elevator. "I hope you find what you're looking for."

"Thank you," I say, limping past him. "You're going to feel silly when you see me on TV, but don't worry. I won't hold it against you. You're just doing your job, right? Perhaps we'll laugh about it one day."

"Perhaps," he whispers.

I step into the elevator, but I can't find the button for floor 34. I shrug and press for the highest floor available: number 14. If floor 34 *does* exist, perhaps it's inaccessible from the lobby. I'll simply ride the elevator as far as it will take me and climb to 34 from the stairwell. I smile, satisfied with my plan, satisfied with my logic, optimistic that this is just another hiccup, another wrinkle in the script. But when I exit the elevator on 14, the corridor is identical to the one I was escorted down two days ago: sterile, door-less, devoid of life and colour. There's a notable difference, though. The strip lights and ceiling tiles above are missing, revealing a canopy of floodlights, LEDs, catwalks, rigging systems and air conditioning units. Was there *ever* a ceiling? Or did I imagine it, assuming it would be in this building, in this scene? I walk up the corridor, feeling exposed as I near the door to Rupert Wreath's office.

I knock. "Rupert? Rupert, it's David. Apologies I'm late. I had some trouble with the receptionist downstairs. Can you believe the guy didn't even recognise–"

But when I open the door and enter the office, Rupert isn't there. Just the anatomy of the room: the desk, the chairs, the plants, the minibar, the full-length mirror, the walls, the window. It's exactly as I remember, except the ceiling is missing here too. Spotlights glare from above, bathing the office in an oppressive red glow that has caused the ferns and evergreens to wilt. Christ. Even I'm wilting. I place the photo album on the desk. I wipe the sweat off my forehead, staring into the mirror behind it. My reflection glares back at me, as if it's appalled, as if it doesn't recognise me. *What happened to you, David?* The reflection shakes its head with disappointment, melancholy. When I turn away from its crestfallen eyes, I notice the sunlight still slicing through the wooden blinds covering the window.

The sun shines on us, David. Consider it a good omen. A blessing from the cloud.

Is it still the good omen that Rupert Wreath promised? I walk towards the window, across the desiccated leaves and petals that litter the carpet, and roll up the blinds. I squint into the burning light. And then I gasp. Instead of the sun, a mounted profile spotlight shines through the glass. "It doesn't make any sense," I laugh, struggling to control my emotions, the volume of my voice. "It doesn't make any *fucking* sense!"

Enraged, I pick up one of the withered rubber plants and bowl it through the window. There is a screaming splash of noise, an explosion of glass, the audible release of tension from this cathartic act of vandalism. I step through the window, walk past the spotlight and touch the horizon behind it. It's a canvas backdrop. Vivid blue with white candyfloss clouds, like the sky in a child's finger-painting.

"That's very interesting," I admit.

I walk around the plywood exterior of the office until I'm on the other side of the mirror, looking into the empty room, across Rupert Wreath's empty desk. Surrounded by jibs, dollies, tripods, wires and microphones, two cine-cameras point through the two-way glass. I ease myself into the director's chair positioned behind them, imagining who sat here, imagining their expression as I unravelled on the carpet, sobbing over Rupert Wreath's brogues. I pick up the clapperboard on the floor: *SCENE 1. TAKE 1. PROD: SICK & BEAUTIFUL. DIRECTOR: R. HAYES.* I nod, allowing this information to resonate.

I'm not certain how much times passes before I climb back through the fake window, into the fake office, and walk to the minibar to pour a gin and tonic. I collapse into the uncomfortable chair I sat in two mornings ago. It feels more bearable, as if my body has readjusted to a crueller existence. I caress the armrest. I smell the aroma of its leather skin. I hover the tumbler under my nose, allow the effervescence of the tonic to tingle my nostrils. I sip, tasting the bitter, sanative notes of the gin. It all seems so *real*. But these are just cheap props, false sensations, components of a manufactured reality. There is no way of knowing how far the stage stretches. Are its borders even measurable? Or is this unreality expanding, like the cloud, cannibalising the kingdom I always assumed I inhabited?

While I ponder this conundrum, men in blue overalls remove the mirror in front of me, revealing the camera equipment behind it. Like phantoms deconstructing a dream, they don't acknowledge or look at me. I'm just another inanimate set piece that can be disassembled and put back into storage. I pick up the photo album and hug it to my chest, watching them carry away the plants, the minibar, the desk in front of me, the chair behind me, the tumbler in my hand.

And then I stare into the black lenses of the cameras.

I don't wonder if they're still rolling.

I wonder when they *started* rolling, capturing this simulation I used to call reality.

I walk back to the elevator, through the dismantling corridor, through the dismantling world, head bowed in silence.

In the lobby the receptionist is stood in front of the exit. Since our encounter earlier, he seems to have recovered his composure.

"David Temple, you said?"

"Yes?" I reply hesitantly.

"That's very interesting."

He pulls an envelope out of the breast pocket of his suit jacket. My name is pencilled on the front.

"An individual delivered this in person yesterday," he says. "He asked us to pass it on if you returned to the premises."

He hands me the envelope and takes two steps back.

"Now, please, sir," he adds emphatically, "*leave us.*"

The receptionist returns to his chair behind the desk, crosses his legs and unfolds his newspaper. He pretends to read it, desperate for this strange episode to reach a definitive conclusion. I can see next week's weather forecast on the back page. Low temperatures. Low pressure. And rain. Lots of rain.

I open the envelope. There is a piece of paper inside. I unfold it. It's a telephone number.

"Thank you for passing on the memo," I say, walking towards the revolving doors. "Apologies, I didn't catch your name?"

"Why, it's Dave, sir."

"Of course it's Dave," I say, tipping my head back, cackling into the spinning face of the ceiling fan. "And why shouldn't it be?"

I find a phone box on Watling Street and tip the shrapnel the receptionist gave me into the coin slot. I thumb the telephone number into the keypad. And then I wait for a small eternity, listening to the abrasive echo of the dial tone. *It's a dead end*, I concede, on the brink of hanging up. That's when it happens. Someone answers.

"Bloom Talent PLC. Agent for the stars. How can I make your dreams come true today?"

The voice sounds defeated, emptied out, dangerously hungover, but it's unmistakable.

"What's going on, Rupert?" I say.

"David? It's you." He sighs, audibly relieved. "Beautiful. You made it. I honestly didn't think you'd come this far. David, we need to talk. Urgently. I can't explain everything on the line. They're always listening. Always watching us. Always waiting. Do you understand?"

"No. I don't understand. Your office– it's a fucking charade, Rupert. It isn't real. Jesus. Please tell me the book deal isn't fake too?"

"I'll tell you everything," he says, "if you tell me what happened to Rachel Garland."

CHAPTER
TWENTY-EIGHT

I agree to meet Rupert Wreath in Apollo Cafe, a greasy spoon on the corner of Hopton Street.

A bell rings when I push open the door. The floor is mobbed with a blur of thick forearms, sweat-shellacked brows, fluorescent coveralls, the clatter of cutlery careening into cheap crockery. Rows of brickies, sparkies, roofers, plumbers, navvies and mechanics are bowed over plastic tables, squeezed into plastic seats, forking fried stodge into their mouths with hushed efficiency. They're fuelling for a day of hard graft, fixing all the things we spent yesterday breaking, like spoilt toddlers smashing their expensive toys. When civilisation finally collapses, they'll take back what's theirs – the city they built with their calloused hands. After the 20-minute slog in the rain from 34 Cannon Street, I'm thankful for the humidity of the cafe, the collective heat of these sentient bodies.

I spot Rupert Wreath. He's where he said he would be – alone, on the table at the back, hidden inconspicuously behind an unfolded tabloid, taking careful sips from a coffee cup. He tenses when I place my hand on the shoulder of his ketchup-stained tracksuit. When he realises it's me, his eyes (raw, exhausted) soften into something even more terrifying – *relief*. But something is different about the hotshot I met on the 34th floor of Paradise Publishing. Something's off-kilter.

"Where's your suit?" I ask.

"Dry cleaners," he mumbles.

Suddenly it hits me. Rupert Wreath doesn't look like Rupert Wreath at all. The wealthy tan has dulled into an anaemic grey. The assured posture has melted into a dispirited slouch. Even the lean torso and million dollar grin have dissipated. I look at the hoop of flesh girdling his chin, the way his shivering beer gut causes the zip on his tracksuit to creep open with every laboured breath, and shake my head sadly.

"What happened to you, Rupert?" I ask.

Rupert Wreath blushes. He turns his attention back to the tepid remains on his plate: pig meat, blood pudding, blackened cinders of cremated toast, coagulated into a grimace of iridescent grease. He forces back one more forkful, lays down his clotted cutlery and wipes his mouth with the sleeve of his tracksuit. Dog ends float in the sludge of his coffee cup. He belches, lights another cigarette.

"Please, sit," he says. I painfully lower myself into the seat opposite him. He sighs. "I'm not the person you think I am, David."

"None of us are," I assure him. "Rachel Garland once told me that we're always acting, playing as characters in undefined roles."

Rupert Wreath cringes, attempting to smile. He removes his flat cap and massages his temples. The mane of blonde hair has vanished too. He props his bald dome in-between two clenched fists.

"This is who I am," he admits heavily.

Wounded, he turns away and stares out of the window. The cloud is pressing its face against the glass, dribbling, slobbering and snogging with a billion lunging tongues. It sounds like it's goading us, mocking us. It wants us to know that it's always watching, always waiting for the next confrontation. It knows that we can't hide in here forever, out of the rain. *It's just a cloud*, I try to persuade myself. Air pressure, precipitation, automated elements. Nothing else. But, really, it's impossible to confirm.

"I haven't been honest with you," he says. "I haven't even been honest with myself. I don't exist, David. I don't even *own* a suit."

Rupert Wreath's head drops. His shoulders quiver with choked sobs. I look around me. Everyone else in the cafe politely ignores this grotesque scene, shovelling down their breakfasts with habitual apathy. He tilts his head back to swallow two oval pills with his coffee, unconcerned by the dog ends and cigarette ash bobbing on its surface. He winces as he massages the medication down his throat.

"Can I tell you a secret?" he asks. "You won't believe a word of it."

"After the things I've seen today," I say, "I might believe anything."

"My real name is Alan Bloom." He clears his throat, repressing a blister of laughter. "My name is Alan Bloom," he repeats (louder, more confident). He cups my hands in-between his own. "Paradise Publishing doesn't exist. And 34 Cannon Street isn't an agency. It's a film studio. Rupert

Wreath is a character. His office is a stage set. His entire life is a construct. And your book deal? It's all fairytale, David. It isn't real. Nothing is real."

I stare across the table, utterly perplexed. I feel the muscles tense across my neck and shoulders.

"You're an actor," I say, very quietly. This isn't a question. This is a statement, a cold acceptance.

"I was, once upon a time," he says, eyes lost in a halcyon memory. "I was an extra in *Creepshow*, *Howling III*, *Warlock*, *Shocker* – I turned down a small part in *Bride of Re-Animator* for that last one. I also performed in a few pornos, most notably as Pool Guy in *Stretch Paradise III*. Until this week, that was probably my most fulfilling work, creatively and artistically. I mean, who *hasn't* acted in a porno or horror movie? It takes virtually no talent. But I'm still proud of my portfolio. And I enjoyed escaping the city, fleeing reality. Nowadays, I focus on building the roster at my agency, Bloom Talent, teaching others the craft. That and a bit of roofing and plastering on the side. Got to pay the bills, David."

"They say teaching is the most noble profession," I mutter, but my thoughts are elsewhere. It's becoming increasingly apparent that I'm one of the only people on the planet who hasn't landed a Hollywood part. Hidden behind a plume of cigarette smoke, I refuse to reveal how much I envy his modest success, his ability to become anybody else. "What made you take on this particular role?"

"Two weeks ago, Bloom Talent got a call about a part in a low-budget horror film," he says. "Late thirties. Six foot plus. Lean build. White and male. Un-famous. They faxed over this article and asked us if we had any actors who fit the profile of this gentleman."

Alan Bloom pulls a sheet of paper out of his tracksuit trousers and unfolds it on the table. It's a newspaper article. The headline says: HOLLYWOOD PRODUCER PUSHED OFF 11TH-FLOOR BALCONY. It's my story about Rupert Wreath's death. I look at the closeup of Rupert on the red carpet, smiling, waving to an unseen audience. And then I look at my photograph of Rachel Garland knelt next to his remains, arm outstretched, contemplating the sensation of touch. I attempt to skim the body copy, but the words are blurred, as if the world around me is losing its focus, losing its cinematic clarity.

I look at Alan Bloom – the ballooned frame, the pockmarked skin, the abyss of authority and charisma – trying to find the resemblance between him and Rupert Wreath, but it simply isn't there. Perhaps it never was. He looks away again, as if he feels vulnerable in his true form.

"I know what you're thinking," he nods. "I'm no oil painting, but you'd be astonished what they can do with makeup and some solid backstory."

"You call that article *solid backstory*?" I laugh. "That's just a farrago of rudimentary details and unchecked facts. Nothing that gives you a sense of who Rupert Wreath really was. I should know. I wrote this trash."

"I didn't just use the article. I also had the script to help me with characterisation."

"There's a script?"

"Of course. That's how I got a real feel for the character. That's how I knew Rupert was unpitying, bombastic, narcissistic, privileged. It's written in the subtext of his motives, the tone of his dialogue."

"Jesus." I close my eyes, take a deep breath, exhale, titter, open them again. "What's it called?"

"The movie?"

"The movie."

"*Sick & Beautiful.*"

"*Sick & Beautiful?*"

"Pretty good, right?" he beams. "Arguably better than the plot. You get that with horror movies, though, don't you? Great title, but the story always seems to fall flat."

It is a great title, isn't it? I want to say, trying not to smile, trying not to let my vanity derail the interview.

It's difficult to ask this next question. It takes a lot of courage.

"Tell me about the script," I say. "What's the premise of *Sick & Beautiful?*"

"Here's the synopsis: an aspiring author, David Temple, is set to realise his dream by publishing his first novel, *Sick & Beautiful*, but his literary agent, Rupert Wreath, threatens to reject it unless he steals the photo album: an insidious relic haunted by an interdimensional demon. That's the conflict. David has to sell his soul to realise his dream. And Rupert has to compel David to do it so he can help him confront the terrible secret buried in his subconscious." Alan smiles. "Bizarre, right? Perhaps a little hackneyed. But I took the gig. The premise sounded like fun. And I knew I could do something interesting with Rupert. I wanted him to be a kind of corporate, toxically masculine rendition of the Sirens, lulling David towards the rocks." Alan pauses. "Did you get any of that in my performance?"

"Perhaps," I shrug. There's a short silence. "Tell me. What did you think of *my* performance?"

"When you crawled across the office floor, eyes flooded with tears, my God, David!" he says. "I thought you were *sensational.* I felt intimidated by your fearless emotion, your effortless stagecraft. You practically carried that scene. I had a blast with you out there. That's until I realised the truth."

Alan Bloom pauses when the waitress comes to our table to top up his coffee and collect his dirty plates. He smiles politely, watching her with narrowed eyes until she disappears through the beaded curtain, back into the mist of the cafe's hissing kitchen.

"It didn't hit me until I was in the dressing room, frowning at my reflection in the vanity mirror," he continues. "Fake tan was streaked down my face like warpaint. My toupee was completely skew-whiff. Even my girdle snapped during the scene. But you didn't notice these wardrobe malfunctions. You didn't even stick to your lines. You just ploughed through, like a real person, as if it was real life. That's when I realised something – *You weren't an actor.* So, I left the note at Paradise Productions, just in case you returned looking for answers. Just in case you really were David Temple."

I take the photo album off my lap, lay it on the table and unwrap it. Alan Bloom cowers. And then he smiles.

"I am David Temple," I say. "And the director's name was Richard Hayes. He's dead because of the entity searching for this object. And my neighbour, Abraham Maher, is dead because gangsters are hunting it too. Even if this photo album isn't haunted, death seems to be inexplicably attracted to it. Richard created his movie so he could give it to me and pass on its curse. And he resurrected Rupert Wreath so he could break me, degrade me. So he could force me to follow his script. It's obvious."

Alan Bloom laughs in disbelief. "It isn't a prop, is it?" he asks, frowning at the photo album. "And you *actually* took it, just like David does in the script. Jesus. This is unreal. It's obscene. I can't believe you're *the* David Temple in the script. And I can't believe that thing is here, on this table, in this cafe. I don't know whether to scream or to ask you for an autograph."

"I don't want you to do either, Alan. I want you to tell me how deep this thing goes, how many people are involved. I need to know where Richard's movie ends and where my reality begins."

"That's impossible to say. There was the director and myself, of course. The executive producers. The cameramen, camera assistants. Lighting technicians. Set designers. Wardrobe. Hair and makeup. Catering. All the other actors who came to the casting for the role of Rupert." Alan Bloom counts on his fingers before abruptly giving up. He shrugs. "Who knows how many?"

"The receptionist?"

"I don't know."

"The whistling janitor?"

"I don't know."

"Your PA, Eve? Eleanor Wither? Leonard Lynch? Docklands Dave?"

"Honestly, David. I don't know."

I gasp, cupping my hand over my mouth.

Is this another scene?" I ask, glaring around the cafe. "Are the cameras rolling right now?"

"Stop," he whispers, pressing the tip of his greasy index finger against my swollen lips (it tastes like chip fat and cigarette ash). "Please. Don't torture yourself. I enjoyed it. We all did. The intensity. It got physical in there. It may have been a studio and I may have been an actor, but that was a real experience. More real than anything we'll encounter *out there*. How else do you explain why we're both here, now, in this moment?"

"Who am I, though, Alan? I'm following the script, just like everybody keeps telling me to, but I'm no closer to knowing who I am or why I'm here."

Alan Bloom unzips his tracksuit, pulls out a copy of my novel, *Sick & Beautiful*, and places it on the table.

"You're the author of the source material, David. It's why you're here – so we could make this movie together. You're an integral part of the creative process. It means that you're involved too."

"You read the book?" I ask hopefully.

"*Sick & Beautiful*?"

"*Sick & Beautiful.*"

Alan Bloom blushes again.

"The director gave me this to help prep me for the role," he says. "I tried to read it, but– well, let's just say it wasn't my bag. The director's adapted screenplay is unquestionably superior to the book in terms of its ambition and focus. There just seems to be more motives, more purpose. I feel as if I can relate to the characters more. Even yours to an extent. Perhaps I'll give it another bash before pre-production starts."

"What pre-production?"

"I'm afraid I still haven't been entirely honest with you, David," he sighs. "Here's the truth. I'm in negotiations with an LA production company about remaking *Sick & Beautiful* with a bigger budget and a reworked screenplay. An award-winning director is attached. We're discussing a few changes, like the continuity errors and resetting the plot in Beverly Hills even though, ironically, they want to shoot in

Shepperton, but I'm confident they'll figure it out. And guess what? They want to recast me as David Temple. At the very least, they'll recruit me as a cultural advisor. But listen. You have what it takes, David. I've seen your work. We know what you're capable of on the stage. Perhaps there's a part for you in this picture too. I can represent you at Bloom Talent. We could be famous, baby."

"You've got it all wrong, Alan," I say. "This isn't my role. I'm predestined to be an author, not an actor." I pause, staring into the embers of his cigarette, wondering if either of us are really here. I pick up the photo album and hug it to my chest. "I know who I am," I add defiantly. "I'm one of the good guys."

"Are you sure about that, David?" he asks. Alan Bloom leans back. "At the casting, the director told me something interesting. He said that David Temple suffers from paranoid delusions. He said that the character is *unreliable*. He doesn't have a firm grip on reality. It's as if he's an actor in his own life, but completely unaware of it."

"That *is* interesting," I admit.

I feel the cafe's angles and edges lose their focus again.

"I haven't enjoyed watching you unravel," he says, voice muffled like a faraway echo. "But I have no regrets about the roles we played in this strange plot. You revitalised my passion for acting. And you taught me the true scope of reality. It's a malleable concept. It can be destroyed, dismantled or reimagined into something crisper, into something beautiful. You've proven that I don't need to be Alan Bloom. And that you don't need to be David Temple."

"Rachel Garland believes our potential is limitless," I say. "She taught me we can be anybody we want to be."

"Beautiful," he says. "That's beautiful."

Alan Bloom looks very serious now. Almost despondent.

"You said the director wanted to curse you with the photo album," he finally says. "Why?"

"For revenge." I smile. "You said that David Temple has a terrible secret in the script?"

"Yes."

"It's my secret too, Alan. And it is terrible. It really is."

Alan Bloom nods, registering this data, taking a long, thoughtful sip of his ash-coagulated coffee.

"It's OK," I say. "Ask the question, Alan. I'm ready."

"OK," he says. "Did you really kill Rachel Garland?"

CHAPTER
TWENTY-NINE

The night of the accident is still invasively evocative.

A memory that refuses to fade or lose its pertinence.

Minutes after I stormed out of the afterparty for *The Passion of Darkly Noon*, a car pulled up on the kerb of Grosvenor Road. When the passenger door swung open, I assumed that I would be greeted by a random act of violence. Instead, I was greeted by Rachel Garland.

"Get in the car, David," she said. "It's the baby. I'm having contractions. I need you to drive me to King's College Hospital."

"I can't drive, Rachel," I said. "I'm at least two dozen times over the limit. Also, I'd argue the baby is more Richard's remit than mine."

"Richard," she replied sharply, "is too busy to drive me. Networking, apparently." Rachel's voice broke. "Please, David. Get in the car. I need this. I need *you*."

As soon as I closed the door behind me, Rachel Garland accelerated across Vauxhall Bridge with terrifying speed. Astonishingly, the route was completely clear. No roadworks.

No gridlocks caused by crashes or collisions. It was as if London's infrastructure wanted to expedite our trajectory. In this car, I felt like we were the last two humans in the city, on the planet, travelling at a supersonic pace. The wipers shovelled rain off of the windscreen with audible exhaustion. I could barely see the road in front of us.

"Are you still flying to California?" I asked.

Rachel Garland didn't reply. We both already knew the answer to this question. I moved onto my next one.

"When are you coming back?"

"I'm not coming back, David. *We're* not coming back. We're moving to the Sierra Nevada. To a town called Paradise."

Rachel didn't need to tell me that *we* meant her, Richard Hayes, the unborn child. I fell silent, imagining this new dream that occluded me: gated residentials, mowed lawns, tanned skin, grinning children, lanky evergreens, distant mountains, lilac skies, innocuous clouds, enervating sunshine.

"But what about the book?" I said. "I can't finish it without you. Have you even considered what it would be like transcribing interviews over the phone in different time zones? It'll be a nightmare."

"There is no book. I'm terminating the project. This is *my* life. *My* story. You don't get to write it."

Rachel Garland smiled, as if she felt relieved to express this. That's when I noticed she had fixed her broken teeth. It was a utopian mouth lined with uniform canines and incisors, like a cul-de-sac of pearly luxury apartment complexes. Funded by Richard Hayes, I assumed, just like the gold earrings and haute couture maternity dress. And whose car is this anyway? I wanted to scream. I wanted to–

I was swiftly jolted out of this rumination when Rachel

clipped a concrete traffic island outside Vauxhall tube station. Something scraped, clunked and detached itself from the suspension, rattling across the bitumen in a shower of orange sparks.

"Jesus, Rachel," I said, twisting in my seat to glare out the rear window. "Perhaps I should drive."

Rachel Garland ignored this suggestion, taking another swig from the gin bottle between her legs. She passed it to me. I hesitated, took it, sipped, passed it back again. And then I buckled my seatbelt. Why is somebody not stopping us? I wondered. Why are the police never around when you *actually* need them?

"There's nothing for you *out there*, nothing for anybody outside this city," I said, pointing out of the open window and nearly amputating my arm on a passing lorry. I pulled it back inside, flexing my hand to check it was still physically attached. "How can you bring a child into this world?" I continued. "After the things we've seen, the things we learnt. You know that the man in the bowler hat will be waiting for you in Paradise. Even if the galaxy collapses and human history is reduced to cinders in a celestial heartbeat, *he* will never stop haunting us or the people we love."

"This creature growing inside me wasn't part of the plan," she said, caressing her baby bump like a crystal ball, as if she was trying to conjure an image of their rose-tinted future. "Falling in love with Richard wasn't part of the plan either. But *he* never said we had to understand the script. He told us just to follow it."

"What plan?" I asked.

"The first night we met, the night Rupert died, was an accident," she said. "Moving in with you, spending time with you, was not. Here's the truth – I did it for research for a role. A script about an expat who falls in love with an addict attempting to publish a novel. The movie got postponed. Cancelled. Rewritten. Postponed again. But filming finally begins in October. In LA. After the baby is born. I'm sorry, David. After everything we've experienced together, you deserved to know the truth."

We careened down Harleyford Street, narrowly missing the bumper of a pivoting night bus as we cut through the red traffic lights on the intersection of Brixton Road, taking wrong turn after wrong turn. Ignoring this near-fatal collision, I rolled up the window (as if *that* could make us safer) and pulled out my notepad and biro.

"What's the movie called?" I asked.

"Please, David–"

"What's the movie called, Rachel?"

"They're still working on the title."

"What casting agency landed your audition?"

"I can't remember."

"Who's the director?"

"I don't know."

"The cinematographer?"

"I don't know."

"The production company?"

"I don't know, David."

I nodded, as if I believed her, but this information felt like another invention, another deviation from reality. I watched my tears fall on the blank notepad like raindrops.

"You told producers and former flatmates you took acting classes at the National Theatre," I said, "but none of the coaches there know your name. You told me you've performed in over 100 movies, but not one talent agency in London or LA can name a single casting you attended, one picture credit you landed. It's as if you're a ghost." Silence. "Just admit it, Rachel," I continued. "Just say the words: *David, I'm not an actor. I never was, even though I dreamt endlessly about being one.* You're just like Richard. Pretending to be somebody else, creating a make believe reality. This whole time, I've been trying to write a book about a character you fabricated. Does Richard care you're not real?"

"Why would he care?" she asked. "Like you said – Richard isn't real either. We love each other for who we are, David. For who we want to be."

I nodded, again disingenuously, as I stared through the windscreen at the shuttered viaducts of Atlantic Road. And then I saw him, in the distance, stood in the centre of the road, rain cascading off the brim of his bowler hat. My eyes widened. My mouth gaped.

"Don't look so shocked, David," Rachel Garland scoffed. "You tried to exploit every tragedy in my life for your precious book, but you're living a fantasy too. You're not a journalist. You're not an author. You're *nothing*, David. If Richard and I aren't real, you're not real either. Being ghosts, being fictitious, is the only trait we ever shared. Pretending to be someone else *is* our purpose. We're like children in many ways – free to create beautiful worlds, able to dream even when we don't sleep."

The man in the bowler hat smiled. And then he waved, as if greeting an old friend. Could Rachel not see him too?

Kill it, I thought. Kill this sick creature. Kill it. Kill it now. Kill it before it contaminates your spirit.

I lurched over the gearstick and grabbed the steering wheel with both hands, swerving the car towards the man in the bowler hat with an authoritative jerk. Time slowed as the tyres howled over the kerb and we mounted the pavement, missing the apparition by inches. I shut my eyes. Rachel Garland screamed. Oblivion enveloped us.

By the time I regained consciousness, a small crowd was gathered around the car, which had moulded itself around one of the steel pillars supporting the overhead train tracks of Brixton station. The traffic had staggered to a standstill as the drivers killed their engines, stepped into the rain and approached the accident. I watched them jostle to the anterior, run their fingers over the twisted bodywork, the crushed bonnet, the smashed windscreen, aroused by the incredible damage.

"I'm sick, David. I feel sick."

The words collapsed through Rachel Garland's lips with mouthfuls of blood as she explored the fresh orifice in her abdomen, which was impaled by the steering column. Her wig was upside-down on the dashboard. I put my hand on her thigh, patted it gently. Both of her tibias were shattered in the compressed leg compartment. Over the chorus of car horns, in the alcoves of my imagination, I could hear the baby crying. I could see it, scarlet, squidgy and naked, curled underneath the clutch and accelerator pedals, born from the velocity of the collision. Or, perhaps, I imagined this.

"It'll be OK, Rachel," I said. "In the end, everything always is. The paramedics will be here soon."

Rachel Garland adjusted the rear-view mirror to study her cleaved forehead. Blood secreted from the wound, down the bridge of her nose. She touched her face, consulting its grooves, its lapels, its textures.

"Beautiful," she said, smiling, her new veneers imbedded in the steering wheel. "I'm beautiful."

"I know you are, Rachel. You're the most beautiful person, the most beautiful soul. I fell in love with you the moment we met." I kissed her, feeling her tepid blood on my lips. "I love you, Rachel. I wrote *Sick & Beautiful* for you. I wanted to share your vision with the world. I wanted us to be forever."

"Don't cry, David. This is just the beginning for both of us."

I held Rachel Garland while she convulsed, until she went limp and settled into an awful stillness. Blood drooled out the corner of her mouth as she rested her head on the steering wheel with a soft thud. I removed her cracked sunglasses – her eyes were open, rolled back, glassy like a broken doll.

"Help us," I sobbed as our audience gave a standing ovation, smacking their palms on the bonnet, applauding our performance with cheers and wolf-whistles.

The man in the bowler hat pressed his face against the cracked window of the passenger door. I laughed (dry retching, choking) as he took a photograph. He was wearing my face, stretched across his grotesque teeth. His putrid breath condensed on the glass.

"I believe there was a time when this scene moved me to tears," he sighed. "Perhaps there is another version of myself in the future or the past that still weeps every time it travels back to this memory. The accident, the gore, the rubberneckers. I've ruminated these details a thousand times. They used to make me feel grateful for my time on this planet. But now?

They make me feel empty. Numbed. Scooped out. They make me feel *nothing*. You know I take no joy in haunting you, David? It's torture."

When I pressed my hands against the window, he splayed his fingers over mine. I stared into his infinite eyes, our faces only inches apart, separated by the glass. In this moment, I felt sorrow for the man the bowler hat. I could see through him, *into him*, the desolation and grief of his capsized soul. I felt a connection. Unconditional empathy. We were suspended in time, the only entities on Earth.

"Help us," I whispered. "You promised her we'd live forever. Please. You know how to stop this."

"Rachel is right," he said. "This, sadly, is just the beginning. So, don't cry, David. She'll be waiting for us in Paradise. I'll take you to her when you're finally ready. It's all part of the script. And believe me – I wish I could stop this. I really do." He smiled. "You can scream now. It's OK, David. Let it out."

Obediently, I closed my eyes and screamed.

At last. The book had its final chapter.

Yeah. The book found its neverending.

CHAPTER
THIRTY

A soliloquy: "After seeing the world repurposed around me – the city landscape, the corridors of Paradise Productions, the cathedrals of flesh that were once the living bodies of Rachel Garland, Richard Hayes and Abraham Maher – I can't be certain if anything exists. Not in any conventional sense. Suddenly, every structure looks like a rickety set piece, littered with underpaid actors and overpriced props. I feel, quite suddenly, *out of context*. Like an opinion or an uncredited excerpt. Perhaps reality has always been like this, and I've only just began to notice its kinks and fallacies."

I pause. "It's like the book," I continue. "There's all these components, but they don't seem to fit together. I'm searching desperately for meaning (every story needs *meaning*), but I can't find it. Just a 270,000-word existential crisis. The text refuses to present any intelligible patterns, as if its content and the violence that defines it are entirely meaningless. I feel the same way about the city's tangled infrastructure: the one-way systems and scaffolding poles, the pylons and washing lines, the thickets of green-windowed high-rises. How much of London's skyline is an extravagant backdrop? It all looks so *fake*. And then there's the humans, dressed like humans, doing and not doing the most mundane human things. How many of these dazed pedestrians are costumed extras? Every crevice of the city is adorned with surveillance cameras that swivel, whizz and whirr from low and lofty angles. It's not inconceivable that this technology captures endless footage of our cruelty to entertain an audience of sadistic alien viewers." I laugh. "Jesus. I'm beginning to sound like Abe."

I sip my gin and tonic, noting the absence of ice and/or slice. I let it go.

"If unknown forces control reality with an invisible switchboard of nefarious knobs, buttons and dials," I theorise, "then this isn't my story. It's *theirs*, the brief owners, the directors and producers, to edit and amend at their leisure. I became so intoxicated, *so complacent*, I failed to recognise I've been existing across two conflicting dimensions: one in which Rachel Garland is still alive and I'm on the cusp of authorial stardom, another where I'm an inept actor starring in Richard's revenge porno. Both of these universes share a common thread – an unhappy unending. The reality, for want of a better word, is inescapable."

Docklands Dave doesn't take his eyes off the fruit machine when I share these notions, but I can tell that he is visibly moved by their clarity. It's the way his posture breaks, the way his gaze softens.

"You couldn't bear the weight of reality," he says. "So, you forged a new one. We all live across multiple worlds, David. Ones where we're beautiful, wealthy, kind, un-lonely, famous, autonomous. Everybody is building their own visions of a private Paradise, swimming across the infinite oceans of their imaginations. Sometimes, demons slither out of those dark waters, copulating with our waking reality, replacing or redefining our memories. We've been on a bizarre journey, you and I. But we're finally enlightened. You followed the clues, and you found the truth – the truth about the accident, Rachel, Richard, *everything*." He lifts his pint. "Congratulations. You made it back to the real world. Isn't it just beautiful, David?"

That last line – I can't tell if Docklands Dave is being sincere or sarcastic. The latter, it seems, isn't in his nature.

"That's the thing, Dave," I say, staring into my tumbler, trying to find the right dialogue. "I'm not interested in the *real world*. I want to go back."

"Go back where?"

"To Paradise. *My* Paradise. The world where Rachel resides, where she visits me, where I can see her smiling, dancing barefoot in the rain. There's something I need before I return, though. It's in my flat. I know that Piggy and Mother will be waiting there for me, for this," I say, holding up the photo album, "but I can't leave without it."

Docklands Dave nods, sips his pint, scratches the stubble on his jaw. He seems to be getting used to the idea.

"Perhaps the journey isn't over," he agrees. "Perhaps you still haven't realised your true role." He smiles. "It's high risk, high reward, but I like it. You're not following the script – you're following your heart."

Docklands Dave sighs heavily.

We agree that I'll need a gun.

We exit the Market Porter and walk down the foggy backroads behind Southwark Cathedral. When we reach Clink Street, Docklands Dave unzips his tracksuit and hands me something wrapped in a polishing cloth – it's a revolver. The grip is bandaged with black electrical tape. The barrel is sawed down to an uninspiring snub.

"It doesn't look like much," I say, lining up the sight. "Where did you get it?"

"It was my father's. From the war." He pauses. "He gave this to me before he left me and Mum. He said it would keep the boogeyman away."

I nod, imagining Abraham Maher aiming this weapon, pulling the trigger, holding it with the hand Piggy gnawed to a bloody stump.

"I'll be honest, Dave. I was expecting something with a bit of *oomph*, a bit more stopping power. Does it even work?"

Docklands Dave shrugs.

"I wouldn't know," he says. "I haven't fired it. I've never fired a gun, in fact."

I hand it back to him, disturbed by the girth of its components, the weight of its aggregate parts.

"This is unbelievable," I mutter. "Christ, Dave. How have you never fired a gun?"

"I don't know what you expected. I'm a pub man. Not a gangster. But have faith, David," he says, kneading my shoulders reassuringly. "Let me teach you how to tote it."

I follow Docklands Dave to Bankside. Just like the snow and hail this morning, this fog has really come out of nowhere, obscuring the structures on the other side of the river, reducing the freighters and tourist ferries on the water to rows of levitating portholes. We finally stop inside the dripping underpass of Southwark Bridge.

"What are we waiting for?" I ask after several minutes pass.

"Our victim," he says, pointing to the silhouette materialising from the fog: a man in a pinstriped suit, clutching a black umbrella and leather briefcase. *Jesus*, I think. He looks like the person I used to be, a ghost of a former life, a former self. "He's ideal for the role," he grins. "Follow my lead, David."

Before the man can pass us, Docklands Dave steps in front of him. Revolver levelled at the chest, Dave pushes him backwards until his elbows are pressed up against the dank brickwork of the underpass.

"Please," begs the victim, holding his hands in front of his face. "Please. I don't deserve this."

Docklands Dave cocks the hammer and digs the barrel into the victim's dimpled cheekbone.

"Please, you don't have to do this," he says, sliding down the wall, curling into a quivering ball.

Docklands Dave stands over the victim, watching him lay out his belongings on the pavement (he doesn't even ask the guy to do it): a leather wallet, a gold watch, a handful of shrapnel, an unclaimed betting slip, house keys, a deck of fags. Hands trembling, he opens the briefcase: it contains nothing of note, nothing of value.

"What do you say, David?" asks Docklands Dave. "Shall we kill him? He's got nothing. *Is* nothing."

When our victim starts to whimper in objection at this prospect, Docklands Dave answers his outburst with a sharp sneaker to the ribcage.

"That's enough, Dave," I say, placing a palm on his muscled back. "I think we're done here."

"I'll tell you when we're done here," he growls, swiping my hand away, digging the barrel deeper.

The victim's eyelids are pursed shut, the palms clasped in unpractised prayer.

"Count to three," orders Docklands Dave, "or I'll transform your face into an open wound."

"Wuh- one," stutters the victim, gulping for words, for courage. "Teh- teh- two–"

But I don't hear three. Docklands Dave has already pulled me into the fog engulfing Bankside, the victim's sobs fading in the invisible distance. We walk briskly up Clink Street, back to the sanctuary of the Market Porter.

"It's crucial to be calm, to be confident," he says, handing me the revolver. "You'll never need to use it if you can act. But you need to be convincing. You have to *perform*."

Sickened with adrenaline, I lean against the outside of the boozer. I tuck the revolver inside the breast pocket of my overcoat (over the heart).

"I fear I might embarrass myself," I say. "What if my enemies aren't afraid of my new hardware?"

"Then you may have to shoot," he shrugs.

As I'm about to step through the doors of the Market Porter, Docklands Dave stops me.

"Sorry, David," he says, "but the landlord says you're not allowed back in here with that thing."

"The shooter?" I ask.

"The photo album. You can't even feel it anymore, can you? It's becoming part of you."

Docklands Dave nods to the idling taxi on the corner of Stoney and Park Street.

"If you insist on returning to your flat," he continues, "you don't want to take the tube or, God forbid, the bus. Your assassins will be watching, waiting. But you can always trust a London cabbie to grant safe passage through the city." He pats me on the back with fatherly affection. "Best of luck."

Docklands Dave turns to enter the pub but abruptly pauses, pivots back. The grace that defines his motions is strained with concern, the composed features askew. He pulls a roll of fifties out of his tracksuit trousers and pushes them into my palm. There's a lot of money here. And no eye contact.

"Thank you," I say, feeling fresh tears manifest. "Tell me, Dave. Why are you still helping me?"

"Your motives, your performance, have truly moved me," he says, splaying his fingers over his heart (he's getting choked up now too). "You remind me what it means to be human. In these sour times, it feels good to be good, to do good. It feels good to share hope. I pray the cloud will let you escape, so you can take that darkness to Paradise. Perhaps your role is to save us, David. Perhaps you really are one of the good guys."

"Perhaps," I say.

We shake hands.

"Until next time, David."

As the taxi pulls out of Borough Market, Docklands Dave disappears in the rear-view window.

He waves.

An angel combusting in the fog and downpour.

CHAPTER
THIRTY-ONE

I ask the cabbie to drop me off at the Beehive on Brixton Road.

It's a simple request. An undemanding route with an accessible destination. But when we arrive, something unexpected happens. When I pull out my wad of banknotes to pay the cabbie, she shakes her head, as if to say, *I don't want your money.* She does this until I put the cash back in my pocket.

"This fare's on us," she says, studying me in the rearview mirror. She looks troubled, as if she wants to tell me something significant. And then she comes out with this: "People tend to vanish when they get on the wrong side of the Paradise Corporation."

"Excuse me?"

"Piggy and Mother operate under the banner of Paradise Flowers," she says, "but that's just a charade. This thing– it's so much bigger. It's *gigantic*."

"What *thing*?"

"The Paradise Corporation. There's also Paradise Hotel

& Spa in Chelsea. Paradise Real Estate in Knightsbridge. Paradise Productions on Cannon Street. Paradise Casino in Piccadilly Circus. Paradise Adult Entertainment in Soho. Paradise Brewery in Walthamstow. Paradise House Recovery Clinic in Surrey. The list, the conspiracy, is endless. Soon, they'll rename the city Paradise. We can't stop it."

"Who are *they*?"

"Who knows? But the Old Bill are in on the *thing* with the *they* too. Big money."

"Why are you telling me this?"

The cabbie shrugs. "Just making conversation, imparting knowledge. It's my role."

"Well, don't worry about me," I say. "I'm going to find the *real* Paradise."

I open the door, slide off the backseat, step back into the fog, the rain, close the door behind me.

"Good luck, David," she says through the window. "We're rooting for you."

Before I can ask her how she knows my name, the cabbie winds up the window and pulls into the traffic. I read the sticker above the taxi's rear bumper – *Choose Paradise Cabs: The Hackney Carriage to your DREAMS.*

"Probably nothing," I mutter.

I pop into the Beehive to flash a double gin and tonic before making my way up Atlantic Road, back towards Eden Estate. I walk past the pillar Rachel Garland and I crashed into six months ago. The pillar is dented, the paint chipped, slightly peeling. Bouquets of flowers are moored around it, withered inside their cellophane sarcophagi. Were they laid here for Rachel? Or do these expired petrol station posies commemorate another victim of this pillar, this city? It's impossible to know.

"See you soon, Rachel," I say, marching with purpose, building pace.

As I approach Eden Estate, I see the mesmeric blink of emergency lights piercing through the fog. Two police cars are parked in the forecourt. There is also a van with *Paradise Removals* tattooed on its tarpaulin hide. Two policemen flank the lobby steps like a pair of stone gargoyles. I stand in front of them, waving warmly, attempting to smile.

"Afternoon, officers," I say. "Awful weather."

"Awful indeed, sir," one agrees.

When I take another step forward, the other officer holds up his hand, signalling for me to stop.

"Apologies, sir," he says. "Strictly no visitors. Renovations are being carried out on the building."

"Relax, officers. I live here."

I dig my housekeys out of my pocket. I jingle them playfully. The policeman looks at his colleague, at the photo album in my arms, at his colleague again. After a short pause, he smiles too. They both do.

"Apologies for the inconvenience, sir," he says, waving me inside.

"It's quite alright," I say, limping past them. As I'm about to call the lift, the doors open and two men in blue overalls walk out carrying Abraham Maher's armchair (still stained with blood). I watch them unlovingly lug it across the lobby, down the steps and into the back of the removal van. They dust off their hands, satisfied with their brutal efficiency.

"That's very interesting," I admit. "Very interesting indeed."

I hit the control panel, quiver to the second floor, exit the lift, hobble up the corridor and study my front door, which has been crowbarred off its frame. Cold air shrieks through the gap. More men in blue overalls pass me carrying binbags and boxes haemorrhaging with Abraham Maher's derelict possessions, but they don't seem to notice me. Not even when I draw the revolver and tiptoe inside my flat, barrel first.

Sitting room. Bedroom. Kitchen. Pantry. Bathroom. Balcony. The flat is empty, but someone has turned it sideways. It was already a tip. But now? It's a catastrophe. Every drawer and cupboard has been ransacked, emptied. Floorboards and carpets uprooted. Mattress and furnishings eviscerated. Sentimental objects obliterated. Shattered glass, feathers and shredded photographs are scattered across the floor like confetti.

I sink into the carcass of the sofa and gaze at the kicked in television set, mourning my material existence, dismantled in one afternoon. We enter the world needing everything – medical staff, day and night care, human clothes, human milk, absolute attention, absolutely *everything* – and exit it again, naked with nothing. I stand up. With my ear flattened against the wall, I can hear the scream of pneumatic drills and the squeak of footsteps inside Abraham Maher's flat next door.

"*They're here*," I whisper. I need to move with conviction, with proficiency.

I hang my overcoat on the back of the front door and moult my clothes and sneakers. Naked, I find my briefcase under the overturned breakfast table and begin filling it, almost at random: half-smoked packs of cigarettes, three printouts of *Sick & Beautiful*, the photo album, twelve roll films, passport, pen, notepad, the remaining drugs (half a baggie of coke, four ecstasy pills, a half-empty baggie of weed, a pick 'n' mix of Abraham Maher's amphetamine, alprazolam and diazepam pills).

Next, I enter the bedroom, slip into a black three piece suit, hang my camera around my neck, pull my overcoat back on, feel the revolver inside the breast pocket. I complete this confident look with Chelsea boots and magenta teashades. Finally, I lift Father's jar of ashes off the top of the TV set which, unlike every other object inside the flat, has survived the bedlam.

Scatter my ashes outside the city. Beyond the reach of the cloud. Take me back home. I still believe in Paradise.

I smile, finally grasping the true meaning of Father's death note.

"I'm taking you home, Dad," I say, kissing the jar, placing it on top of the briefcase. "All I need now are Abe's car keys. Then we can get going. We can catch up with Rachel. Give me two ticks."

I take a deep breath, step onto my balcony, step over the railings. I look up at the cloud, down at the forecourt, and let that chilly calmness consume me. I close my eyes and savour this moment, this sensation, allowing my hands, my feet, my instincts, to guide me across the breach. When I open my eyes again and realise that I've made it, that I'm on Abraham Maher's balcony (wonderfully dressed, crouched low), I look through the window, into the sitting room.

"Incredible," I mutter.

Two women in blue overalls slather the walls with coats of white emulsion. A policeman holds the front door while removal men exit the flat with Abraham Maher's personal effects, only to re-enter with something chic, something with taste. They're erasing him from the face of the faceless city, filling the abyss of his existence with leather furniture, earthenware ceramics, glossy tabletop magazines, tall vases exploding with honeysuckles and tuberose. Rejuvenated with money, the flat sparkles like a show home in the gated commuter belt of Elysium. There's no denying it. The place has never looked better. The attention to detail is *magnificent*. There's even a man in the far corner of the room, on his hands and knees, varnishing the restored floorboards. He whistles, mopping the sweat from his forehead with a handkerchief. Where have I seen this character before? And then it hits me. It's the whistling janitor from the lobby of Paradise Productions, assuming a new role: the whistling handyman. And guess what? He's doing it well. Yeah. *This guy*. He's really in his element.

    I turn away from the window and gaze into the fog, into the rain. After viewing the exorcism of Abraham Maher, I feel my confidence draining, my body lagging. I can't supress the feeling that I'm next. It's only a matter of time now. Soon, the Paradise Corporation will erase me too. When they find me (and they will, because the margins of error are growing increasingly narrow), they'll chuck my corpse into a mass grave in the Purley Way or into the canals of Merton Abbey Mills. They'll sell my refurbished flat (*and* make an enviable profit). Burn my post. Erase my NI number. And that will be the end of it. The end of David Temple. I'll be engulfed by the salivating mouth of the city, as if I never existed. I feel helpless, unbuckled from reality.

    "I knew you'd come back for me, David."

    I hold my hands in front of my face, expecting a swift blow to the skull from a dull object, but when I peek between my fingers, I see Osiris sheltered beneath the windowsill. "Jesus," I whisper. Knots of fur hang off his emaciated frame. His eyes are cloudy, the ears chewed, bloodied, wilting like dying flowers. He looks terrible, *smells* terrible, yet a smug smirk is still framed between those drooping whiskers. He nuzzles his bald head around my boots. I recoil with disgust, afraid I might contract his disease.

"I didn't come back for you, Osiris," I say, enjoying his swift physical decline (it couldn't have happened to a nicer mog). "I came back for Abe's car keys. And then I'm leaving London. I'm a ghost."

"Forever?"

"Forever."

"You think the cloud will let you leave?" he asks, inspecting the underside of his scabbed paw. "You think *they* will let you leave? Also, do you even have a Scooby Doo where Abe hid his keys?"

A Scooby Doo – Cockney rhyming slang for *clue*. Another new phrase. Where did Osiris learn this one? I wonder. A British crime film? Somewhere set in the East End? This locution irritates me, but, ultimately, he's right. I don't have a clue.

"I'll tell you where the keys are if you do something for me, David," he continues, examining his other paw, apparently in no rush.

"What's your proposal, Osiris? I haven't got all day."

"Take me with you," he says. "There's nothing left for me here, for either of us."

"After the way you tormented me and Abe with your sick games?" I laugh. "Give me one reason why I'd take you with me."

"Because that's what the old man would have wanted."

Don't forget to feed Osiris. He's a very special kitty.

"Perhaps this is all part of the script," I say after a short pause. "Perhaps Father said these words to prepare me for this moment."

"Perhaps," he agrees.

"We have a deal," I finally say, tickling Osiris under his blistered chin. He narrows his swollen eyelids and stretches out his neck, like an iguana basking in afternoon sunlight. I wince as a hank of wet fur slithers off his jaw. I can see maggots wriggling underneath. I try to ignore this. "Tell me where Abe hid the car keys, Osiris."

"Under the flowerpot on the windowsill," he says. "The one nearest to the balcony door."

"Finally, some luck," I gasp, relieved. I look up at the cloud and smile. "This might *actually* work. We might make it."

"It wasn't luck, David."

"What do you mean?"

"Abe said someone told him to hide the keys there."

"Who?"

"I think humans call them *angels*. But you call him something else."

It visited me in a dream. It told me my purpose. Can you guess what it is? To hide my car keys. Can you believe it, David? My purpose in this life, on this planet, is to hide a set of fucking car keys. It's like a sick joke, but it promised it would all work out, that it would all be over soon.

Abraham Maher's revelation reverberates through the back of my mind, replaying over and over and over again. Is it possible the man in the bowler hat told him this to help me? Perhaps he is doing what he always promised: ushering me towards Paradise. It's all just so perplexing, so ambiguous, *so him*. Whatever his motives are, I can't let them distract me. *Drag yourself together, David*, I console myself. Focus. Be unafraid. *Be too fucking cool.*

I tip the flowerpot and slip the keys hidden underneath into my pocket. When I take a final peek through the window, my heart stammers, increasing in tempo. Piggy and DC Scythe are stood in the centre of the sitting room, trading taut, one-two-word affirmations. Piggy leans on his knees with his ear to her vermillion lips. He makes the removal men squeezing past him look like dolls carrying doll house furniture, made with tiny tools and tiny hands. DC Scythe is holding something. It's a printout of *Sick & Beautiful*. She flicks through the pages, apparently reading sections at random. They frown and giggle as she does this, occasionally shaking their heads in bewilderment. I turn away from the window again, feeling wounded.

"It's time to go, Osiris."

I climb back across the balconies, enter my flat, open the briefcase and have a quick (but vital) bump of coke using Abraham Maher's car key. Instantly revitalised, I pick up the briefcase, Father's ashes and Osiris, checking the corridor is clear before I exit the flat and sprint to the lift. I press the button and listen to its painful ascent from the ground floor. Sweat collects on my forehead. My vision flickers. And then a voice behind me asks: "Room for one more?"

When I turn around, it confirms the obvious – that I should have made my exit via the stairwell.

"You've got it," I reply, stepping into the lift.

I press the button for the ground floor. As we begin our

descent, a peculiar chemistry pervades the carriage. I'm stood by the control panel, cradling my itinerary while Osiris writhes and yowls in my arms, ploughing his claws into my shoulder. DC Scythe is stood next to me, smoking a cigarette, reading *Sick & Beautiful*. She sniggers, lips clamped shut, attempting not to let the laughter escape, but it's apparently impossible. It comes tumbling out (the laughter), all at once, causing her knees to arc while she manically tee-hees into the vinyl floor tiles.

"I'm sorry," she says, wiping a tear away from her eye. "It's just this– It's just–"

And she's off again. I force a smile, attempting not to let my pain or embarrassment surface.

"It's quite alright," I reply. "What are you reading, if you don't mind me asking?"

"I'm not even sure how to describe it." She pauses. "I suppose it's a bit like bad porn."

"I did the best I could with the resources I was allocated. Rachel Garland ensured the book would be a disaster, but I've come to realise that I need to accept some of the blame for the final product. I know that my own flaws, my own errors throughout the creative process, contributed to its failure."

DC Scythe nods, studying me with modest curiosity. The way my feet shift nervously, the way my eyes dart behind my sunglasses, struggling to elect a focal point. Do these small details intrigue her?

"You look familiar," she says. "Do I know you from somewhere?"

She continues to examine me, waiting patiently for an answer. I look at the floor, searching for respite, but it isn't there. *This is it*, I think. I wait for the unbearable tension to snap with precipitous violence, but the moment doesn't culminate. *Jesus.* What's the hold up? Has it ever taken this long to descend two storeys? As I'm about to break down, to confess everything, the doors finally open and DC Scythe steps out of the lift.

"Actually," she says, "you can't be the person I thought you were."

"Why's that?" I ask.

"Because he's already dead," she says, exiting the lobby, vanishing into the fog.

I limp across the forecourt, up Loughborough Road, towards Abraham Maher's VW Beetle. It's exactly where I left it on Christmas Day: on the double-yellow lines outside the Hero of Switzerland, parked at an inconceivable angle. It's flat-tyred, coated with rust, festooned with tickets, clipped of its side mirrors by vandals or passing traffic, but the car is *here*, largely intact, ready to execute its function.

"Good to see you, old friend," I say, patting the corroded emerald roof. "I'll be back in two ticks."

Cat, urn and luggage in-hand, I pop into the Hero of Switzerland to sink a swift gin and tonic before trying my luck turning the engine. When I step back outside, I smile, surprised with the repose that washes over me. My fingertips tingle with numb serenity, an introverted peace.

"Afternoon, David."

"Afternoon, Piggy."

"Did you really think we would just let you go?" he asks, sat on the bonnet of Abraham's car under his umbrella. "Mother knew you were telling porky pies. But she also knew you'd lead us back to the photo album. That's why we kept you alive, David. So you could perform your designated part."

Piggy points to my briefcase.

"Are you going on a trip?" he asks.

The briefcase suddenly feels unfathomably heavy, as if its contents are expanding, pulling me towards the pavement, towards the molten core of the planet.

"I'm going to Paradise," I reply.

"Is the photo album in there?"

"Yes."

"I thought so," he says. "Father Gladioli was right. You really can feel it, even when you can't see it. My God. That sensation. It's quite frightening. How have you been able to endure it for this long?"

When Piggy takes his weight off the car, the front bumper lifts off the tarmac with ardent relief.

"First," he says, "you're going to put that moggie on the pavement. And then you're going to come with me. Mother is very upset with you, David. Very upset that you lied to her. But if you bring her the photo album, she may find it in her heart to forgive you. It's what mothers do, after all."

"OK," I say, placing Osiris on the wet paving slabs. "I have a gun," I add.

"So do I," says Piggy.

Piggy and I draw our weapons with mirrored urgency. Piggy aims his longer, thicker shooter at the centre of my forehead, while I point my pocket rocket in his general direction (hip-height, side-on, a bit like a cowboy). I feel myself exuding a cool confidence with this revolver (its heft, its black metallic opulence). I am a weapon. Streamlined, deadly, exempt from fear. Piggy examines it with sincere bemusement.

"Does that thing even work?" he asks.

"Supposedly," I reply.

I feel my arm tremble under the revolver's weight. My courage is waning, regressing.

Am I a weapon? I wonder. Am I a *purposeful* weapon? Am I even a purposeful object?

"It's time to accept that you've fulfilled your role, David. You were always destined to be an errand boy, nothing more. This, I'm afraid, is where your narrative ends. This *is* your Paradise." Piggy smiles. "And Rachel won't be waiting for you."

I pull the trigger, sending a bullet through the centre of Piggy's windpipe. I flinch, astonished that the revolver is loaded, astonished that it *actually* works. Osiris doesn't flinch. He doesn't even blink.

Clutching his neck, blood ejaculating between his fingers, Piggy collapses with a heavy thud, sending a tremor through my skeleton. He looks at me with amazement, red bubbles gurgling out of the hole in his trachea. I shoot him twice more in the chest. The wound blooms like a rosebud.

"Get in!" I bellow to Osiris, unlocking the door, slinging the urn and briefcase onto the passenger seat. I can hear the wail of sirens, perhaps as near as Barrington Road. "We haven't got much time."

Osiris obediently hops onto the backseat. Before I slide behind the wheel, I look at Piggy one last time. Eyes closed, lips slightly parted. And then, on sheer impulse, I pick up his bowler hat and slam the door. I grin in the rear-view mirror. It fits perfectly. It almost looks stylish.

When I turn the key, the dashboard ignites, blinking and ticking with a constellation of bad news. Faulty braking system. Faulty airbag. No oil. No petrol. No kinetic energy forwards or backwards. No hope. Osiris seems unconcerned by the desperation of our situation. He's already asleep, stretched out on the backseat like an abused hunting trophy.

After a few more enthusiastic twists of the key and a rugged plunge of the choke valve, the heap finally comes to life. The exhaust pipe reverberates, spluttering smoke, drooling pinguid resin on the tarmac. The air conditioning vents deluge the cockpit with carbon monoxide. The radio spills broken words out of the speakers like the phantom of a yodelling pisshead. It's a woman's voice.

Quickly, David. Before Piggy wakes up. Before the cloud stops us. I'm waiting here for you.

"I'm coming, Rachel," I say, releasing the handbrake, pulling into the road.

After a brief period of acceleration, we brake at the traffic lights on the intersection of Akerman and Loughborough Road. In the rear-view mirror, I see Piggy sit up, rubbing his eyes as if he has just awoken from a small coma. He strokes the stubble on his bald dome, wondering what happened to his bowler hat. Sickness washes over my body like a wave of frozen water. I whistle, drumming the steering wheel, watching Piggy rise to his feet. I fidget in my uncomfortable seat as the springs spear into the soft flesh of my bruised carcass. I alternate the speed of the windscreen wipers. I twist the knobs and dials on the dashboard to no avail. I roll down the steamed windows. I roll them back up again. I simultaneously shiver and perspire. Piggy has spotted us. He's walking towards the car now, picking up speed. One hand splayed around his bleeding trachea, a light jog turns into a canter. And then a full sprint. Why does nothing work in this decrepit machine, in this decrepit reality? I wonder, thumping the wheel. Piggy is three cars away now, galloping on all fours. I tell myself to relax, stay calm, be cool. *Have faith in the script.* If it happens, it happens.

But it doesn't. Phenomenally, the traffic lights turn amber, allowing me to floor the accelerator and speed up Akerman Road, just before Piggy can curl his trotter around the door handle and haul me out of the vehicle. I slap my fist on the dashboard, whooping hoarsely, tears swelling in my eyes. The tailback divides, the infrastructure relents, just for me. Has the city finally given me its blessing?

In the rear-view mirror, I can see Piggy in the centre of the road, the traffic unable to manoeuvre around his enormous frame.

He's smiling, blood staining his teeth.

He mouths something. It's the same words, over and over again.

Don't go to Paradise.

PART THREE
PARADISE

CHAPTER
THIRTY-TWO

As we speed towards outer London, outer space, the foggy city fades in the rear-view mirror. Slowly, civilisation slumps and haemorrhages. It's frightening to watch, but I'm bleakly hypnotised. It's like a scene from a postapocalyptic horror movie.

High-rises and multi-storey council flats level out into suburban semis. Asphalt playgrounds and concrete car parks decay into a turbulent blur of verdant pastures. Lampposts and pylons bloom into evergreens and distant manacles of extraterrestrial wind turbines. The windscreen wipers whinge and squeak under the endless rainfall. I drive towards the horizon, convinced that soon, at any moment, the car will collide into the backdrop of an astronomical stage set. But the scenery and junction signs keep rolling past in an unnerving exhibition of reality. An accident on the hard shoulder – ambulance lights, a buckled motorcycle, a severed leg clad in torn leather, tyre marks the hue of blood from the outside lane to the concrete barricade – serves as a visceral reminder that I'm still at the mercy of the cloud's malefic fits.

I reach Welling. Dartford. Rochester. Canterbury. Dover. And, finally, the water.

Oily suds crash and froth against the port's mossy berths, whipping up the scent of salt and raw sewage. Squawking seagulls mindlessly drift over an endless blue abyss. It moves me. I haven't seen anything like it since my childhood. I revisit the memory: I'm maybe nine years old, walking across a beach. Sand sticks to the soles of my feet. Waves break, roll back. The wind smells like seaweed. I'm holding a woman's hand. She wears a floral dress. I look up at her face and smile. It's her. It's Rachel Garland. And in the distance, stood on the water, is the man in the bowler hat. A silhouette on the shimmering horizon, waving and smiling, dressed in black.

I push this vision out of my mind as I enter the port, joining the queue of traffic in front of the ferry. When I finally roll the car up the ramp and onto the parking deck, I cut the engine and climb the stairs to the ferry bar, cradling my cat, my bruised ribs, gasping at the top of every landing. The vessel splutters to life. Above, the smokestacks chug and billow. With Osiris curled up on the chair next to mine, I wash down two of Abraham Maher's tablets with a double gin and tonic, watching the coastline evaporate.

"Incredible," I whisper, staring through the window.

I can finally see the edges of the cloud. A levitating cotton swab, fattened with the sullage of our species. Serrated beams of light shatter across its pulsating contours. It spits and slobbers across the shrinking landscape. Over the rumble of the engine, I hear it convulse with laughter. It's remarkable. Almost beautiful. I have no doubt it still has the power to capsize the ship, dragging my frame under the water. Slouched behind my sunglasses, I refuse to let my mind and muscles relax until the cloud is out of sight, until I'm certain that this creaking vessel, with its metal decks and metal entrails, has broken away from the magnetic embrace of the cloud's violent compass.

Exhausted, mildly tipsy, I sink deeper into my chair. And then I sink into a deep sleep filled with turmoil, tumbling under darkness. When I wake up (it doesn't take long), the ethereal relief granted by the pills and alcohol transforms into stomach-curdling seasickness. I order a bottle of red, but the choppy channel and cheap plonk somehow only make it worse, intensifying my sea-legless ailments. I close my eyes and cling onto the edge of my table, smoking cigarettes, attempting to style out the nauseating waves of nautical torture. I check Father's pocket watch, desperate for this insufferable voyage to arrive at its destination – the Port de Calais.

Nightfall blackens the sky as the car ramp snogs the mainland. I climb back into the Beetle, turn on the engine, turn up the radio, swallow two ecstasy pills and drive. I just *drive*. But as the journey wears on and the adrenaline kicks in, I feel increasingly inclined to drum up conversation with Osiris. All manner of questions come to mind, from the painfully mundane (*Would you like me to crack the window open an inch, Osiris?*), to the earnest and profound (*Do you agree that the only way to end suffering, disease and violence is to wipe out humanity, Osiris?*). He looks up, but he doesn't answer. In fact, he hasn't said a word since we left the city. He sleeps. He stares through the rear window. He sheds more fur, more skin. But he doesn't speak. Perhaps he isn't in the mood to answer my bizarre questions. And that's OK. I'm starting to enjoy his quiet company. In silence, I steer south, letting the uppers carry us.

Boulogne. Rouen. Marmouillé. Alençon. Le Mans. Tours. Poitiers. Aunac. And, finally, Paradis. Paradis it seems – as the car gags and rolls to a standstill, the petrol, battery and brake lights blinking with unanimous despair – is my terminus. Yes. Paradis is where this story ends.

"We're home," I whisper.

I look at the flatlined dashboard. And then I look at Osiris in the rear-view mirror, sat upright on the backseat. Suddenly, another questions pops into my head. I can't shake it. It needs to be asked.

"Is that you in there, Dad? If it is, I want you to know that I love you. Please. Just give me a sign."

No answer.

As soon as I open the door, Osiris bolts through the gap, across the tarmac and down a narrow alleyway. I scream his name with my hands cupped around my mouth (*Osiris! I'm sorry! Osiris?*), but he's already out of sight, already gone. Feral and freed from humanity. Perhaps I had exhausted my usefulness now that he has escaped to Paradis. Or perhaps his survival instincts took control. It's a wonder he hung on this long. "I love you, Dad," I repeat as I climb out of the car.

Holding my briefcase and Father's ashes, I walk alone, up the deserted street, towards the burning sun, leaving the car behind me.

There is a boulangerie, boucher, mairie, tabac and small supermarché, but their shutters are rolled down, the doors inconspicuously locked. When I peer inside, the shelves are empty, the clerks and customers absent. I run my finger across the bonnet of a car parked on the side of the road. It's covered in a layer of scarlet ash. "Where are the traffic wardens?" I ask aloud. "And, for that matter, all the gardeners and arborists?"

I add, studying the weeds and vines that colonise the cracks in the tarmac, the walls, the buildings. A dead dog (no collar) lies on the pavement, haloed by flies, bloated by the heat. I feel for my camera, crouch down, take a photograph. Even the dog walkers and dog owners have vanished. It doesn't make any sense. I rise to my feet again.

"Hello?" I ask the dead world. "Is anybody out there?"

No answer.

Feeling the ecstasy dissipating, I pause outside a cinéma on the corner of the street. I gaze at its boarded windows, the rivières of cracked lightbulbs. Once upon a time, those neon signs must have lit the night like fireworks. I examine the movie posters pasted on its walls, bleached by the sunlight, imagining what they could have been (French horrors like *L'Abîme des Morts-Vivants*, *Les Raisins de la Mort* or, perhaps, *3615 code Père Noël*). It could have been the Prince Charles from another time, another reality, haunted by the shadows of our past. I push forward, leaving these notions behind me.

And then I see it: a chapel opposite a derelict chateau. Is this the chapel from Abraham Maher's war stories? The chapel in which he encountered the man in the bowler hat, the one Father burned to the ground? I cautiously approach the door and peer inside. But there are zero corpses or spectres. No ghostly priests or grieving grandmothers. Just empty silence, the scent of aged bibles and rotting wood, a cavalcade of scantily clad saints bedecking the walls and alter. I step inside. In this chapel, it feels almost– what's the word? *Peaceful.* Yes. It feels peaceful in the lonely chapel. Its details gently reminds me that bad things never happen inside a sacred place. But is this true here? I wonder. In a place that has absorbed so much pain. In a place that can regenerate itself from its ashes, healing like an infected wound. In a–

Outside, I hear a wind chime crooning in the breeze, a metal gate sighing on its rusted hinges, beckoning me to exit the chapel. When I do, I see them. The sunflowers. They're everywhere. Lining the street, erupting through roofs and windows, the fissures in the pavement, the bonnets of parked cars. Endless rows, stretching beyond the town, all the way to the horizon. Have they been here this whole time? Or have they only just emerged, awakened by the sound of my despair? I walk past them, feeling their black eyes spiking invisible holes through my body.

Eventually, I arrive at a hôtel on the edge of Paradis. Enveloped by the sunflowers, the relentless silence, I pass the abandoned cars in the abandoned forecourt and mount the stairs that lead to the abandoned lobby. I listen to my footsteps echo in the unsettling serenity. I ring the bell on the front desk, wondering what phantom its hollow siren might summon from the hallways.

"Bonjour, monsieur."

I flinch, drawing my revolver and spinning around to confront the figure behind me. I stand there, mouth open, utterly stunned.

Hands linked behind her back, Eleanor Wither is stood in front of me.

"Ellie?" I say, looking into her eyes. "Ellie, it's me. David."

But she doesn't recognise me. The forlorn expression, the decisive posture, the shabby suit and shiraz-stained incisors – *it's her*. Everything is identical, but it's possible Eleanor Wither doesn't even recognise herself. Out here, has she forgotten who she is? Who she was? Whoever this person is (a funhouse reflection or a doppelgänger from another dimension), she is determined to perform her role.

"En quoi puis-je vous aider, monsieur?" she asks, unphased by the revolver still levelled at her chest.

A fly crawls over her face and disappears into the collar of her shirt.

"I- I'm- I've- I'd like to book a room," I finally say, attempting to sound authoritative.

The hotelier nods politely, walks behind the desk and opens the register in a cloud of pale dust. She carefully turns its yellowed pages – they're all blank, as if Paradis suffers from a year-round off-season.

"Très bien," she says. "Pour combien de temps?"

"I'm staying indefinitely," I reply, pulling my wad out of my pocket and dumping it on the desk. The hotelier studies the wrinkled banknotes with mild disinterest before shaking her head, just like the cabbie.

"C'est tout bon," she says, smiling broadly.

When I slip the money back in my pocket, the hotelier closes the register and unhooks a set of keys hanging on the rack behind her. She drops the bundle into my palm – suite 34, on the second floor.

"Bienvenue, David," she says. "Bienvenue au Paradis."

CHAPTER
THIRTY-THREE

It's difficult to translate what it's like in Paradis.
It's only been one day, but I feel like I've always been here, waiting in this moment.

In Paradis, it's like walking onto the other side of a backdrop, where the set meets a different reality. With its ruthless, uninhabitable landscape and mephitic atmosphere, out here (outside the city) is like another planet. The cloudless sky looks like a bottomless pit you could float and tumble into, an endless fall into pristine, baby blue oblivion. And the sun isn't yellow like in a child's finger-painting – it burns bright red, the hue of oxygenated blood, ancient violence. The raging daylight is an inconceivable sensation: to freeze and melt all at once, shivering in the shade, sweating under sunshine.

Out here, nature has taken back control. Coarse knots of green and violet ivy strangle the slate houses and tangle the slats of their shutters. Tree branches break through window panes, displace terracotta roof tiles. Swarms of hornets and blood-lusting insects pinball through the sky like drunk football hooligans, whipped into venereal hysteria by the flora's technicoloured blossoms. And the sunflowers. They encircle Paradis like sentries, expressionless, emotionless, casting long shadows.

Out here is having an awful effect on me. I sneeze until I get migraines and uncontrollable nose bleeds. My sinuses are so swollen and caked with coagulated blood and mucus I can't sleep, breathe or bump what's left of the coke. I'm losing my peripheral vision (eyes shot, insufferably itchy, forced shut). Every patch of skin is plagued with burns, boils, hate bites, cold sores, breakouts. The wildlife aggressively thrives and flourishes while I slowly wilt and wither. Maybe (just maybe) the cloud was protecting us all along. The only way to placate nature's onslaught is through a steady diet of drugs.

But there's a problem. The coke is virtually gone, utilised to fuel my sleepless, breakneck run from Calais to Paradis. I smoked the last joint this morning. And I carelessly dropped the remainder of Abraham Maher's pills down an autoroute rest area urinal (screaming, weeping, juddering my clenched fist at the sun). All I have left are two ecstasy pills. These are dark times indeed. And you don't get dealers out here. In fact, out here, you don't get *anybody*. Perhaps this troubling drugs deficit will force me to adapt, to evolve, doing that thing that made humanity so successful and famous, but it's unlikely. I lack the energy, the perseverance or creativity.

If anything, I've *de*volved, regressed, physically and emotionally deconstructed. I'm terrified to venture beyond the lobby steps or the veranda that haloes the hôtel. Overheated, totally delirious, I watch the sunflowers sway in the lifeless breeze. A slur of black under a sea of bleeding orange. The uninhabited houses, their vacant windows, stare back at me without feeling. Where *is* everybody? I wonder. Lamplight and the neon signs of corner shops, casinos and offies do not hum or glow. Cars don't even drive through Paradis, heading somewhere new. Humanity, it appears, has evaporated under the oppressive, slow-motion tempo of this publess purgatory.

But even if I can't see or hear human life, I constantly feel as if someone, *something*, is present, watching me, absorbing my personality, my physical appearance, my past and immediate memories. I feel myself becoming hollow, more forgetful, *more abstract*. Did my life inside the city ever exist, or have I always been out here, dreaming another reality? The only certainties are these unanswered questions and my unsubstantiated recollections, floating through empty rooms and empty worlds.

The only place I feel safe is the deserted hôtel bar, but that safety comes at a cost. The measures are criminally small. There are no fruit machines. No tabs. No lock-ins or regulars. Just a cob-cloaked television set (no video player) and an unplugged cigarette machine with *HORS SERVICE* taped across its sternum. It's as if they don't want you to get drunk. It's simply not part of the culture. They don't have landlords out here either. It's just me and Eleanor Wither's stunt double, the hotelier, running her ruin like clockwork.

Over the past 24 hours, I've watched this strange character serve me drinks, hoover dead hallways, plumb pipes, gut gutters, tune up the engines of the abandoned cars in the forecourt and water the overgrowing plant pots and hanging baskets that decorate the portico and lobby, bravely exploring the world beyond the bar's brass beer taps. She whistles while she performs these endless odd jobs, but the hôtel, it seems, never gets any less dusty, any less derelict or haunted. The building has a spirit of its own, refusing to comply with the vague patters of human activity. Sometimes I hear doors slamming in distant corridors, shuffling feet and running taps behind locked doors, but as far as I can tell, the hotelier and I are the only tenants. It's just us and the echoes of civilisation.

Now, she stands motionlessly behind the bar while I work a bottle of house red with Campari chasers, trying to rework *Sick & Beautiful*. I sweat under the weight of this excruciating task. I tap my pen on my glass, glaring accusingly at the opening paragraph of my manuscript, waiting for letters to transform into purposeful words, structured sentences, coherent paragraphs, and so on. But nothing materialises. I have no ideas, no solutions to improve the prose, to give the story clout, continuity. I have nothing. I look at Father's jar of ashes on the stool next to mine. And then I look away again, ashamed, as if I can feel his disappointment pervading its transparent walls.

Rachel Garland. Richard Hayes. Abraham Maher. Alan Bloom. Sultan Gillespie. Even Piggy and DC Scythe. They were all right about me. I'm not cut out for this. I lack the drive, the ability.

"Maybe I'm not a writer."

I flinch, surprised with my honesty, the weight of this admission in this empty space. It feels good to verbalise it, to hear it outside my head. It feels good to feel *something*.

"Ellie," I say to the hotelier. She looks up and smiles. "Do you remember the conversation we had in your office on New Year's Day?"

No answer.

"It was the morning after I met Rachel," I continue. "I told you that my job was ebbing away my creative talents. And do you remember what you said to me, Ellie?" Silence. "You thought that I was burnt out. That journalism can sap the soul. But here's the thing – perhaps I had no creative talents to begin with, Ellie. Perhaps there was never any soul to sap."

No answer.

"Perhaps," I say on her behalf. "Perhaps."

When the hotelier starts to flick off the lights and turn the stools upside-down on the bar, I look at the daylight sloping through the leggy windows, and then back at the hotelier, utterly perplexed.

"You're shutting up shop?" I ask.

"Oui, monsieur."

"In the middle of the afternoon?"

"Oui, monsieur."

"Jesus," I say, closing my eyes, pinching the bridge of my nose between my thumb and forefinger. I take a deep breath. "How close is the nearest boozer?"

"Roufec. Vingt kilomètres."

"Fine. Is it open?"

"Non, monsieur."

"What are my other options?"

"Angoulême. Trente-deux kilomètres."

"Is that one closed too?"

"Oui, monsieur."

"Well– when are they open?"

"Demain, monsieur. Huit heures."

I pull out Father's pocket watch. The glass is cracked, but the hands still tick and tock studiously.

"But that's" – I say, peering closer – "that's 19 hours away."

"Oui, monsieur."

"I don't have 19 hours," I say, gripping the hotelier's arm.

She smiles, devoid of emotion.

"Je suis désolé, monsieur."

But how can she be sorry if she doesn't understand? In the city, the pub is your church. A haven where strangers congregate to deliberate the sickness and the beauty of the day, bent into wooden furniture as uncomfortable as any cathedral pew, eating salted snacks as tasteless as any communal wafer. I can feel the muscles in the hotelier's wrist tense as I pull her in closer, *tighter*, struggling to process my thoughts.

"I've already emptied the minibar," I explain. "There are no buses or black cabs. I've exhausted all my options. *He's coming for me. And I don't know how much time I have left.*" There are tears in my eyes now. "Please. *I need this.*"

"Oui, monsieur," she agrees gravely. She shrugs, very slowly. "Je suis désolé."

"Could I leave Paradis if I wanted to?"

There is a long pause.

"Je suis désolé, David," she finally says.

Hopelessly guttered on the plonk – overwhelmed by the heartburn, the transdimensional jetlag – I dissolve into a blabbering, blubbering shipwreck. An inconsolable washout incapable of maintaining balance on his teetering barstool.

I pull myself together, just long enough to ask the hotelier: "Do you have a phone?"

"Oui, monsieur," she says. "À la bibliothèque."

Holding the almost-empty bottle of wine in one hand, *Sick & Beautiful* in the other, I sulk out of the empty bar, through the empty lobby, down an empty corridor, past an empty dining room (the plates, glassware and cutlery laid symmetrically on empty dining tables for the hôtel's non-existent diners) and into the empty library, walled by shelves of books not written by authors named David Temple.

There's a book in everybody, everybody says. Just like a heart, lungs, blood, bones, soul. So, where's mine? I wonder. Where's my book? Where's my soul?

I sink into a tattered reading chair and pick up the phone on the coffee table beside it. In a pool of pink lamplight, I listen to the ring-ring of the dial tone.

"Hello?"

"Did you read that copy of *Sick & Beautiful* I gave you?" I ask.

Docklands Dave laughs. It's a laugh that suggests he's astonished, completely unprepared for this phone call.

"I didn't," he says. "I couldn't. The book is incredibly long, but still, somehow, feels incomplete."

"Did the landlord read it?"

"He wept, David. He called it poetry. He said it was a shame about Richard Hayes. He clearly had real talent."

"Richard?" I ask, puzzled.

"The author of the book," he says. "The tabloids are predicting it'll be a posthumous bestseller."

I look at my manuscript. Below *Sick & Beautiful*, typed in bold, it says: *Written by Richard Hayes*.

I laugh too, lost for words. I rest the manuscript on my lap, remove my teashades and feel my face – tracing my fingers over my swollen jaw, the papillae on my arid tongue, the lacerations criss-crossing my forehead and eyebrows, the queues of spidery hair – wondering if I still exist in a shape I could recognise. It seems that everyone's doing it: not just writing novels, actually *publishing* them. And everyone, the library emphatically but silently belabours, is doing it better than me (David Temple, polymath of failure).

There is an excruciating pause before Docklands Dave clears his throat, audibly emotional.

"David," he says. "I don't know how to tell you this, but two days ago you were shot dead outside a pub called the Hero of Switzerland. One bullet in the throat. Two more in the chest. Gang violence, according to the news."

"That's impossible," I say.

"The papers said you killed Richard Hayes too. When they found your body, you were wearing Richard's face like a mask. And a bowler hat. And get this: they think you killed someone else called Rupert Wreath. Allegedly you pushed him off a balcony one year ago, on New Year's Eve. Someone called Detective Constable Scythe is heading an investigation to uncover the true extent of your crimes." Docklands Dave pauses. "Don't you get it, David? Your role was never to be the author – you're the director, the photographer, the man in the bowler hat. You always have been. And you always will be. Even if you haven't murdered those people, you will, in the future or the past."

I nod to myself, metabolising this information.

"Can I listen to the rain?" I finally ask. "Dave, you couldn't fathom how much I miss that cloud's corrosive drizzle."

Docklands Dave sighs.

"For years," he says, "I've dreamed about sailing west, upriver, starting over in Richmond or Twickenham. But I know the cloud will never let me go. Sometimes, I watch it from the shore. If I listen hard enough, I can hear it weeping, sniggering. It wants me to know that it could capsize my home, drown me in my sleep, haul me into the undertow. The cloud controls everything. Everybody knows it, but they refuse to confront it. The truth is too ugly. Too unsettling. Now it wants more. It wants everything. And it's too late to fight it. Whatever it's plotting up there, it didn't want you or the photo album spoiling its fun. You never beat it, David. It let you escape. It extracted you like a tumour."

I laugh, gazing up at the mildewed ceiling.

"You're starting to sound like your father," I say. "Abe believed the cloud had an agenda too."

"Listen to it, David," he says. "Just listen."

And then I hear it. The rain. I can smell its damp freshness. I can feel it streaking down my cheeks like teardrops. It grows louder, perforating my consciousness like a tsunami of television static. I feel like I'm drowning.

"Hark at that weather, David," he whispers. "It may be the worst we've ever had."

The line goes dead.

I light a cigarette.

Hugging the tone-deaf handset, I shiver myself into a restless, sweating slumber.

CHAPTER
THIRTY-FOUR

Tomorrow is New Year's Eve, assuming measurements of time still apply in Paradis.

Exactly one year ago, Rachel Garland and I met in a nightmare: the one with the television, the man in the bowler hat, the wave of molten static. This memory, like the memories of Mother and my urban reality, are beginning to ebb, to lose context and focus. Yet Rachel still swims like an astronaut across the oceans of my dreams, trawling the seabed of my subconscious, refusing to be forgotten.

What's my most acute memory of Rachel Garland? The answer is obvious: the night we watched *Braindead* in the Prince Charles. We sat in the back row of Screen One. Outside, it was chilly, raining, an unremarkable January backdrop. The violent imagery of the movie's closing scenes – in which the monstrous stomach of Vera Cosgrove gapes open like a mouth to devour her son, Lionel – inspired me to say: "Rachel, I think I'm in love with you."

How long did she pause before she answered? It felt neverending.

"We only say the words, *I love you, I need you*, when we're low and when we're high," she finally said. "We wade through the darkness searching for love's artificial sweetness, a measure of bliss that helps us savour our sentience, but love– it's sick. True love? It's torture. It makes us slaves to hope. I'll never forgive you for reminding me how suffocating love can feel."

I pulled out my notepad and biro to write this down. *True love = torture.* It wasn't the answer I wanted, the answer I *needed*, but it was still another great soundbite for the article. Maybe even pull quote material.

"Perhaps that's the man in the bowler hat's secret," I suggested. "We escape death *with* love. We live forever *through* love." I wrote this down too, impressed with this rare exhibition of balladry. "It's the central theme to humanity's narrative. It's the resolution. Love transcends our physical bodies. It transcends time itself."

"Perhaps," she said, but she sounded unconvinced.

Rachel loathed it (love), but I always suspected that her views were more complex. *I'll never forgive you for reminding me how suffocating love can feel.* I chose to believe that this was her way of saying, *I love you too, David*, but it was impossible to know. Instead of asking her for clarity, I said: "Did you know that *Braindead* holds the record for the most fake blood ever used on a stage set?"

"I didn't," she replied, but this time she sounded disappointed, underwhelmed.

Did she want me to say something more substantial, something that related to the preceding dialogue? I turned back to the screen, chewing popcorn. Rags of septic flesh slid off the skull of Vera Cosgrove. Blood exploded from her stomach as Lionel, fist first, burst free, born again. The creature staggered backwards and crashed through the caving roof, into fire, smoke, bottomless nothing.

Staring in the mirror of my hôtel room en suite, this is how I feel now: a creature sculpted out of plastic flesh and toy blood. My skin is fissured like papier-mâché, split open like condom rubber. I'm stuffed with sawdust and animal organs. An oozing bin liner filled with rotting meat and low-budget prosthetics, every artery clogged with corn starch, syrup and food dye. Almost nothing recognisable is left. Just a defective machine ready for the scrap-heap. This realisation, this sorry sight, reminds me of Father's words.

Death. It happens to us all.

So now death is here, contaminating my fading anatomy, why am I so underprepared for it? I couldn't have predicted any of the events that drove me towards this grim finale, but death itself? That was always going to happen. It was always sprinting forwards. Perhaps it's because I always visualised my death being more conclusive, more resolutely un-alive. Something more like Mother's and Father's.

I pick up the jar of ashes next to the sink, unscrew the lid, tip the grey contents into the toilet.

"Welcome home, Dad," I say, pulling the chain. I watch the muddy water swirl and vanish. I imagine the plumbing carrying Father through the sewers, all the way to the ocean, into the gentle waves kissing the beach Mother and I explored in my decaying memory.

I glare at my appalling reflection before sneezing into a deluge of tears.

"Don't cry, David. Your father would have been proud of you. Just look how far you've come."

Rachel Garland is sat on the foot of the bed, watching me grieve in the mirror, shedding cold sweat. She has the photo album open on her lap as she writes something on the inside cover with my biro. I smile. It reminds me of the first time Rachel visited my flat and leafed through my own photographs, sharing her strange observations, her unnatural perspectives. But now she looks like she did after the accident: legs shattered, forehead split open, the cavity in her abdomen drooling blood. She is covered in flies and spiders. We both are.

I turn away from this image, focussing on the watercolour framed above the bed: a landscape of a golden beach, white cliffs, an emerald ocean, poached clouds, blue sky.

Looking at the painting, I ask: "Rachel, am I dead?"

"Not dead, David. *Reborn*." She smiles with an undisguised sorrow. "This is who you are."

"But *who* am I, Rachel?" I turn back to my reflection. "Who are you, you sick fuck?"

I throw my fist into the mirror, yelping with pain as my broken fingers crunch inside their filthy dressing. I pick up one of the shards that crashes into the sink. And then I guide the sharp edge into my jaw, desperate to see what's hidden underneath. I dig enthusiastically until I feel the glass slip through the flesh with a sickening pop, scraping across the molars on the other side. I hack the soft meat off both cheeks, pulling away rashers of tissue and skin. Blood gushes down my chin and neck, soaking my shirt and overcoat. I whimper with pain. And then I laugh. I laugh so loudly Rachel starts doing it too. I survey the ridges of my new face: the sunken eyes, the displaced nose, the hideous smile stretching ear-to-ear. I snigger, straightening my bowler hat, hanging my camera around my neck. I do a twirl, bow, doff my titfer. Rachel giggles.

"How do I look?" I ask.

"Beautiful, David. You finally lost that awful mask."

"*Beautiful*?" I laugh. "I'm not so sure."

I wash back the last two ecstasy pills with another glug of wine. Fire, almost instantly, combusts inside my chest like a supernova. I collapse into the bathroom tiles, shaking and bawling.

"Don't feel sadness, David," she says. "You're going to be on the television. Just like you always promised you would be." She smiles. "The show is starting soon. Make sure they can't disturb us."

I nod, obediently collecting myself off the floor.

I hang the *NE PAS DÉRANGER* sign on the outside of the door. I lock it, draw the chain. And then I draw the curtains, blanketing the room in darkness. With waning strength, I heave the wardrobe and chest of drawers across the room and push them against the door, barricading the exit. Gasping with exhaustion, I sit on the bed next to Rachel, facing the television. She hands me the remote control. I press the power button. The TV set fizzes to life.

"Incredible," I murmur.

I gaze at the monochrome image projected on the screen: it's me, sat on my sofa, in my flat, the night before Rachel and I first met. My reflection stares back at me, perplexed and horrified. I crawl towards the television. My past self, after a moment of hesitation, does the same, slithering across the floor, pressing his hands against the glass. I splay my fingers over his. We watch each other. We wait.

Have I always been the audience? I wonder. How long

have I been reliving the tragedies of this expired reality, over and over again? I remember the words I told my past self in the Prince Charles, the night before the fake interview with the fake agent, in the fake agency, for the fake book deal.

It feels like I've been sailing through your memories for aeons trying to find her. Sunlit beaches, hospital wards, derelict hotels, labyrinthian corridors, the insides of crashed cars. It's been like a bad dream, but it can't last forever. Surely not? That would be too cruel. It's a vulgar joke, too insidious even for my tastes. But I still have faith in the script. I have faith that, in the end, it'll all work out.

"It wasn't a dream," I whisper, looking at Rachel Garland. "It was a warning." I turn back to the television. "Don't go to Paradise!" I scream at my reflection. I thump my fists on the glass, repeating the words, accentuating their syllables. "Don't go to Paradise, David! Don't go to Paradise! Don't–"

My past self points to his ears, as if he can't hear me. I collapse into a fit of laughter, choking and sobbing on the floor. *I can't hear me*, I realise. But I can hear the rain salivating against the windows. Finally, the cloud has come back home. *It's come to watch the show.*

"Do you understand now, David? You can't alter the script. It's too late. It's always been too late."

"But what if it isn't? You once told me that our potential is limitless. What if we have the potential, *the autonomy*, to stop this horror show, Rachel? Rupert, Richard, Abe – they don't need to die. We don't need to die. And the man in the bowler hat? He'll just be another bad dream."

"If we stop this thing now, we never meet, David. This moment won't exist. *We* won't exist."

I look at Rachel Garland. And then I look at my past self,

into his hopeful eyes, attempting to remember who I was, who I am. I try not to weep. I try to pretend that I'm unafraid, in control, *too fucking cool*. I try to bury true love. I try to–

"I'm sorry, David."

I punch through the glass and drag my screaming reflection out of the television set. I assault his body. I wrap my hands around his neck, his genitals. I push my fingers into his mouth, his eyesockets. I pull the jaw away from the skull. Waves of static crash through the screen, drowning us, the room, the universe, in liquid fire.

"Don't cry, David. It'll all work out. In the end, it always does."

We synthesise, disintegrate, perish.

The embers of reality trail behind us like the tassels of a child's tricycle.

Deconstructed, physically displaced, I accept every fatal, flawed frailty.

We're sick and beautiful.

Sick and beautiful, in love and alone.

This book is printed on paper from sustainable sources managed under the Forest Stewardship Council (FSC) scheme.

It has been printed in the UK to reduce transportation miles and their impact upon the environment.

For every new title that Matador publishes, we plant a tree to offset CO_2, partnering with the More Trees scheme.

For more about how Matador offsets its environmental impact, see www.troubador.co.uk/about/